The
Before Christmas

New York Times Bestselling Author
BRENDA NOVAK

USA TODAY Bestselling Author
DAY LECLAIRE

MOLLY O'KEEFE

When anything is possible…

Bundle up and get cozy with three new stories from *USA TODAY* bestselling authors Jennifer Greene and Merline Lovelace and reader favorite Cindi Myers.

Baby, It's Cold Outside

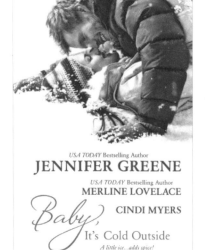

USA TODAY Bestselling Author
JENNIFER GREENE

USA TODAY Bestselling Author
MERLINE LOVELACE

CINDI MYERS

Baby, It's Cold Outside

A little ice...adds spice!

In stores January 2010!

HARLEQUIN®

www.eHarlequin.com

ISBN-13:978-0-373-83736-6

PHANTH1109IFC

EAN

The Night Before Christmas

New York Times Bestselling Author
BRENDA NOVAK

USA TODAY Bestselling Author
DAY LECLAIRE

MOLLY O'KEEFE

HARLEQUIN®

TORONTO • NEW YORK • LONDON
AMSTERDAM • PARIS • SYDNEY • HAMBURG
STOCKHOLM • ATHENS • TOKYO • MILAN • MADRID
PRAGUE • WARSAW • BUDAPEST • AUCKLAND

PLEASE RECYCLE · THIS PRODUCT IS RECYCLABLE ·

Recycling programs
for this product may
not exist in your area.

ISBN-13: 978-0-373-83736-6

THE NIGHT BEFORE CHRISTMAS

Copyright © 2009 by Harlequin Enterprises S.A.

The publisher acknowledges the copyright holders
of the individual works as follows:

ON A SNOWY CHRISTMAS
Copyright © 2009 by Brenda Novak.

THE CHRISTMAS BABY
Copyright © 2009 by Day Totton Smith.

THE CHRISTMAS EVE PROMISE
Copyright © 2009 by Molly Fader.

CONTENTS

ON A SNOWY CHRISTMAS   9
Brenda Novak

THE CHRISTMAS BABY   131
Day Leclaire

THE CHRISTMAS EVE PROMISE   215
Molly O'Keefe

ON A SNOWY CHRISTMAS

Brenda Novak

Dear Reader,

I found the research for this novella very interesting, probably because I live close to the Sierra Nevada. I had no idea there were so many crash sites there, but it stands to reason. They're such a rugged range. As sad as it is to think about the people who have gone down in these planes, I came across several stories of survival, which were very uplifting, especially the one about the boy who lasted several days alone—until rescuers could reach him—that is mentioned in the story. It's amazing what people can do even in difficult circumstances!

I hope you enjoy Maxim and Adelaide's story. Sometimes the best things come out of the greatest tragedy.

I love to hear from readers. Please visit my home on the Web at www.brendanovak.com and sign up for my mailing list so that I can alert you whenever I have a new book out.

Merry Christmas and happy reading!

Brenda Novak

CHAPTER ONE

Tuesday, December 16

ADELAIDE FAIRFAX HAD been apprehensive about taking this flight from the very beginning. For one thing, she preferred not to be in such close proximity to her election opponent. Maxim Donahue, the man who'd filled her husband's state senate position via special election two years ago, was working on his laptop across the aisle and slightly in front of her. He was the only other person on the seven-seater Cessna except for the pilot and, although he refused to show it, he couldn't be happy that she'd been the one to claim Franklin Salazar's endorsement at their meeting this morning. A very wealthy developer, Franklin would not only be a generous campaign benefactor, he'd be a strong influence on other key supporters.

But, despite the awkwardness of their association, it wasn't being cooped up on a private plane with Donahue that'd tempted her to stay in Tahoe and forgo the governor's fundraiser in Los Angeles. Neither was it the Christmas music that filtered through the speakers, reminding her of a season she preferred, for the third year, to forget. It was that she'd always hated flying. The newspaper article she'd read last week, detailing the shocking number of uncharted plane wrecks in the Sierra Nevadas, didn't help. This range contained some of the highest mountains in the northern hemisphere—craggy, rocky peaks that soared above the timberline.

Those same craggy peaks were now lurking somewhere below them in the blizzardlike weather. How close, Adelaide didn't know. But she had a feeling it was too close.

She knew the instant they were going to crash, but because of her fear, she couldn't really describe it as a premonition. It was more of a gut instinct, a sudden prickly sensation that told her something terrible was about to happen—the same sensation she'd experienced right before she'd received the call notifying her of her husband's fatal car accident.

She opened her mouth to ask the pilot if everything was okay but didn't have a chance to voice the words. One of the powerful downdrafts they'd been battling almost since takeoff jerked the plane, and it lost altitude at such a rate her stomach jumped into her throat.

Senator Donahue looked back at her, his expression, for once, devoid of the contempt he typically reserved for her. It was an honest "Oh, my God" moment when their eyes met and they understood without speaking that the primary they both wanted to win so desperately the following June no longer mattered. Chances were they wouldn't see Christmas.

THE IMPACT OF THE CRASH rattled Adelaide's teeth and threw her against the harness of her seat belt, like a one-two punch to the stomach and chest. At the same time, a heavy object fell from above, striking her on the temple. It hit hard enough to disorient her, but she didn't lose consciousness. She sat, eyes wide open, staring at nothing but darkness. The Christmas music was gone, replaced by a low hissing sound.

The smell of gasoline registered simultaneously with the pain she felt from the landing. She had to climb out, get away from the fuselage. But how? If there were emergency lights, they hadn't come on.

Could she find the exit? If she did, could she open it? She was shaking so violently she doubted she had the strength to move even a small piece of luggage out of her way.

How had this happened? The pilot had promised they'd be able to get through. And God owed her a small break, didn't He? She'd barely been able to function since Mark died. The coming election, and her decision to enter the race—what should've been Mark's race—had given her a reason to go on.

Ironically, it was also thanks to the coming election that her life was now at risk.

She struggled to get her bearings, but the creaks and groans of the plane and the heavy dust-filled darkness worked against her. Never had she imagined herself in such a situation, where survival depended entirely on her own ingenuity and instincts. A pilot, a flight attendant, a firefighter—she'd always assumed there'd be Someone In Charge in case of an emergency. Someone *else*.

Had the senator or pilot survived? What were the chances?

Not good, surely. She didn't hear anything—no movement, no groans. Was she completely on her own?

She held her breath. The howling wind gusted into the cabin as if a hole had been ripped in the metal, or the hull had broken apart. Maybe she wouldn't need to open the door. Maybe she was mere inches from freedom and didn't know it. But if she made it out alive, how long would she survive in conditions like this? Were there any emergency supplies on board? Flares?

I'm going to die.

That realization made her shake. But what did dying mean, exactly? As a foster child who'd been bounced around so many homes she'd lost track, she hadn't stayed in touch with any of her "parents." She had no children. She'd already turned her business over to the woman who'd worked for her almost from the beginning, so she could campaign.

For the briefest of moments, she allowed herself to fantasize about seeing Mark again, touching him. He'd been the one constant in her life, the only person who'd ever made her feel loved. She missed his appreciation for fine wine and good books and old architecture and modern art, missed the way he laughed and made her laugh. Was he still the same in some other dimension, maybe living in heaven, as so many organized religions taught?

The possibility calmed her. If heaven existed, maybe she wouldn't be alone for Christmas, after all. Lord knew she'd trade her money, her company and her hopes of winning a state senate seat for some kind of contact with Mark—would do it in a heartbeat. No more forcing herself to meet each new day without the husband she'd lost. No more aching loneliness. Only someone with a fierce will to survive could come out of an accident like this. And that wasn't her. She'd fought enough battles. It was better to give up right away, let go—

A moan interrupted her thoughts. She was almost reluctant to acknowledge what that moan meant. Another survivor complicated her desire to slip away without a struggle.

It had to be Maxim Donahue, she decided. He opposed her in everything.

But it wasn't Donahue. The sound came from the pilot. She could tell because Maxim called out to him a second later, his voice so scratchy and strained it made her wonder if he'd been seriously injured. "You…okay, Mr. Cox?"

Cox. That was the pilot's name. They'd been introduced when Adelaide came on board, but she'd been too busy keeping to herself to concentrate on someone she'd likely never meet again. A friend of the governor's had provided the plane and the pilot. Governor Bruce Livingston wasn't about to let bad weather beat him out of what he had planned for his biggest fundraiser of the year. He'd invited Donahue as a way to show his continued support; he'd invited her as a way to reach her wealthy supporters. She knew it was a calculated move, but her acceptance was every bit as calculated. Although most folks expected the governor to stand by Donahue, her inclusion in this event signaled that he wouldn't be entirely opposed to seeing her take over. It was a perfect strategy—playing the middle ground, as Livingston did so well.

"Mr. Cox?" Donahue called, a little louder.

The moaning stopped. "Get out…now!" the pilot rasped.

Other than that hissing she'd noticed earlier, silence fell, as absolute as the darkness.

"Adelaide?" Donahue said next.

It was odd even in such a desperate moment for this man, who'd only ever addressed her as *Ms.* Fairfax— lately with a starched courtesy that bordered on rudeness—to use her first name. But at least he sounded more coherent than he had a minute or two before. She knew that should've brought relief. Instead, she experienced an unmistakable reluctance to give up her hope of seeing Mark again.

"Hey, you still with us?" he persisted.

Don't answer. She knew what she was in for, couldn't face it. They'd freeze to death even if they got out.

And yet, despite all the odds stacked against them, despite the possibility of Mark waiting for her in heaven, the drive to go on, to live, finally asserted itself.

"I'm here." Unfortunately. Why couldn't it have happened quickly? Why couldn't it be over already?

"Where's here?"

In her seat. She hadn't budged because she'd assumed it was pointless. She didn't know where to go or what to do. Her head hurt, and a wet substance rolled down the side of her face, but it couldn't be tears. She was too shocked to cry.

"Answer me, damn it," he snapped while she was puzzling over her own reaction.

The force of his demand, and the same instinct that had led her to answer the first time, drew another response. "Where I was when w-we crashed."

That information was enough to guide him to her. A moment later she felt him touch her. His hands ran over her head, her face and then her body. They moved briskly, purposefully—and they missed *nothing.*

Mark... The yearning nearly overwhelmed her.

"I don't feel any major injuries," he said. "Can you walk?"

Not Mark. Mark's replacement. Mark's old acquaintance turned political enemy. "I th-think so." Why weren't his teeth chattering? How could he remain calm, even through *this?*

She should've expected it. She'd often said he was made of stone. His wife, already ailing with cancer, had committed suicide two years ago, six months after Mark's death. But Maxim Donahue had never shown so much as a hint of regret. She could still remember the implacable expression he'd worn when he appeared on television on a completely unrelated matter only days after Chloe Donahue's funeral.

Adelaide had always resented him for the ease with which he'd been able to return to business as usual. He made carrying on look simple. Probably because he cared about nothing as much as his own ambition. That was part of the reason she'd decided to run against him. What Donahue had said about her late husband provided the rest of her motivation.

"Let's get out of here," he said.

The pilot didn't utter another sound. *Cox.* Adelaide knew she'd never forget his name again. Not if she lived to be a hundred.

"Wh-what about M-Mr. Cox?"

Light appeared. At last. But it wasn't the emergency lights. It was the blue glow of flames licking across the cockpit. The flicker illuminated the slumped figure of the pilot.

"Get your hands out of the way!" Maxim Donahue shoved her fumbling fingers aside, unlatched her seat belt and half dragged her to the door, where he pulled the barely visible emergency latch. But the door wouldn't open. They were trapped. Unless they could discover where that wind was getting in….

Grabbing her shoulder, he shoved her toward the back. "Find the opening. I'll get Cox."

Find the opening. Adelaide could feel the wind, the

cold, even the wet snow seeping through the wreckage, but her head injury left her dizzy, stupefied. She couldn't think. Especially when she heard Donahue behind her, his gruff voice carrying a terrible note of finality. "He's gone." -

"Gone?" she repeated, unable to absorb his meaning.

He didn't clarify. He pushed past her and kicked at the walls and windows. But the fire in the cockpit yielded more smoke than light. Flames stole along the floor, threatening to destroy the only hope they had.

Adelaide's nose and throat burned. And the sticky substance, the blood, coming from the wound on her head kept running into her eyes. She wiped at it and blinked and blinked and blinked, but it made no difference. She couldn't see. She couldn't breathe. She couldn't imagine how they'd live another five minutes.

Suddenly, the plane shifted, and a great gust of ice and snow blew back her hair.

Donahue had found an opening. He'd widened it. That brought a poignant burst of hope. But at the same time, metal screeched against rock, echoing miserably against the night sky. Then the plane tilted at a crazy angle and the floor beneath their feet gave way.

CHAPTER TWO

THE FRIGID BLAST of air that represented escape hit Maxim Donahue just as the plane plummeted down the side of the mountain. Had he not already lunged for the opening, he would've experienced a second crash—and Adelaide Fairfax would've gone down with him. As it was, the movement of the plane jerked her so hard he nearly lost hold of her. Numb from the cold and blinded by swirling snow, he wasn't sure he'd managed to pull her out until her hand patted its way across his chest as they lay, prone, in the snow. Maybe she wanted to confirm that he was still with her. Or maybe she was just seeking warmth. They were both going to need it. He wondered if they'd last long enough to be rescued.

"I'm here," he yelled above the raging storm. "You okay?"

"That depends on how…you define okay." The wind made it difficult to communicate, but at least she seemed to be making sense. The shock of the crash had caused her to react with a sort of stunned lethargy. He was under the impression that she'd still be sitting in her seat if he hadn't unbuckled her restraint and prodded her to get moving. But that didn't surprise him. There'd actually been studies showing that only a small fraction of the people involved in plane wrecks got themselves out.

Another small percentage grew hysterical. The majority did neither. They simply stayed put and allowed themselves to die.

A bang resounded far below, indicating that the plane had come to rest.

The pilot was still inside.

The image of Cox's body, now probably as mangled as the twisted metal that encased it, made Maxim sick. But he couldn't change what was, couldn't turn back time. His only choice was to do what he'd done with Chloe's death—bury the shock and grief in some other part of his brain so he could function. If the panic he held at bay ever took root, it'd spread so fast he wouldn't be able to stop it. Just as Adelaide had remained buckled in her seat, watching flames devour the cockpit, he'd find himself lying in the snow, unable to move or even think. And if ever he needed to keep his wits about him, it was now. Together with a wing and some other debris from the crash, which looked more like props in a movie, they were a few feet from the edge of a steep precipice. The wind whipped at them feverishly. If they weren't careful, those gusts would toss them over the side just like the main body of the plane.

Why had he put himself in this situation? *Why* had he listened when Cox insisted they could beat the storm? They should've stayed in Tahoe as they'd initially discussed. Instead, Maxim had succumbed to the pressure of Governor Livingston's phone call. But only because he'd *wanted* to make the party. He couldn't slow down, couldn't stop working. That would give the emptiness in his life a chance to catch up with him.

"What are we going to do?" Adelaide called.

The irony of being caught in this situation with the one

person he disliked more than any other hit him, and he began to laugh.

"What's so funny?" she asked. "We're stranded on the side of a cliff in one of the worst storms to hit the Sierras in a decade. We're going to die up here, and you're laughing?"

He felt no obligation to explain. "I've finally pushed fate too far," he muttered instead.

He doubted she'd heard his reply, but she must've understood a little of what he was thinking because she shouted, "Who do you figure will win the primary if we're...not there?"

There was only one person with any real prospects. Luke Silici, who worked for the governor's office, had been making noises about running for the senate, until Adelaide stepped up and surprised everyone. Then, feeling she'd get more party support than he would, he'd backed off at the last minute. "Luke Silici will enter in your absence. The die-hard conservatives won't have a prayer of producing someone who can beat him. Not this late in the game. That's why they pressured *you* to run against me. You were their best shot. Not that I believe you could've taken me."

She shouldn't have had a chance. He was the incumbent. But Adelaide had her husband's tremendous popularity on her side, the sympathy factor, the support of key Republicans who possessed the power to swing a large number of votes, and the success of her multimillion-dollar energy conservation company, which established her business acumen. She'd even stolen the Salazar endorsement.

He expected her to come back at him, listing those assets as proof that retaining his seat was far from a given—and welcomed the argument that would start. This was his first opportunity to privately confront the stunning widow who'd pulled her support from him the moment he began to oppose legislation her husband had favored. If they were about to die, he could say whatever he wanted, knowing he wouldn't be quoted in the *Sacramento Bee* the following morning.

But Ms. Fairfax didn't return fire. She merely said, "They didn't have to pressure me."

Those six words put him in his place and removed the distraction he'd so eagerly embraced.

"We have to find shelter or we'll wish we'd gone over with the plane," she said and made a move to get up.

"Not so fast." He yanked her down by her expensive wool coat and rolled onto his hands and knees. That was when he realized—as inappropriately as he was dressed for winter survival in a fifteen-hundred-dollar business suit—her apparel included a skirt. Although her legs had proved quite a diversion when he was boarding the plane, the panty hose and high heels that showed them off so well would give her little protection from the elements.

How could this have happened? He was freezing his ass off, staring at nothing but snow, and still couldn't believe he was stranded in a blizzard instead of on his way toward the fundraiser, where he'd hoped to convince the majority of his party, once and for all, that Adelaide Fairfax didn't have what it took to win against the Democrats come November.

"What are you doing?" she asked as he surveyed the mountain.

They had to continue shouting. "I'm trying to figure out where we should go in order to increase our chances of survival."

"Are you w-worried about an—an avalanche?"

Her teeth chattered as she spoke. Her coordination would start to suffer next. Mild hypothermia began with uncontrolled shivering, impaired coordination and blue lips. It could progress quickly to more serious problems and eventually death. Anyone who'd seen a survival movie knew that.

Death seemed to wait at the end of every avenue. He was astonished that they'd both escaped this far. Cox hadn't been so lucky.

"That's exactly what I'm worried about," he said, speaking more loudly.

"Are we in an—an avalanche area?"

Evidently, she wasn't much of a ski buff. "Any steep mountain covered with snow can avalanche. But they occur most often when new snow falls onto cement pack."

"Like it's doing now."

The wryness in her voice encouraged him. He hoped it meant she was tougher than she seemed. She'd certainly done well navigating the predominantly male world of business. But the way she'd reacted in that plane had him worried. "You got it, ace. The wet, heavy snow sitting on top of the hardened ice slides right off, especially when it's steep."

"Great. So if we d-don't want to go hurtling to the b-bottom of the canyon, what should we do?"

"Move carefully and get on stable ground."

"Say that again?"

"We need to find a safe place to build a shelter!"

"Out of *what?*"

"The only thing we've got—snow." Fortunately, he'd

been an Eagle Scout and knew about snow caves. He'd had to build a total of three in his lifetime, on various campouts. Of course, those had been for fun, for practice. And it'd been twenty-seven years since he'd built the last one.

She cupped her hands around her mouth. "What about the p-plane? Maybe we can f-find some emergency supplies in the wreckage."

She was right. Legally, the pilot would've had to carry certain articles. But it wasn't as if the plane or the pilot came from Alaska. California was known for its predominately mild weather. Had the members of the state legislature concerned themselves with winter in the high Sierras when they considered emergency gear legislation?

Maxim hadn't seen any such bill since he'd been in office. He could only pray that they had.

"Regulations would demand some sort of supplies, but who knows how well the owner or pilot complied. Or if those supplies went over with the main body of the plane." It was very likely they had. The pilot himself had gone over, hadn't he?

Maxim didn't want to think about that. Christmas was next week. What kind of holiday would Cox's family have? And what about the two of them? *Any?* Probably not. But he didn't believe it was advisable to extinguish all hope. Adelaide was losing body heat faster than he was; it wouldn't help to discourage her. "We'll look, but first we'll get warm and wait out the storm."

"Sounds g-good."

Not as "g-good" as waking up to discover this was just a nightmare, that he could still look forward to seeing his daughters next week when school ended. But at least he wasn't alone. He'd found it ironic to be stranded with Fairfax's young widow. Now he was grateful for her company. Because the only thing worse than being stuck out here with her was being stuck out here alone.

CHAPTER THREE

MAXIM HAD NO IDEA how long it took them to dig the cave. He couldn't see his Rolex, couldn't see much of anything. He wasn't even sure they were tunneling in a safe spot. They hadn't had the time, the visibility or the mobility to look around. They'd found what appeared to be a level spot and started digging. It was either that or continue to brave the cold without any shelter, which wasn't a viable option. If they didn't warm their extremities soon, they'd lose them to frostbite.

At least the physical nature of the work kept them somewhat warm. They covered their hands with the sleeves of their coats and took turns using a metal piece from the plane to scoop snow.

Adelaide had fallen silent almost as soon as they'd begun. Maxim knew her legs and feet must be even more frozen than his, but there wasn't anything he could do about it. Not until they had some way to block the wind.

"I wish we had supplies to build a fire," he said. It was a lame comment, but he wanted her to interact with him.

His efforts to draw her out didn't help. She said nothing. He only knew she was still alive because he had to let her take over with the shovel every now and then or he'd begin to sweat, heightening the danger of acute hypothermia. She needed to keep moving more than he did, anyway.

She attempted to further their progress, but her movements grew slower and more uncoordinated as the minutes ticked by. He was losing her.

The panic that struck at that thought didn't correspond to the way he felt about her in regular life. In the campaign, he'd forced himself to stick to the issues, but it hadn't been easy in the midst of her more personal attacks. Especially because her husband had done some unconscionable things and no one knew it, except Maxim and Harvey Sillinger, his campaign manager. Harvey was angrier than a junkyard dog that he wasn't allowed to expose what he'd learned. But Mark Fairfax was dead. The only person who'd be hurt by his duplicity was the wife he'd left behind.

Destroy the squeaky-clean image of her late husband, and you wipe away her power. This is a fight, man! Go for the jugular! She's running on the popularity of a man who pretended to have integrity but didn't. Harvey made this argument almost daily. Maybe they could remove the threat Adelaide posed by leaking a few carefully chosen details. But it would also destroy the positive memories she had of her husband, and Maxim refused to stoop that low. He knew what Mark's death had cost her. At the time of his funeral, he and the Fairfaxes had been political allies.

"Keep digging!" he snapped, hoping impatience would have some effect since persuasion hadn't. "Now! Hurry up!"

The added intensity seemed to work. At first. After the next few scoops, however, she grew completely unresponsive no matter how much he shouted.

"Shit!" he yelled to no one in particular. They were out of time.

Maxim gauged the depth of the hole. It wasn't as deep as he would've liked. They couldn't be too close to the walls or ceiling, or the snow would melt, and he couldn't have that. They had to stay as dry as possible. But staying dry would be a moot point if Adelaide couldn't make it long enough to take advantage of the shelter.

Stripping off his raincoat to cover the floor of the cave, he set their makeshift shovel near the opening so they could dig their way out if they got blocked in. He was supposed to leave a hole, but the metal plug was the best he could do under the circumstances.

If Adelaide had considered the possibility of being buried alive, she didn't mention it. She backed inside when he told her to and didn't resist when he began stripping off her clothes.

"Stay with me." Going by touch alone, he fumbled with the buttons on her suit. "I'll get you warm. Do you understand? Are you aware of what I'm telling you? Hang on."

The shallowness of her breathing alarmed him. He could barely feel it against his cheek. And what he felt wasn't as warm as it should've been. He was afraid her core temperature was dropping. He'd never felt a woman's skin that was so cold, so deathlike. Even Chloe had been warm when he'd found her....

"The outside temperature can fall to seventy below in a storm like this." He hoped his voice would give her something to concentrate on in the dark. "This cave should make it a whole hundred degrees warmer." He carefully removed her wet skirt. "That sounds practically tropical, doesn't it?"

Shivering, she held her arms close to her almost naked body. "N-no."

It wasn't the answer he'd been hoping to hear, but it proved she was coherent. "Talk to me, Adelaide. You can't go to sleep. You know that, right?"

He didn't think she'd respond again, but more words came…after a long delay. "That's all I w-want to d-do."

"If you sleep, you die," he said. "And we've got to get back home. We have an election battle to wage—against each other."

"S-somehow…the n-nomination doesn't…m-matter… anymore."

"I'll remember you said that once we're both safe and warm."

Thanks to the narrow confines of the cave, Maxim had trouble taking off his suit jacket. His button-down shirt wasn't any easier because his numb fingers couldn't seem to loosen his tie.

"W-what…are you…doing?" she asked.

"Only what I have to."

At last, he untied the damn knot. He wrapped his tie around his wrist, in case he saw some use for it later, and started to peel off the rubber boots that protected his Italian leather shoes.

"M-Maxim?"

"I think that's the first time you've ever used my first name," he said.

"Are you g-getting naked?"

"Yes. As fast as I can."

"Okay."

He laughed. "Somehow that wasn't what I expected you to say."

He took off her sensible pumps, which seemed anything but sensible in this situation, and slipped his socks, which were dry thanks to the overboots, on her feet. Then he put the overboots on over them, to insure they stayed dry, and pulled his leather shoes back on his own feet.

"Does that help?" he asked.

She didn't answer.

"Adelaide?"

"I'm f-fine. We'll be fine."

"That's the attitude," he said, but he sensed it was more of a capitulation than anything else. She didn't want him to bother her anymore. She preferred to be left alone. So she could drift into unconsciousness?

"You can't sleep," he reminded her and wondered what to do about her bra. Leave it on or take it off? It didn't seem wet, but if he was going to die, there were worse ways to go than pressed against the soft body of a woman.

In the end, he couldn't justify taking that liberty.

Leaving the bra on, he drew her into his arms.

"Oh! That feels g-good."

Her comment made him wish he'd removed her bra. Then it would've felt that much better. Having her even partially undressed was enough to bring his libido roaring to life. It'd been too damn long since he'd been with a woman, and he wanted to live while he could. What else would they do for the next several hours? They couldn't sleep—and nothing else had as much potential for distraction.

But the same vigilant conscience that wouldn't allow him to remove her bra wouldn't allow him to do anything else, either. Not when he suspected she wasn't thinking clearly.

When she wedged one slim leg between his thighs, he knew he wasn't thinking clearly, either. This was Adelaide Fairfax, his nemesis. She'd been stealing his endorsements and financial backers right and left, and hammering away at his Achilles' heel—his voting record on taxation issues—since September. Yet the feel of her against him provoked a sudden recklessness that made him want to roll her beneath him and make love to her more desperately and feverishly than he'd ever made love to a woman. The anger and resentment he'd felt toward her for the past four months only made that desire more potent. His grudging admiration of her beauty and equally grudging respect for her poise created a powerful drive to possess— and it happened more quickly than a match dropped in gasoline could burst into flame.

THEY WERE DEFINITELY making use of their clothing but they weren't actually wearing much of it. While Maxim's water-resistant coat protected them from the snow beneath, his suit jacket and Adelaide's wool coat covered them like blankets. She had on only her bra, panties and nylons; he was still wearing his boxers. But Adelaide wouldn't have cared if they were completely naked. It didn't matter that he was her enemy. He was warm. And he even smelled good.

She pressed her frozen nose into his neck and breathed in the scent of soap. Maxim Donahue was built like a Giorgio Armani model—long, lean and spare. He dressed like one, too, in expensive tailor-made suits he wore as easily and comfortably as other men wore sweat suits.

His pulse beat against her lips, rhythmic and steady. She'd just count the pounding of his heart until help arrived. Then she'd be whisked away and would never have to be alone with him again.

But a rescue team wouldn't get anywhere close to them until after the storm. And she had no idea how long that would be.

Her feet were still so numb she couldn't feel them.

"Adelaide?"

She didn't move. "What?"

"You're not falling asleep, are you?"

"Of course not." But she didn't see how she could avoid it. She didn't have the strength to lift her eyelids.

CHAPTER FOUR

"HEY." MAXIM SPOKE into Adelaide's hair, next to her ear, but she didn't move. "You still with me?" he said, more loudly.

When her head lolled on his arm, he grew alarmed enough to shake her. "What are you doing? Wake up!"

No answer.

With a curse, he leaned on his elbow. A moment before, he'd caught his own mind wandering, blanking out as if preparing for sleep. It'd happened so fast he almost wondered if he was the one who'd slipped away and was now hallucinating. "Listen, we're not...giving up, okay?"

She mumbled a few words. They weren't coherent, but at least they proved she was alive.

Thank God!

Closing his eyes, he let go of the breath he'd been holding. "If they find us...like this...they might...take a picture and...and put it on the front page of *The Bee*. Can you...imagine the caption?"

He hoped his comment would cause a reaction, and it did. "They'd better *not!*"

"They could. We have to remain conscious, make sure they don't."

"We'll...be...conscious."

Not if they didn't do something to stay awake. Less than sixty seconds later, he felt the tension seep out of her body.

"Adelaide, come on." Come on *what?* Where was he going with this thought? It took a moment, but at last he remembered. "We have to…to keep dalking."

"Keep…what?"

He was having trouble enunciating. He had to capture each word, chase it around in his head, then drag it to his mouth.

"T-talking." There, he'd said it. But the effort was wasted. His warning brought no response.

"Adelaide, fight…please." The sexual desire he'd felt earlier was completely gone. Now he wished for that spike of testosterone, for the flare of physical strength it had given him. In its place sat a hard knot of dread, but it was muted like everything else seemed to be. It certainly wasn't enough to overcome the sluggishness bogging him down. And with the storm still raging, they had a long wait ahead.

"Shall…we sing…some Christmas carol?"

No answer.

"Jingle bells, jingle bells, jingle all the way—" He stopped. That was all he could remember, which was ridiculous. He wasn't any kind of Scrooge. He liked Christmas. But apparently he hadn't paid much attention to the lyrics of even the more popular songs in quite some time. Probably because he didn't usually sing, didn't have what he would consider a voice. So he settled for something more repetitive and less vocally demanding. "Ninety-nine bottles of beer on the wall, ninety-nine bottles of beer, take one down, pass it around, ninety-eight bottles of beer on the wall."

His words ran together as if he was drunk. He tried to sing more clearly, hoping Adelaide would join in, but she didn't. Only the flutter of her heartbeat, which he could feel when he pressed his lips to her throat, gave him hope—until that heartbeat became erratic, weak.

Feeling her heart wind down finally triggered the release of some much-needed adrenaline. Suddenly, he could think. Almost as important, he had the energy to move.

"Adelaide?" He kissed her throat, her jawline, her cold lips. "Hey, you're naked…with…the enemy."

Forgetting the scruples that had kept him circumspect and discreet, he unfastened her bra and slid his hand up to cup her breast. He didn't care about right and wrong anymore. He cared only about saving her life. To do that, he needed to rouse her to some level of awareness. "Can you feel me touching you?"

She moved, which encouraged him.

"Do you like it?" Parting her lips with his tongue, he kissed her while his fingers sought the more sensitive parts of her body. He wasn't having fun. He was too frightened. But he was putting everything he had into trying to interest her—or at least anger her. As far as he was concerned, either reaction would work. He simply needed to evoke an emotional response. Even a small rush of adrenaline could keep her lucid.

"Mark?"

He went still. She was out of it, all right. She thought he was her late husband.

He opened his mouth to correct her. But he feared despair would set in if he did. She was trapped on the side of a mountain, in the middle of a terrible blizzard, with little chance of survival. With him, a man she hated. But only when she knew who he was.

"Yeah, it's me." He cringed at the lie but didn't regret telling it when it worked better than he would've guessed. For the first time since the crash, he sensed some fight, some real strength in Adelaide. She was weeping now, but she clung to him, kissing him so passionately he began to experience a flicker of the desire that had crashed over him when he'd first encountered her barely clad body.

God, what am I doing?

He was saving her life, he told himself and, at her urging, slid his hand down her flat stomach to take off her panty hose.

IT WASN'T MARK, and Adelaide knew it. But that didn't mean she had to accept it.

Shutting out the reality, she concentrated on Maxim's mouth, his muscular chest, the thickness of his hair—and told herself it was the husband she'd lost. Sure, his kiss seemed a little different than she remembered, but it was so good she didn't mind. He showed more emotion, and the groan that rumbled from deep in his throat let her know he wanted her. The way he handled himself—handled her—was slightly more commanding. She liked it better. *Because it's been so long.*

"I love you," she whispered through tears she couldn't seem to suppress.

He stopped moving. She imagined him staring down at her, even though neither of them could see. "Is something wrong?" she asked.

"Adelaide—"

She pressed a finger to his lips. She didn't want him to ruin it. She had her husband with her. That was all that mattered. Maybe he'd disappear in a few minutes, leave her as alone as she'd been before. But at least she'd have this final memory—a better parting than the one she'd agonized over for so long—to carry her through whatever came next.

"Tell me you love me," she whispered, craving those words more than any others.

He hesitated.

"Mark?"

"You know it's true." Although he'd spoken a little too gruffly to make it entirely believable, there was no mistaking the sincerity in the words that followed. "You're the most beautiful woman I've ever laid eyes on, Adelaide Fairfax."

She chose to focus on that instead. *You're the most beautiful woman I've ever laid eyes on...*. Wrapping her fingers around the proof of his arousal, she couldn't help smiling at his sudden intake of breath. The passion that had begun to wane in their marriage was back. Her doubts, her insecurities, they were stupid. Wasted energy, just as he'd always said. "Feels like you're ready."

"I'm ready. But—"

"Shh." She regretted ever breaking the silence. She'd only wanted to clear the air between them, hated that he'd died before she could apologize for the accusations that had sent him storming from their home. "Just make love to me. Tell me I'm all you ever wanted. Tell me that never changed."

"You're taking my very soul," he murmured.

"Don't fight it." She meant that teasingly, but he seemed to take her response at face value. His hands and mouth found her again, drawing a greedy response from every single nerve—until she was so sensitized she quivered at his lightest touch. She wanted to be with him completely, craved the old sense of connection they'd known when they were first married. But he resisted her attempts to take their lovemaking that final step.

"What are you doing?" she asked, confused by his hesitancy. "I want to feel you inside me. *One more time.*"

"Adelaide, I can't. I'm not Mark. You know that, don't you? I'm—"

"Shh!" Couldn't he take what she was willing to give him and spare her the harsh reality? It was her last night on earth; this was all she asked of it. "I don't want to hear what you're saying."

"It's the truth. I can't do this unless..." He seemed to struggle to find the right words. "I have to know you're okay with it, that I'm not taking advantage of you."

"We're taking advantage of each other," she said and arched into him, seeking the fantasy that had enveloped her only moments before.

Stubbornly, he clung to his resistance. "You're sure?"

She let her kiss answer for her, let it coax him to succumb, to forget that she was pretending he was someone else. And it worked. His restraint snapped. She felt it go.

Mumbling words she couldn't quite make out—*heaven help me* or something like that—he rolled her beneath him.

CHAPTER FIVE

THEY DIDN'T DIE that night. But when Maxim opened his eyes the next morning, he was almost disappointed to be breathing. They were still stranded, still freezing, and still without much hope. He'd also made love to his election opponent while allowing her to fantasize that he was her dead husband. How sick was that?

Even sicker was the fact that he'd enjoyed it.

What had he been thinking? Certainly not of waking up with her in the morning.

But it didn't matter. So what if they'd made love? The experience had been so passionate and intense, so all-consuming, it had kept them *alive*. Best to leave it at that.

Adelaide was beginning to stir. He felt his body react when her breast brushed his arm. Her softness brought memories of their earlier intimacy and a surprising desire for more. But he was in no hurry for her to achieve full awareness....

He'd tried to tell her he wasn't Mark, and she'd responded as if she understood. But who could say what was really registering and what wasn't?

He pressed a thumb and finger to his eyes. Then something else occurred to him. He could no longer hear the wind. Had the storm abated?

Maybe the worst was over. Maybe the rescue crews

were on their way. If so, it wouldn't be long before they were both taken home, and then they could forget what had happened here.

Fresh air rushed in when he removed the piece of metal he'd wedged into the corner. As light streamed in with it, he felt a desperate urge to escape the confines of the cave—and the physical reminder of the line he'd crossed last night. But a groan told him Adelaide was awake. He glanced over to see her watching him warily.

"Tell me we didn't," she muttered.

Now that he could see her, it wasn't difficult to spot the dried blood on her right temple. She'd been hit by something and had probably suffered a concussion. That explained a lot about her behavior, making him especially glad he'd identified himself properly before taking their lovemaking all the way. "Now you're asking me for more lies?"

"Can't we consider it an extension?"

He would've smiled at the wryness of her response, but he was still worried that he might've gone too far last night. He wasn't exactly sure *how* it'd all happened. The passion was suddenly there. It had brought them together. Was it entirely his fault that they'd made love? He didn't think so. He remembered trying to stop himself, but she'd been pleading with him to continue.

Still, that bump on her head made him nervous.... "Works for me," he said, "as long as you understand the reality."

"Which is…"

"You need me to explain it?"

"I thought you were Mark."

"No, you *wanted* to think I was Mark, and I let you. There's a difference."

"So you were doing me a favor."

"That's a good way to look at it," he said with false cheer.

She rolled her eyes. "You're so self-sacrificing."

"As a public servant, I aim to please."

"Do you do those kinds of favors for all your constituents?"

"Now you're going to attack my reputation?"

She seemed to realize that she was being purposely contentious. "It's freezing," she said with a sigh. "Any chance we can seal the hole until we hear a helicopter?"

"You're kidding, right? We have to get out, do whatever we can to make it easy for the Civil Air Patrol to find us."

"Do you always have to be so big on reality?"

This time he did smile. "Put on your coat and crawl out so I can get mine."

She didn't answer. Neither did she move. "I can't believe it," she mumbled, and he knew she was busy replaying the "favor" he'd done her. He'd told her he *loved* her! But that was when he thought they'd never see daylight again.

"If it helps, we had no choice," he said. "If we hadn't gotten so…involved, we probably wouldn't be alive right now." Their activities had certainly warmed *him*.

"I didn't realize what I was doing."

He focused on widening the hole. "That scares me, and you know why. Are you going to keep it up?"

"No." She burrowed under the coats. "You might push me off a cliff if I do."

"I won't kill you after going through *that* just to save you." He grinned to himself.

"You're all heart."

When the hole was finally big enough to crawl through, he tossed the piece of metal he'd been using outside. "Are we going to stay in here and stress over the fact that we—" he wanted say "had sex" to make it as impersonal as possible, but what they'd done wasn't impersonal at all "—made love? Or can we forget about it, like we should, and move on?"

"You're willing to forget about it?" She popped her head out from under the clothes, seeming more embarrassed than angry. Maxim could understand why that might be the case. But he couldn't hold the request she'd made last night against her. He'd read about the disorientation that often resulted from a knock on the head, not to mention the effects of hypothermia. Without those two elements, he doubted she would've have been able to pretend. Playing the role of Mark had been a stretch for him, even in the physical sense. Her husband hadn't been much bigger than she was.

"I'm willing to forget about it," he said. "Are you getting out or not?"

"There's just one more thing."

He was sure he'd regret asking, but she'd piqued his curiosity. "And that is…?"

"What about birth control?"

"What about it?" He hadn't used any. It'd been so long since he'd had to worry about it that he didn't even own a condom, let alone carry one around in his wallet, which was in his briefcase on the plane, anyway. "Birth control hardly seemed important when I thought we were going to die."

"And now that we might live?"

It was taking on a whole new significance. "What are the chances?"

"Considering...everything, they could be pretty good."

Just what he wanted to hear. Not only had he made love to Adelaide Fairfax while letting her pretend he was Mark, he might've gotten her pregnant.

Shit... That was the absolute last thing he wanted. He loved his two children, but they were grown. And he and Adelaide weren't even friends.

Swallowing a sigh, he refrained from sharing those thoughts. He knew it was better not to show her how upset he'd be if their encounter resulted in a pregnancy. "I see."

"So...you didn't get fixed after you were finished having kids?" she asked.

There'd been no need. His wife had had her tubes tied during the cesarean section performed at Callie's birth. "No."

Adelaide's face fell. But a moment later, she set her jaw, and he knew he was looking at the shrewd business-woman who'd taken Fairfax Solar public. "Then I'll make you a deal."

Surprised by her sudden calm, he raised an eyebrow. "What's that?"

"You tell no one what happened up here..."

He liked it so far. "And..."

"And if I'm pregnant, you let me keep the baby and pretend it isn't yours."

He wasn't sure he'd be able to do that, not after being a parent and knowing what it was like. But there were other considerations he felt more comfortable voicing. "You're running for office. How will you explain a pregnancy when you're not married?"

"Maybe Mark made a deposit in a sperm bank before he died," she said with a shrug.

"Is it true?"

"No."

I love you. She'd been crying when she said that. Her emotion had reminded him of what he'd felt before his own marriage disintegrated, made him want to experience again that same level of intensity. "You regret not having children when you had the chance?"

"I never had the chance. Mark was infertile."

Maxim had always assumed it was her, that she'd been too wrapped up in her career to want a child. "You could've adopted."

"We were looking into it."

And then her husband had died.

"Anyway, I wouldn't have asked for this, wouldn't have planned it," she went on. "But if it's already happened because of last night—"

"Last night won't amount to anything," he interrupted.

"You don't know that."

"Let's wait until we're sure we have something to worry about before we start making difficult decisions. Right now, we need to concentrate on getting off this damn mountain."

"Help will arrive soon." She shoved her blond, shoulder-length hair out of her face and, for a moment, he was transfixed by her blue eyes. Even in this cave, he could make out their startling color. "With the storm over, Yosemite park rangers or…or CAP rescuers will be able to track the plane's emergency locator transmitter beacon," she said.

He wished he could be as confident. "*If* the signal went off."

"It went off. The ELT is activated automatically on impact."

"Not if it was cushioned by too much snow. And

even if it went off, we're in some pretty rugged mountains, Adelaide."

Her full lips, which she'd used so artfully last night, twisted in distaste. "Don't call me that."

Offended by her tone, as well as her refusal to let him address her by her first name, he studied her—and tried to tell himself he didn't like what he saw. That what had taken place last night hadn't changed the way he felt.

"You can try to distance yourself all you want, but it won't change what happened. Anyway, as I was saying, the signal could easily bounce from ridge to ridge, making it difficult to track. Or maybe the fire burned so hot it destroyed the box containing the equipment. Even if that's not the case, the ELT is so far down the mountain, who knows what they'll think when they find it."

She curled up. "Surely they'll search above it."

"Maybe they will, if they have time before the next big storm. Regardless, we can't sit back and wait. We have to search for supplies, light some flares, make a fire, do anything and everything possible to survive another night, if it comes to that."

She didn't react to his mention of another night. "Is there any chance Mr. Cox is still alive?"

"None." He scowled to tell her he didn't want to be reminded of the pilot, but she didn't give up.

"You're sure?"

"I'm positive. But you can see for yourself. We have to hike down there. If anything's left of the plane, we might find some food. Eating and drinking will help us keep our body temperatures in the safe zone."

"Fine." She rubbed a hand over her face. "Where are my clothes?"

"They're wet. That's why I took them off."

Their eyes met, making him wonder if she was reliving the same memories he was.

"If you want me to thank you for that, I don't think I can," she said.

"I'm not asking for your thanks. Just answer one question."

"What's that?"

"Are men so interchangeable?"

A muscle flexed in her jaw. "I don't know what you mean."

"It seemed easy for you to accept a replacement."

"Well, it wasn't. It required a great deal of effort to block out your true identity. But I managed. Otherwise, I wouldn't have enjoyed it," she said, but she pulled her gaze away as if she feared he might read a different response in her eyes. Then she dragged her coat around her shoulders and crawled out—and he tried not to look at the bare bottom she accidentally flashed him as she wriggled through the opening.

CHAPTER SIX

ADELAIDE'S HANDS and feet were freezing, despite the sun. And her coat wasn't meant to be worn without a layer of clothing beneath. After three hours of struggling to get down the sheer cliff to where they thought they saw the shadow of the fuselage, she wished she'd braved putting on her wet bra and underwear. The rough wool fabric chafed, and since Maxim was leading the way, his hand often went up her coat to help her down. The descent was steep enough that she didn't complain about him touching her bare thighs—she wanted to feel secure during the climb—but she knew what he had to be seeing whenever he glanced up.

"This is humiliating," she grumbled.

"At least we're alive," he said.

"That's easy for you to say. I'm not staring at *your* ass every time I look up."

He laughed so freely it made him seem younger—and even handsomer, which was really something, since he was already one of the best-looking men she'd ever met. The media agreed; reporters often compared his charisma and appearance to John F. Kennedy, Jr.'s. Tall, dark and handsome, Maxim also came from money and was considered a real "catch."

"You don't have anything to say to that?" she asked

when it became apparent he wasn't planning to continue the conversation.

He studied their options for farther descent. "I'm not stupid."

"What's that supposed to mean?"

"It means nothing I say is going to help. I can't say I don't mind seeing your bare ass or you'll think I'm getting some sort of sexual gratification out of it. And I can't say I do mind without making you even more self-conscious."

"It leaves me with no dignity."

He maneuvered onto a rock outcropping a few feet lower in elevation and turned back for her. "You had too much of that to begin with." His hand went up her coat again, and he gripped her thigh while she secured her footing.

"How can anyone have too much dignity?" she asked once she'd reached the ledge he was on. It was so cold that their breath appeared in small, foggy puffs.

"You manage it quite well."

She tilted up her chin. "You think I'm too stiff?"

"Not stiff, exactly. Unapproachable."

"Some people would say that about you."

"Those people don't know me."

"I could say the same."

"That's because no one knows you."

"I have friends," she argued.

He peered below. "Friends or acquaintances?"

"Friends! Franklin Salazar is my friend. I just received his endorsement, didn't I?"

"Franklin isn't your friend. I wouldn't even call him an acquaintance. He just liked your, ah, assets. Tough for a guy to compete with that."

"You're saying I got his endorsement because of my *figure?*"

He climbed down farther. "I'd be more specific, but you might slap me."

"He endorsed me because he knows I'll fix the damage you've caused since taking over," she snapped.

"You're kidding, right? It's taken me this long to clean up the mess your husband made."

She'd been waiting for his help, but now she didn't move. "Don't you dare talk about Mark! He's not here to defend himself."

He sighed. "Fine. Mark was perfect. It's just the rest of us bastards who have flaws." He blew on his hands. "Are you coming or not?"

"No."

"What's the matter?"

"I need my bra." He had all their clothes rolled up and fastened with his tie, which he'd hung around his neck and tossed over his shoulder so he could carry them as a bundle. She wasn't sure why he'd bothered bringing them along. She expected to be rescued before they had the chance to dry out. "Give me my panties, too," she added as an afterthought.

Lines of impatience appeared on his forehead. "Will you quit worrying about things that aren't important? I'm not so impressed with what you've got that I can't forget about it, okay? Your clothes are soaked."

The "I'm not so impressed with what you've got" stung more than it should have. "You didn't have any complaints last night."

"It was *dark* last night. It didn't matter whether it was you or anyone else in that cave."

Surprised by the harshness of his response, Adelaide blinked at him.

He seemed to soften but didn't apologize. Dropping

to his knees, he found her bra and her lacy red Santa panties, her one concession to Christmas, and handed them to her.

She put them on while he retied the rest of their clothes. Her things were as wet as he'd said but she was already so cold and numb that she could barely tell the difference.

"Let's go." He stretched out an arm toward her, but she refused to lean on him any longer. He didn't owe her anything. Just because they were stranded together didn't mean they had to be friends.

Waving him away, she said, "Go ahead and see if you can find the plane. Or, better yet, find some help. I'll get there when I can."

He shook his head. "We should stay together."

"The blizzard's over. We'll be fine. Just tell them where they can find me if you reach them first."

"Adelaide—"

"Don't call me that," she said again. Every time he did she heard his voice from last night: *You're the most beautiful woman I've ever laid eyes on.* Even though she'd known it wasn't really Mark who'd whispered to her in the night, the use of her name had made those words personal. She'd believed they were spoken in sincerity. But that couldn't be true. Maxim didn't appreciate anything about her. The whole experience, every bit of it, had been staged for the benefit of survival.

"Well, regardless of what you prefer I call you, I'm not leaving you behind," he said. "So you have two choices. You can let me help you so we can travel faster—which is critical since the weather can change within minutes. Or you can climb down on your own and I'll wait a few yards ahead before continuing."

"Maybe I'll be the one waiting for you." Without giving him a chance to stop her, she started down from her side of the ledge.

It didn't turn out to be a good decision. All that white snow was blinding, and the canyon yawning so far beneath made her dizzy. But she felt for the safest toeholds she could find and kept moving. She didn't need Maxim Donahue; she didn't need anyone. Ever since her husband and parents had died, she'd learned how to soldier on alone.

"Adelaide, stop!" Maxim warned.

She ignored him, ignored everything except the tricky climb.

Staying where he was, he leaned over the ledge. "Look, if you want an apology, I'll apologize."

She wished he'd go down his own way and leave her the hell alone.

"I'm sorry, okay?" he called. "Will you hold still until I can reach you? You're scaring the shit out of me!"

That wasn't true, either. He only cared about himself. She would've told him so, except she was breathing too hard to speak. Clinging to the icy mountain took a lot of effort, more than she'd expected.

Spotting what appeared to be a fairly secure route, a path of bare rocks jutting out of the ice and snow, she paused for a moment to catch her breath. If she could get to the next plateau, she'd have a chance to rest and recover. Maybe she would prove that she was capable enough and Maxim would go on without her. Then she could sit and wait, or climb down at a more comfortable speed. Right now she felt the pressure to move quickly and efficiently, to show him she didn't need his help. But her fingers and toes were numb, and the wind kept whipping her hair into her eyes.

"Not that one! There's nowhere to go from there," he shouted.

She recoiled and glanced up to see him staring down at her with an intensity that told her he didn't think she'd make it.

"You're right…you—you might want to go the other way." She laughed as she clung to the mountain.

The wind howled through the canyon below. "You can do it," he said. "Just be careful. Those boots are too big for you."

She should've given them back. He was going to need them.

A dusting of snow fell on her as he moved. "One handhold at a time, okay?"

"I've got it," she breathed but she doubted he could hear. She was talking to herself. She had to make a small leap and hope she could reach the ledge. It was the only way to progress; she couldn't stay where she was. Her strength was running out.

Concentrate. Almost there… With a deep breath, she jumped.

She might've made it. Her fingers touched the edge of the rock, but before she could grab hold and pull herself up, a gust of wind made her coat balloon like an umbrella, throwing her off balance just enough that she grasped nothing but air.

MAXIM HAD NEVER FELT more helpless in his life. As Adelaide fell, she didn't scream. She didn't thrash around. She just slipped down the mountain and out of sight.

God, she even died with dignity.

He clenched his fists, hoping and waiting for some

sign that he was wrong, that she was still alive. But he heard nothing except the words he'd spoken earlier, rattling clumsily in his head: *I'm not so impressed with what you've got that I can't forget about it... It could've been anyone in that cave.*

Turning his face toward the rocks, he squeezed his eyes shut. He'd caused this. She'd given her heart and soul last night because she'd been pretending he was Mark, and he'd thrown them right back in her teeth. But only because he couldn't justify what he'd felt as easily as she could. He'd had to acknowledge who it was moaning in his ear, and the eagerness of his reaction made him wonder if he'd ever hated her as much as he wished.

Forcing back the terror that made him colder inside than out, he scrambled down to the place where she'd fallen.

It was a difficult climb, but once he'd traveled ten feet or so, he could see beyond the bank of snow that had hidden her from view. She hadn't fallen all the way to the bottom; she was lying on an outcropping of rocks.

But she wasn't moving. She looked small and pale, as white as the surrounding snow, especially with her dark coat torn open to reveal the smooth skin he'd touched last night.

He spotted red almost immediately. Was that her underwear? Or was it blood?

The thought that it might be blood created a hard lump in Maxim's stomach, a lump that got heavier the closer he came to her. She was scratched up; he could see that easily enough. But...he watched for movement, any hint of life—and saw her hand twitch.

She might be badly hurt, but she wasn't dead. The minute he reached her, she opened her pretty blue eyes and said, "Did you come...for your boots?"

CHAPTER SEVEN

ADELAIDE FELT LIKE an idiot for causing Maxim and herself so much additional trouble. She'd let sensitivity and pride urge her to act rash and now she had scraped knees and an abrasion on her stomach to show for her icy slide down the mountain. Worse than that, she'd hurt her leg and could only limp, which meant she had to rely on him even more.

He didn't complain. He didn't say much of anything. He was too determined to get them to where they were going. Every hundred yards or so, he'd leave her in a safe spot, scout out what he planned to do next, then come back for her. She argued with him several times, insisting he take his boots and go. He could move so much faster without her and send the rescuers back, she told him. But he refused.

She was glad he hadn't relented when they finally found the plane. Although the fire and the crash had done significant damage, it wasn't as bad as she'd assumed it would be. The tail had been sheared off, leaving a jagged hole that exposed part of the interior, the nose was smashed and the charred walls and upholstery smelled terrible.

But there was some good news. They could climb inside to avoid the worst of the wind. They had the comfort of knowing that if there was a working emergency beacon, they were now much closer to it. And they could take Mr. Cox home with them and make sure he received a proper burial.

Not that Adelaide wanted to spend much time in close proximity to his remains. Maxim must've felt the same because he pulled the frozen corpse out and moved it some distance away.

The absence of that morbid reminder of what had almost happened to them—what could still happen— filled Adelaide with relief. Until she saw Maxim return wearing the pilot's snow boots and carrying his parka.

"Take off that wet coat and put this one on instead," he said, tossing it to her.

She slid over so it wouldn't brush against her as it landed, drawing a frown from him.

"We have to be practical or we won't make it." The gruffness of his voice told her he wasn't any happier about appropriating Cox's clothes for his own use. She couldn't fault him for doing it, but neither could she follow his suggestion. The idea of borrowing from the dead made her ill.

"He'd want you to have it," Maxim said.

"Why would he?" she asked. "He didn't even know me."

"As a pilot, he was responsible for your safety. And it's not as if he'll miss it."

She shook her head. She knew she was being impractical, but she couldn't help it. Her hand recoiled every time she tried to reach out. "No."

He studied her but didn't insist. A moment later, he started rummaging around, gathering up items that might prove useful.

Because the plane had landed upside down, Adelaide sat on one of the overhead compartments and removed Maxim's rubber boots so she could warm her toes. Her leg throbbed from her fall and her stomach growled with hunger, but if anything else hurt, she couldn't feel it. She was too cold.

"We're in luck," he said. "There's a lot of stuff here that didn't burn."

She thought they could use a little *more* luck, like a helicopter hovering overhead, but there was nothing to gain by being negative. So she kept her mouth shut.

Maxim made a few other comments as he searched the various compartments that would still open; Adelaide sat there quietly.

Finally, he stood as tall as he could in the cramped hull and waited until he had her full attention. "What're you thinking about?"

She eyed the parka. *Mr. Cox lying in the snow without his coat.* "I'm thinking this is some Christmas."

"How were you planning to spend the holidays?"

Adelaide hadn't decided. Since Mark's death she generally volunteered at a homeless shelter on Christmas morning, to remind herself that she should be grateful for what she had. Then she went to her former in-laws' for dinner. But visiting the Fairfaxes wasn't the same without Mark. His older brother had remarried and had an obnoxious stepson who loved to bait her on political issues. Mark's mother's health was deteriorating, so she was getting cranky and inflexible and spent most of the dinner berating her stepgrandson. And Mark's father remained as uncommunicative as ever. These days, Adelaide felt like a stranger when she went there. Until she got stranded and couldn't see anybody even if she wanted to, she'd actually been thinking she might work as if it were any other day. She'd told herself she'd get more done without all the interruptions. "With Mark's family, I guess."

"You're still close?"

"It's only been two and a half years." *Only?* Those two and a half years had seemed like an eternity. But that response saved her from having to answer more directly. They'd never been close; they were simply all she had. "What about you?" she asked.

"My kids are expecting me to be home."

"Do you have dinner at your place?"

"Yeah." He surprised her with a disarming smile. "I'm hoping I've got a few more years before either of them marry and Christmas becomes a negotiation."

Adelaide could picture the domesticity of the scene— the roaring fire, the eggnog served in wineglasses, the laughter over dinner—and had to suppress a twinge of jealousy. The Donahues no longer had Chloe, which was heartbreaking. But they still had one another. "Who does the cooking?"

"I've hired someone to help."

"A woman?"

He glanced at her. "Yeah, a woman. Does it matter?"

She wasn't sure why it seemed important to clarify that. "I've just…had trouble finding the right person to help me with the same kind of thing," she said, but she didn't really need anyone to cook or clean. She wasn't home long enough to get her house dirtier than what the maid service could manage each Saturday. The dry cleaner handled most of the laundry. And it didn't make sense to hire a cook for one person who was gone most of the time and had a microwave available when she wasn't. She'd just thought it would be nice to have someone waiting for her at the end of the day.

She'd once interviewed a few applicants, but it seemed far too pathetic to pay for a warm smile, a "welcome home" and a TV companion. So she usually stayed at her office until she was too tired to do anything except listen to the news before bed.

"A friend recommended her to me," he explained.

"She doesn't mind working on Christmas?"

"Look what I found!" He held up a first-aid kit.

"That's great," she said, but she didn't see how a few bandages would make much difference to them. Either they'd be rescued before they froze to death—or they wouldn't.

He rooted around some more while she continued to ponder the woman who cooked his Christmas dinner.

"So...does she?" she asked when the conversation lapsed.

He was on his stomach, riffling through a compartment that was so smashed he couldn't get much out. "Does she what?"

"Mind working on Christmas Day."

"I guess not. She doesn't have to. It's her choice."

"Doesn't she have family of her own?"

"She's never been married."

Adelaide's feet were beginning to tingle and burn. They hurt—but she hoped the return of sensation was a good sign. "Does she eat with you, too?"

"Yeah. Then we exchange gifts and she goes to visit some distant relatives."

Adelaide drew her knees to her chest. There was something about this cook woman that bothered her, but she couldn't put her finger on why. "So you get her a gift?"

"Of course. Wouldn't you?" He groaned as he strained to pull out a blanket.

"How old is she?"

"Maybe if I had a hatchet…"

"How old is she?" Adelaide repeated.

"At least twenty-five."

"So she's not matronly Alice from *The Brady Bunch*." He laughed. "Definitely not."

Definitely not? "What'd you get her this year?"

"I'm not sure. I think my daughter picked out a nice purse."

"Nice" meant expensive, at least in Maxim Donahue's vocabulary. Adelaide had never seen him wear anything that wasn't the best money could buy. She wondered what this young housekeeper would think of receiving a Gucci or Dolce bag. "Sounds like she does a fine job."

He didn't answer. He'd found a box of matches and was trying to light one. "Damn, they're ruined."

No fire. No heat. No help.

Adelaide pressed the heels of her hands to her eyes and brought the conversation back to Christmas dinner. "What time do you usually eat?"

"Midafternoon. You?"

She ignored the question. "That means she stays with you most of the day."

He straightened as much as possible in the upside-down aisle of the shattered plane. "Why are you so interested in my housekeeper?"

Adelaide pulled her coat tighter. "It just seems…like an odd situation."

"It's not odd. She cooks and I pay her."

"And she spends most of her Christmas with you, even though she's only twenty-five!"

He angled his head to look at her through the crack between two suspended seats. "Okay, now I see where you're going. But don't get too excited, Candidate Fairfax. You'll have nothing to report to the press when we get back, because I'm not having an affair with the hired help."

"I'm not digging for dirt!"

"Then why would you care if my housekeeper is young, attractive and unmarried?"

Adelaide forgot about her prickling feet. "You didn't tell me she was attractive."

"Well, she is."

"*How* attractive?"

Victory lit his eyes. "My housekeeper, Rosa, is nearly three hundred pounds, at least fifty-five years old and stays with us because she's supposed to. She's live-in help. Except for the relatives I mentioned, the rest of her family remained in Chile when she immigrated— legally—thirty-five years ago."

Adelaide rocked back. "You set me up! What a jerk!"

A wicked grin curved his lips. "You knew it was me last night and you enjoyed it, anyway, didn't you?"

"I don't know what you're talking about," she grumbled.

"In the cave," he said. "I'm saying there were moments you enjoyed our lovemaking even knowing I wasn't Mark. You—"

"Stop it." She scowled. "You're deluded."

He lowered his voice. "Am I?"

"Of course." She met his eyes because she wanted him to believe her; she wanted to believe what she was saying, too. Crediting all that passion to fantasy made everything so much...simpler. But she was having too many flashbacks. His hands cupping her face with palms too large to be Mark's. His mouth on her breast, warming her just when she thought she'd never be warm again. The sounds he'd made, the words he'd whispered. It was all unique to him.

"Would it hurt so much to admit it?" he asked.

She didn't answer.

"I knew it was *you*," he added.

"But it could've been anyone, remember?"

An expression of chagrin wiped the subtly coaxing smile from his face. "Could've been, but wasn't."

"I thought we decided to forget about last night, pretend it never happened."

"Some of us are better at pretending than others," he muttered. He was trying to hang a blanket across the opening to keep out the snow and cold.

"Was there a lot of blood?" she asked as she watched him.

"I don't know what you're talking about."

"Mr. Cox."

The blanket he'd anchored on one end fell, forcing him to start over. "No."

"What killed him?"

He sighed but shifted to the other side. "A head injury, I think. I didn't want to look too closely."

She could understand that. He was wearing the man's boots. "Right."

"We have a total of four blankets. Well, three," he corrected, "if you don't include this one."

"That's better than none," she said, but she couldn't manage any enthusiasm. She had yet to hear the swoop of a helicopter, which meant the Civil Air Patrol or whoever was out there searching for them, probably wouldn't make it today. Temperatures were falling as it grew dark. And the wind was picking up.

Remembering the hopelessness they'd faced immediately following the crash, she shivered. In an hour or so they'd lose what little sunlight they had.

"What time is it?" she asked.

He checked his watch. "Almost four."

They'd been in subzero weather for nearly twenty-four hours. "How're your feet?"

"I don't know," he said with a shrug. "I can't feel them. What about yours?"

"They burn." She chafed them, hoping to relieve the pain. "Did you ever hear about that little boy, back in the eighties, who survived in these mountains for five days? He did it alone. Both his parents died on impact."

"I'd rather not remember that, thanks."

"He made it out. They found him."

"He lost his legs."

"He's now a successful businessman."

"So you were being optimistic in bringing it up?"

No, she was considering how she'd deal with something so traumatic, if she could deal with it. "Here, let me help—"

He lifted a hand. "Stay where you are and keep covered."

"But it's snowing again." Which would make the crash site that much harder to spot, even if rescuers could get a helicopter in the sky.

"Other than hunkering down in here, there's nothing we can do—at least not until morning." He finally managed to block most of the opening, which cut down on the wind. "We'll be okay," he said over his shoulder as he finished.

She nodded, but that wasn't enough for him. Squeezing through the narrow passage, he crouched in front of her and raised her chin so she had to meet his eyes. "We'll be okay…Adelaide." The way he said her name made it a challenge. He wanted to see if she'd object to his use of it, but she didn't. It still brought memories she'd rather forget, but he'd done too much for her; she had no right to complain about anything.

"Okay."

A day's beard growth—something she'd never seen on him before—covered his lower jaw, and his hair fell across his forehead in windblown tufts. She liked him this way. In a suit, he was too suave, too perfect, too…formidable. Or maybe it was just that she preferred a more rugged form of masculinity because she dealt with men in suits every day.

"Great."

"I— Let's take inventory, see what we have." She pulled out of his grasp.

He didn't immediately move. She could feel his gaze lingering on her but pretended not to, and he eventually turned to his cache. "We've got a sleeping bag, some wool blankets, a pair of snowshoes, two boxes of matches—which are no good because they got wet— half a dozen colored smoke bombs—which we can't light because we don't have matches—and rations."

"Rations?" Adelaide didn't think she'd ever been so hungry.

"Looks like military stuff."

"So it's freeze-dried?"

"Some of it." He opened a brown cardboard box the size of a large shoe box. "We've got bottled water, Cup-a-Soup, hot-chocolate mix, biscuits, cooked rice, granola bars, crackers and cheese, chewing gum, chicken pâté, orange-drink powder, a tin of tuna fish, fruit snacks, pork and beans and some condiments."

"That's a lot to fit in a box that size."

"They're not the largest portions I've ever seen." He slanted it so she could take a peek inside. "But we should have enough."

Maybe. That depended on how long they had to survive out here.

CHAPTER EIGHT

THEY'D EATEN THE PORK and beans for dinner and then drank some water, but now that the sun had gone down, they sat in the pitch-black, chewing gum and talking to keep their spirits up. Adelaide was across the aisle from him in the sleeping bag. He was wrapped in the blankets. But it was getting so incredibly cold he knew they'd soon have to huddle together. He would've suggested it already. They'd both be more comfortable if they gave in and made the most of what they had in each other. But he was afraid she'd assume he was using their situation as an excuse to touch her again, probably because he wanted to touch her again and shut out the desperation of their situation, the same way they had last night.

"Do you miss her?" It was Adelaide who broke the silence that had fallen since Maxim had said he didn't think this storm would be as bad as the last one. The rising wind seemed to contradict him, but he felt it was more important to remain positive than to acknowledge reality.

"Who?" His mind was on his girls and whether or not they'd been notified that he hadn't reached L.A. Megan and Callie were in school at San Diego State, but they'd be home next week, just in time for Christmas.

"Chloe," she said.

Her mention of his late wife drew him back to the conversation. "Why do you want to know?"

"I guess I'm wondering whether you're as impervious as you seem."

Impervious wasn't the right word. But this wasn't a subject he had any desire to discuss, so he tried to dodge it by answering her question with one of his own. "What do you think?"

"It's hard to tell. You don't reveal much emotion. Unless you're angry. I can always tell when you're angry."

He hadn't realized she watched him closely enough to be aware of his personal habits. He'd made an art out of pretending he didn't notice her. For the most part, he even tried to convince *himself* of that. What she called "anger" was actually frustration, because he felt envious of a man he didn't even respect.

"How can you tell?"

"There's a muscle in your jaw that tightens, and your eyes glitter with hate," she said.

Not hate—determination. She was wrong again. But at least he wasn't as transparent as he sometimes feared. "When have I been angry around you?"

"You're always angry when you're around me," she said with a laugh.

Apparently, she had no idea how hard he worked not to betray the fact that he was attracted to her. When they were in a room together, he had difficulty looking anywhere else. It was as if he could feel every breath she took, no matter how many people were crowded between them. It wasn't until she'd decided to run against him that he'd begun to dislike her. When she jumped into the race, he'd been almost as relieved as he'd been worried.

"I think you're mistaking preoccupation for anger." He tried to sound as indifferent as possible.

"Maybe."

He couldn't tell if she believed him or not.

"Are you going to answer my question?" she asked.

"About Chloe?"

"Yes."

"I miss her for the sake of my children." He hoped that would suffice. When it came to his late wife, his emotions were too confused to analyze. Her perpetually negative outlook had made him unhappy. But they'd had children before their marriage completely fell apart so he'd decided to stick it out in spite of her instability and neediness. And then she'd been diagnosed with cancer and somehow he'd felt responsible, as if wishing to be rid of her had made it come to pass. Trying to turn pity and compassion into love hadn't succeeded. He'd fallen short, been unable to do it, even for his children. Sometimes he still felt as though he wore a scarlet letter on his chest—a *C* for callous.

"You weren't in love with her."

"My decision to stay with her had nothing to do with my political aspirations, if that's what you're driving at."

"You stayed because of Megan and Callie?"

He doubted she'd believe him, but it was the truth. "Yes."

"That's how you made carrying on after her death look so easy."

Guilt washed over him. He hadn't been capable of mourning Chloe the way he'd wanted to, the way a husband should mourn the loss of his wife, especially one who'd died in such sad circumstances. He'd never even hinted that she was a burden. And yet he couldn't deny that there were moments when he recalled how much she'd changed after the birth of their second child, how difficult she'd become, and was glad to have her gone. She must have known he was merely tolerating her or she wouldn't have taken her own life.

What did that say about him?

"Just because we didn't share the same closeness you and Mark did doesn't mean it was easy to watch her suffer. When I learned what she was facing, I would've traded places with her if I could."

She didn't respond right away. When she spoke, she didn't question what he'd said, as he expected. She made an admission. "Mark and I were having problems when he died, too."

The frank honesty of those words surprised him. Did she know about Mark? Did she suspect? "What kind of problems?"

"I'm not sure exactly. He got so wrapped up in politics he grew almost…secretive." She gave an awkward laugh. "I was beginning to wonder if he was seeing another woman."

It wasn't another woman that'd taken Mark away, but Maxim had no plans to divulge what he knew, especially to Adelaide. He remained silent.

"I felt he was forgetting everything we'd promised each other, you know? Everything we'd once been to each other. We'd started off so strong, had so much fun together."

Being aware of the truth made it awkward to talk about Mark, but it didn't stop the jealousy that sprang up out of nowhere. "He was probably just busy, stressed," Maxim muttered. "You know how it is in politics."

"You think so?" she asked as if she valued his opinion. He knew what she wanted to hear. "Of course," he said but winced at the lie. Only a fool would cheat on a woman like Adelaide, but Mark had been a fool, and more.

As it grew noticeably colder, Maxim thought about getting in that sleeping bag with her. He wanted to keep her warm, but it felt as though they were the only two people on earth, and that made barriers of propriety hard to maintain. It was difficult to worry about tomorrow when he wasn't sure he'd make it through today.

He talked about the election, what the governor must think now that they'd gone missing, what they'd be doing if they'd stayed in Tahoe, what his girls were taking in school. He was trying to keep their minds off the cold, but it wasn't long before she interrupted.

"Are…are you g-going to stay over there all n-night?"

Her teeth were starting to chatter. He couldn't let her lose too much body heat before joining her in that bag, but he was afraid his body would give away the fact that the intimacy they'd shared before hadn't been *strictly* a matter of necessity. He'd wanted to make love to Adelaide Fairfax for a long time. He'd even dreamed about it on occasion—like after that chamber mixer they'd both attended in Roseville a couple of weeks ago.

"I'll come over in a minute," he said.

"Okay."

He waited for his arousal to disappear, but every time it did, the thought of joining her brought it back.

"Maxim?"

He was leaning forward, resting his head in his hands. "Yeah?"

"W-what about now?"

He knew that asking required her to sacrifice her pride. She'd rather pretend she didn't need him. For some reason, she tried not to need anybody.

Busy contemplating what to do, he didn't respond, which prompted her to ask, "Hey, are you still there?"

At the panic in her voice, he closed his eyes. "Of course I'm here," he said and took her hand. "I'm not going anywhere."

"Oh. Right." He expected her to let go, but she didn't. She wound her fingers through his. "But…you d-don't want to sh-share this bag with me?"

What the hell, he decided. Why worry about an erection? If he wasn't hard already, he would be the second he touched her.

"Sure." Silently cursing his unmistakable reaction to her, he felt his way over. With the dampness that seemed to permeate everything, their clothes hadn't had a chance to dry. He was still in his boxers and she was in her underwear, but he stripped off his coat and Cox's boots and climbed in. Then he used the blankets to cover the bag.

At first, Adelaide was timid about curling up against Maxim. They remained stiff, lying next to each other without speaking or moving. But as the minutes passed, she snuggled closer, eventually wrapping her arms around him. She could feel his erection pressing boldly against her abdomen—everything about Maxim Donahue was bold—but she didn't react to his arousal. And he kept his hands to himself, letting her take what she wanted from his body without asking for anything in return.

Adelaide tried to be appeased by that, but she quickly realized one-sided cuddling wasn't very satisfying. "Do you think you could act a little less…unwilling to be here?" she whispered.

He complied by shifting so she could lie on his shoulder, and she grew warm. She expected him to relax and drift off to sleep, but he didn't. His erection remained firm and ready, an ever-present reminder of what they'd shared last night. Soon she caught herself changing positions so she could feel the pressure of it.

"Adelaide?" He spoke her name gruffly.

"Yes?"

"Any chance you could hold still?"

"Sure," she said, embarrassed. But her embarrassment lasted only as long as her restraint. Reckless abandon seemed to be taking over. It started with a burning sensation low in her belly and was spreading through her veins, making her heart beat faster and faster, urging her to get on top of him....

"They'll be here in the morning." His voice sounded strangled, and she could feel the muscles in his arms and shoulders bunch as she straddled him.

"What if they're not?" she whispered, moving to make the contact even more erotic. She knew what he wanted, and she was willing to give it to him. Why was he so reluctant? It wouldn't be their first time....

"They will be," he insisted.

"This could be our last night on earth."

She thought he understood her point when his hands slid lower, curved possessively around her buttocks. But then he said, "I can't pretend to be Mark again. If I make love to you, it'll be because you want *me,* not him."

So that was the problem.

Suddenly, all the desire that'd been pounding through her drained away. Not because she expected Maxim to be someone he wasn't. She hadn't been thinking about Mark. She'd been eagerly exploring a body that was nothing like her late husband's. She'd forgotten all about him.

But that was exactly what was bothering her. She

couldn't believe it was possible to forget him so easily, especially with his worst enemy.

Sliding off Maxim, she turned away, trying to figure out how she could be so disloyal to the one man she'd promised to love forever.

CHAPTER NINE

HE'D DONE THE RIGHT thing, Maxim told himself. Their lovemaking would have no meaning if she was merely pretending again, and he wanted her too badly for a meaningless encounter. But that didn't stop the disappointment that rolled through him when she moved off him.

It's better this way. Why, he couldn't say from one second to the next, not with her rear pressed into his lap, which seemed to interfere with his thinking. But he tried to believe he'd made the ethical choice. The night would pass. They'd get home. And then he'd be glad he exercised some restraint.

Meanwhile the minutes dragged by like hours and he couldn't relax, couldn't sleep. He kept replaying those few moments after she'd asked him to hold her. She'd been so eager to touch him, so eager for him to touch her. She'd even climbed on top of him! Why had he forced her to reconsider?

Because he was trying to be fair. Because he'd wanted her to offer herself without any coaxing...

Closing his eyes, he struggled to shut out the appealing scent of her hair, but it filled his nostrils every time he drew a breath. Had she gone to sleep? He was pretty sure she had. She hadn't moved in a long time, ever since she'd turned her back to him.

Confident that she wouldn't know the difference, he allowed himself to curve more fully around her. He wanted to touch her breast but didn't go that far. He merely kissed her bare shoulder.

"I'm sorry," he murmured, but he wasn't sure why he was apologizing. For being unable to accept less than everything she had to give? For knowing that the man she loved with such devotion was a liar? For his outspoken criticism of Mark, which had put her on that plane in the first place?

Maybe he was apologizing for it all.

PALE TENDRILS OF LIGHT threaded their way through the windows of the Cessna's carcass. It was morning. It had been for some time, but Adelaide remained still. She didn't want to wake Maxim. She preferred to luxuriate in the secure feeling of his arm anchoring her to him and the memory of him kissing her shoulder last night.

I'm sorry. Why had he felt the need to apologize? He hadn't done anything more to her than she'd done to him. They'd both been slinging insults over the past several months. Besides, the race didn't seem to matter anymore.

So what had motivated those softly uttered words? They were so…uncharacteristic of him. He was tough, demanding, uncaring, ambitious—wasn't he?

Definitely. But if that was all he was, why would he care whether or not she pretended he was someone else? Was it pride?

She'd chosen to think so, until his apology had made her reevaluate. She hadn't been able to categorize it under any of the bad qualities she'd assigned to him. She was convinced he wouldn't have said what he had if he'd realized she was awake.

So who was Maxim Donahue? Was he really as bad as she believed him to be?

Moving carefully, she maneuvered herself to face him. He didn't wake; he just stirred, then drew her against him as if they were regular and familiar lovers.

She laid her ear on his chest and listened to his heartbeat, praying that the steady rhythm would soon be drowned out by the rotary blades of a rescue copter. But she was afraid rescuers wouldn't be able to spot them. Judging by the obscure quality of the light, the latest snowfall had nearly buried the plane. Was the emergency transmitter working? Was the storm over?

It was crucial that they get up and do everything possible to make their position more visible. But if rescuers arrived today, these might be the last few minutes she'd ever spend in such intimacy with Maxim Donahue.

She didn't want to trade them away too soon....

"You okay?" he asked.

Apparently, her movement had awakened him, after all.

She tilted her head back to see his face. The shadow on his cheeks had darkened with another day's beard, making him look less like the man she'd spent the past months disliking and more like the man she was coming to know in a whole new way. "We made it through another night," she said.

"I told you we would. How's your leg?"

It'd been sore since she injured it, but preparing the wrecked plane as a shelter hadn't required much effort from her. Although she was fine for now, she was pretty sure her injury would complain more loudly when they got out and starting digging. "I'll live. Well, maybe," she added with a laugh. "How'd you sleep?"

"I've had more restful nights. You ready to get up?"

She didn't answer. Instead, she held his face between her hands and stared into his eyes as she ran a thumb over his lips. "Did you mean it?" she breathed.

A certain wariness entered his expression. "Mean what?"

"That I'm the most beautiful woman you've ever laid eyes on?"

He said nothing.

"Or was that part of the act?"

He looked away. "What does it matter?"

"It matters."

When his gaze returned to hers, she no longer needed verbal confirmation. She could see it in his eyes. The always-in-control, forever-aloof Maxim Donahue had lifted the mask he normally wore to let her see the passion that simmered behind his cool exterior. And that sent an intoxicating flood of warmth and desire flowing through her.

Moving slowly, so he could stop her if he wanted, she pressed her lips to his.

They were warm and dry at first, but then they parted and his tongue met hers.

Someone moaned. She was almost positive it was her. But he moaned, too, the moment his hands found her breasts. He pulled off her bra so he could caress her, and she closed her eyes as his mouth left hers to trail small kisses down her throat.

MAXIM COULDN'T HEAR for the pounding of his heart. Until the crash, he hadn't been with a woman since Chloe—and their lovemaking had lost its luster years before she was diagnosed. He felt younger than he'd felt in a very long time, more excited than he could ever remember. Somehow, nothing seemed to matter except being with Adelaide.

"You feel…amazing," he murmured.

She was breathing too hard to answer; the rapid rise and fall of her chest told him that. But she wasn't unresponsive. Her hands clutched his hair, guiding his mouth to her breast, and he groaned again when he realized she tasted as good as she felt.

He shoved her panties to her knees so he could eventually move lower. But he wasn't quite ready for that. Lightly pinning her down, he explored more leisurely what he'd rushed through the night before.

"What is it you want?" he whispered when she began to writhe against him, gasping. "Tell me, Adelaide, and I'll give it to you."

"You know…what I want."

He was hoping to hear his name. "Tell me, or I'll stop." He held his hand still, as if he'd make good on the threat, and she took his mouth in a fierce kiss.

"I want you, okay? I want *you*," she said against his lips.

"Now?" he teased.

She gulped for breath. "Now!"

Somehow, in the tightness of that sleeping bag, he managed to get rid of his boxers. He had no idea when or where they went. The same was true of her panties. Then he and Adelaide were touching and tasting each other in a frenzy like he'd never experienced.

The next few minutes didn't last as long as he would've liked. They were too desperate for each other. But never in his life had he enjoyed five minutes more.

Adelaide didn't say what he'd been longing to hear, not even when he had her trembling on the brink of climax—but it wasn't much later that they heard the helicopter.

ADELAIDE SAT in the backseat of the chopper across from Maxim. She had a blanket wrapped around her and was staring out the window at the swirling snow. The pilot and his partner had said they'd found them just when they were about to turn back. Apparently, the ELT had gone off but had stopped working after only a few minutes, and the severity of the storm system hadn't allowed them to search more than three hours yesterday, two this morning. If the Cessna hadn't fallen into such a wide crevice, the helicopter wouldn't have had room to land or time to wait for them to climb down into the clearing. The rescuers hadn't even been able to recover Cox. It was too risky to go after him until the current storm had passed.

That news hadn't made Adelaide happy. She'd argued that they should take Cox to his family right now. But once it started to snow, she seemed to realize the helicopter pilot was right and let the subject go. The truth was, they were damn lucky—lucky to be alive, lucky to have gotten out when they did, lucky to be home in time for Christmas.

Maxim hoped his girls hadn't assumed the worst. He hated the thought of what they must have suffered, believing he was dead. They'd already lost their mother.

The wind tossed the helicopter like a cheap toy. Feeling airsick, Maxim glanced over to see how Adelaide was coping with the bumpy flight and noticed how tightly she clasped her hands in her lap. She didn't speak, didn't complain, but she was clearly nervous. After what they'd been through, he didn't blame her. He was anxious, too.

Briefly, he considered trying to comfort her by squeezing her arm but refrained. She wouldn't even look at him. Now that they'd been rescued, neither of them knew what to think of the time they'd spent together—or the physical intimacy between them. The fact that they hadn't used birth control seemed far more important now than it had before, however. Was Adelaide carrying his baby? Was she worried that she might be? What would they do if she was?

Closing his eyes to shut out the blinding white of the snow, which made him dizzy, he told himself there was no use worrying until he knew for sure, and tried to put it out of his mind.

"We'll be down in ten minutes," the pilot announced, speaking through the earphones he'd given each of them.

"Sounds good to me," Maxim responded and the guy in the passenger seat sent him a thumbs-up.

Adelaide didn't comment. But she thanked the pilot once they landed. She shook Maxim's hand and politely thanked him, too—as if they were still professional acquaintances. Then a paramedic helped her across the tarmac to an ambulance.

There was a second ambulance waiting for Maxim. Although he would've preferred to ride along with Adelaide, it made sense for him to have his own transportation. As opponents, they shouldn't share an ambulance or anything else.

They should never have been on that plane together.

But, except for what had happened to the pilot, Maxim couldn't bring himself to regret it.

CHAPTER TEN

HARVEY SILLINGER SLAPPED a file folder on Maxim's desk. "Now you've got to do it," he said, his eyes burning with exhilaration.

Maxim scowled at the intrusion. This was his first day back at work since the crash. He wasn't sure he was ready to deal with his campaign manager's intense personality. Christmas was in three days—his daughters would be arriving tomorrow. He'd wanted to spend a few quiet hours at campaign headquarters clearing off his desk before the new year. He'd thought he'd be able to do that when he walked in at eight and found Harvey so absorbed in a telephone conversation that he barely grunted hello. They'd already spoken several times since the rescue, had nothing pressing to discuss, and Harvey was the only one in the office. Maxim's other employees and volunteers were off for the holidays.

It should've been a low-key, catch-up morning, but nothing about his campaign manager was ever low-key. A longtime political veteran, Harvey lived to one-up his opponents. That was initially why Maxim had hired him. He'd wanted a heavy hitter and had planned to do all he could to retain his senate seat. Maybe he'd even wanted to prove something to Adelaide. But he was learning that Harvey had no sense of when he'd gone too far.

"What are you talking about?" Maxim asked.

Harvey motioned toward the file next to the mini Christmas tree some volunteer had placed on his desk. "I have the e-mails," he stated with obvious satisfaction.

Maxim could guess where this was going, but he'd already told his campaign manager that he didn't want to follow up on what they'd uncovered about Mark Fairfax. He was even more reluctant to hurt Adelaide now than he'd been before—for reasons he refused to disclose to Harvey and preferred not to think about himself. "Tell me this has nothing to do with Mark Fairfax."

"You're kidding, right?" Short and stocky but bursting with frenetic energy, Harvey leaned closer and lowered his voice. "I have correspondence here that proves Fairfax was having a very sordid affair when he died—" he paused for effect "—*with a male intern.*"

"Oh, God," Maxim muttered and dragged a hand over his face.

Harvey thumped the file, nearly knocking the Christmas tree to the floor. "Fairfax sent these messages to a boy of eighteen," he said as he caught it. "They're so explicit there's no way anyone can argue about what was going on." He chuckled. "Read them yourself. He had one hell of a dirty mind. It'll be a shock to everyone."

Especially Adelaide. "Why are you still at this?" Maxim asked, rising to his feet. "I told you I didn't want to know any more about Fairfax. We're running this campaign, *my* campaign, on the issues."

Harvey stiffened, glaring at him. "A political campaign is never about the issues. You know that. At least you did when I came on. It's a sales job, pure and simple. And I'm the best salesman in the business."

"Then sell—but forget Fairfax."

"You're saying personal integrity isn't an issue?"

"The man's dead!" Maxim said. "The only person this will hurt is the wife he left behind!"

"You mean the wife who's trying to take your job?" Harvey yelled. "Who just stole the Salazar endorsement? You hired me to win this campaign and now you're tying my hands? I don't get it! You're the one who came to me with the tip on Fairfax. You're the one who wanted me to see if there was anything to it."

Maxim had received a voice-mail message from an anonymous caller who'd accused Fairfax of a lot of things, including bribery and a vague charge of sexual misconduct. Maxim had been interested in finding out whether or not he'd taken bribe money from some of the developers in the state. He knew it would reveal why Mark had changed positions and thrown his support behind certain projects. But he'd never expected the crazy accusation of sexual misconduct to take them where it had. A homosexual affair with a boy of eighteen? "I wanted to prove he was corrupt, but—"

"But we found something even more damning!"

"More sensational isn't necessarily more damning."

"Everyone takes bribes these days. Not everyone plays hide the salami with teenage boys."

"Stop it." Maxim scowled, but Harvey wouldn't back off.

"He solicited sex from the young men who volunteered to work for him. That's big news, Maxim, and people need to know."

The "need to know" line warned Maxim that Harvey was out of control. "The man's dead," he reiterated. "No one needs to know anything about—" he gestured at the file "—*this*."

Harvey began to stalk around the room. "I can't believe it! I thought you were reluctant because you didn't want to be perceived as desperate, grasping at straws, lowering yourself by accusing a dead man."

Maxim had said all that and more, but keeping what Mark did a secret had always been about Adelaide, not the campaign.

"I thought you wanted me to pull back because we didn't have enough proof," Harvey went on. "So I get you proof, *unimpeachable* proof. This puts Fairfax and his widow right in our crosshairs. And you're not *happy* about it? What am I missing here?"

Maxim shoved the file away and managed to knock the Christmas tree off the desk himself. "No, I'm not happy. I want you to shred every last e-mail and wipe away whatever's on your computer. And don't you *dare* breathe a word of this to anyone." This time he leaned forward. "I mean it, Harvey."

Apparently realizing that he wouldn't relent, Harvey stopped pacing. "I'm only doing my job."

"Your job is to help me win."

"Without this, you'll lose. You're giving her every advantage!"

Maxim threw up his hands. "Then so be it!"

Shaking his head, Harvey kicked the miniature Christmas tree to the other side of the room. "I'm out of here. Why sully my reputation with a loss that we could easily avoid?"

Clenching his jaw in an attempt to control his temper, Maxim carefully modulated his voice. "Harvey, it's Christmastime. Don't you have family somewhere? Can't you just…take a few days off?"

Harvey propped his hands on his hips. "Do you think you might change your mind if I do?"

Maxim imagined Adelaide hearing about her late husband's gay affair and knew changing his mind was out of the question. "No."

"Then why bother?"

"We might be able to strategize other ways to succeed."

"No. I don't pull punches, even if my opponent is a woman. I'm not that sexist," he said with a sneer. "And I can't stay if you won't use the advantage I'm giving you."

Maxim shoved a hand through his hair. Harvey was giving him an ultimatum? "Innocent people will be hurt, Harvey."

"The blame for that lies with Fairfax, not me." He reached for the file he'd dropped on Maxim's desk but Maxim snatched it up before he could touch it.

"No way are you taking this."

With a curse, Harvey turned on his heel and marched out.

"You'd better keep what you've found on Fairfax to yourself," Maxim called after him, but Harvey made no commitment one way or the other. He collected his briefcase and slammed his office door as he left.

Maxim sank into his chair. Would he read about Mark Fairfax and the intern in the paper tomorrow? Harvey had to have some way—favorable to himself, of course—of explaining why he was no longer heading up the Donahue campaign.

So where did that leave Adelaide?

ADELAIDE SPENT MONDAY morning shopping, which was what she'd done during the weekend, too. She was filling Sub-for-Santa orders for a local charity. She still had some difficulty getting around on her injured leg, but at least it was merely bruised and not broken. Shopping gave her something to do. After being stranded in the mountains with Maxim, she didn't feel like going right back to work. She'd decided to take two weeks to focus on the holidays, to allow her mind a rest from the campaign and the confusion she felt now that she knew Maxim better. Before the crash, winning that senate seat had meant everything to her. It'd given her a reason to go on. Now she wasn't even sure she wanted to stay in the race. But with so many people counting on her, she couldn't withdraw and lay off all her employees, especially at Christmas. Besides, she didn't know what she'd do with herself if she didn't spend the next months campaigning. She'd already bowed out of her solar business, put Rhonda Cummings, who'd worked with her for years, in charge, and Rhonda was doing a fine job.

Maybe she'd continue—but at a less frantic pace. If she didn't win the primary in June, she wouldn't be disappointed. She actually preferred Maxim to win. Now that she knew him and liked him, it was easier to forgive the comments he'd made about Mark's lackluster performance. He'd misjudged Mark. He didn't know him that well.

So would she go back to the solar business? That seemed the logical choice, but the idea didn't excite her and certainly wouldn't make Rhonda happy.

Maybe it was time to do some traveling. She'd always wanted to see Europe, Australia, Alaska. She'd pictured Mark at her side, but maybe Ruby, her former neighbor and closest friend, would want to go.

No, Ruby had just opened a dress boutique downtown. She couldn't leave it.

Once again, Adelaide seemed to find herself in no-man's-land....

Her cell phone rang as she was standing in line to buy a video game system. Setting her bags on the floor so she could reach her purse, she fished out her phone and checked caller ID.

She didn't recognize the number but answered, anyway. "Hello?"

"Adelaide?"

Maxim. She would've known his voice anywhere. "Yes?"

"How are you?"

"Better. You?" She tightened her grip on the phone. Crazy as it was, she'd missed him. He hadn't contacted her since they'd been home.

"I'm okay, I guess. Listen, do you have plans for tonight?"

She might've thought he was asking her out. She'd been yearning to hear from him. But the reluctance in his voice made her leery of assuming too much. She sensed that he didn't want to be making this call. "Is this where you try to convince me to drop out of the race?" she teased.

The question seemed to take him by surprise, as if it hadn't occurred to him. "Are you open to that?"

"Probably not."

He sighed. "Too bad."

"So this isn't about the primary."

"No."

Then he was worrying that she might be pregnant. She'd bought an over-the-counter test that boasted almost immediate detection, but she hadn't been able to bring herself to use it. It was more comfortable to live in denial, at least until she'd adjusted to the possibility.

But maybe there was a reason he needed to know now. Maybe he was going to ask the tall blonde he sometimes brought to political events to marry him....

Adelaide cringed at the jealousy that thought evoked. The fantasies she'd had of Maxim during the week she'd been home told her she'd developed a crush on him, but she trusted it wasn't more than that. "I'm free. Where would you like to meet?"

"Would you mind if I came over after dinner?"

After dinner. He wasn't trying to parlay this into any type of date. She interpreted that to mean he regretted what had happened between them and hoped she wasn't pregnant.

She felt her shoulders slump. "No. I-I wouldn't mind." They had to face reality sometime, didn't they?

There was a brief pause. "Will we be able to speak privately?"

How would he react if she was pregnant? *Let's wait until we're sure we have something to worry about before we start making difficult decisions* gave her no indication. He knew she'd want to keep the baby; she'd already told him as much. Would he pressure her to get an abortion instead?

She swallowed hard. "We'll be alone."

"Great. I'll see you tonight."

He was gone without a goodbye.

"It's your turn," someone said, nudging her from behind. She was holding up the line.

Gathering her sacks, she paid for the game system and headed down the center of the mall and out to her car. Her leg was aching too much to do any more walking— and she'd lost interest in shopping. She had to take that pregnancy test. It wasn't fair to keep Maxim in suspense if he needed to know, and she could use the intervening hours to cope, whatever the results.

If she wasn't pregnant, she'd put the plane crash behind her. And if she was, there'd be no forgetting the crash because it would change her entire future.

CHAPTER ELEVEN

ADELAIDE STARED at the unopened pregnancy test she'd just put on her bathroom counter. She'd actually bought three more on her way home. They were sitting in the sack at her feet, held in reserve to ensure an accurate reading. Over the past week, she might've gone through the motions of getting ready for Christmas, but the possibility of a baby had been constantly at the back of her mind. Although she'd dreamed of becoming a mother, she'd put that hope out of her life when she'd learned Mark was infertile. She'd asked him, over and over again, if they could eventually adopt, but he'd been opposed to it. He'd said there was too much risk involved, that they had a good life and he didn't want to spoil it.

She'd talked him into it in the end, but she'd gotten the feeling he'd only relented to placate her, to ease some of the tension that'd crept into their marriage. And by then it was too late. A month later she was attending his funeral.

Oddly, she didn't feel the gut-wrenching loss that normally accompanied any thought of her late husband. Did that mean she was learning to live without him? Or was it the hope of having a child that buoyed her spirits?

If she was pregnant, it would be more than a little ironic that it had happened with Maxim....

"Get this over with," she said aloud.

The face that looked back at her from the mirror was flushed with excitement, even fear. But it wasn't until she reached for the box that she knew for sure which way she wanted the test to go.

"Please, God, let me be pregnant," she murmured. At forty-one, she didn't think she'd have many more chances.

MAXIM HATED THE THOUGHT of what he had to do, but he didn't see any alternative. He had no doubt that Harvey was going public. There wasn't any way to stop him. He wouldn't have as much to gain but, for Harvey, the notoriety of destroying Fairfax's reputation and ruining Adelaide's chances to win the primary would be enough. He'd see it as an opportunity to build his own reputation as unrelenting and successful at all costs. Maxim had to tell Adelaide before she found out from the media.

But…how?

He had no idea. She'd blame him, and she had every right to. If he hadn't passed that anonymous tip on to his campaign manager, Harvey would be as much in the dark as the rest of the world.

He'd thought about the situation all day, but he still didn't feel prepared as he drove to her house, which was located in Carmichael, along the American River.

Adelaide owned a big rambler with a sizeable yard and a gorgeous view. Although it was in a neighborhood of other expensive homes, the mature landscaping gave the property a sense of seclusion. He knew because he'd been there before. When Mark was alive, he and Adelaide had hosted a political fundraiser.

Now that he stood on the doorstep next to a huge poinsettia, staring at a Christmas wreath, Maxim found it difficult to make himself knock. But he knew he had no choice.

She answered wearing a snug-fitting pair of jeans, furlined boots and a classic beige sweater. Her blue eyes seemed even bigger with her hair pulled back.

Seeing her again reminded him how attractive she was, but he'd only forgotten it in the anxiety of the past few hours. Before that, before talking to Harvey this morning, he'd pictured her almost every time he closed his eyes. It'd been all he could do not to call her.

"Hey." He gave her a smile he didn't feel.

"Hi." Opening the door wider, she let him in.

The inside of Adelaide's house hadn't changed. As soon as he stepped over the threshold, Maxim wished he'd picked a different place to meet. He could remember speaking to Mark in this very room, could see their wedding picture hanging on the wall.

He hated how much Adelaide idolized her late husband. He knew it would make the next few minutes all the more painful.

He hated it for other reasons, too....

"Can I get you a drink?" she asked.

"No, thanks." He couldn't pretend this was a social visit. Always a believer in doing the hard things first, he planned to jump right in, but she spoke before he could begin.

"Is this about the blonde you sometimes bring to political events?" she asked.

The blonde? He thought back, trying to figure out who she meant. Then he remembered. She must be talking about Liz, a woman he'd met at the gym. They'd dated occasionally, before Liz had gotten engaged to her personal trainer. But it had never been serious. She wasn't nearly as intelligent, capable or attractive as Adelaide. He'd known that from the beginning, had always been more attracted to the woman across the room than the one on his arm. "No."

She seemed to relax a little, which surprised him. She'd been worried about Liz?

"Oh. Well…" She motioned to the nearby sofa. "At least sit down."

Because she'd very likely be throwing him out in the next few seconds, he decided to remain standing. He wished he could touch her, maybe take her in his arms as he broke the news. But that would only make what he was about to say worse.

"That's okay," he said. "Listen, I'm sorry to bother you so close to Christmas. You probably have a million things to do, but…"

For some reason, he couldn't get the words past his lips. He didn't want her to hear that her husband had cheated on her with another woman, let alone a man. No, a *boy*.

His mind raced, trying to find some other way to break the news, but she interrupted him by touching his arm.

"Does this have anything to do with the fact that…that we didn't use any birth control when…well, you know."

He froze. What was she talking about? He'd assumed she would've done a pregnancy test by now and that he would've heard if their time together had resulted in a pregnancy. There'd been no communication between them in over a week. "I thought—I mean, you're not, are you?"

Her chest rose. "Actually—" she offered him a smile so hopeful it made him catch his breath "—I am."

Maxim felt as if someone had just punched him in the gut. "What'd you say?"

Concern and insecurity entered her eyes, eyes that were normally clear and decisive. "Are you sure you don't want to sit down?"

"No. You're pregnant. Isn't that what you just told me?"

She seemed close to tears, but didn't cry. She nodded.

Unsure how to respond, he considered what he'd come to say and knew he couldn't tell her now. He was going to have a baby with this woman. And, oddly enough, he wasn't as unhappy about it as he'd told himself he'd be. A baby gave him hope that, even with everything working against them, they might be able to create a relationship. He wanted that, wanted *her.* He just wanted her to love him in return—with all the passion she'd felt for Mark—and wasn't sure that was possible.

The silence stretched out as he weighed his options.

"Are you terribly upset?" she asked.

She was watching him intently. If he cared about her as much as he was beginning to believe, the way he handled the next few minutes would be very important. "No, I'm not upset."

Her smile grew more genuine. "Really?"

"Really." But he wasn't even remotely willing to let her claim the baby was Mark's. Would she try to insist? "What would you like to do about it?" he asked.

"I want to keep the baby."

"I realize that." He was wondering what she wanted to do about *him.* "Where do I come into the picture?"

He watched her throat work as she swallowed. "I don't want you to—to feel forced or…or trapped. I understand that this occurred because of…extenuating circumstances. If you'd prefer not to be part of the child's life, I'll handle it on my own. I don't need any help." One of her hands moved to cover her abdomen, an instinctively protective gesture.

That didn't reveal how she felt about him. But the fact that she wanted this baby, *his* baby, made him inexplicably happy, although he couldn't imagine why. He wasn't a young man anymore; he'd turn forty-four in April. He'd thought he was beyond all this. And yet…it felt like a second chance—for both of them. "There's no way I'd ever support you telling anyone that my baby is Mark's," he said.

"We could say I was artificially inseminated and I don't know who the father is. That would provide the most protection for your career—no breaking news story that you impregnated the enemy." She laughed but it didn't sound as indifferent as she'd probably meant it to.

"Do you really think I'm that shallow?" he asked.

She didn't respond.

"We're talking about a baby, Adelaide. *Our* baby. My career doesn't come before that."

"That's how you feel?"

Could this really be happening? With Adelaide? "That's how I feel."

"So what do you propose, er, suggest?" she asked.

He stepped closer to see if she'd back off, but she didn't. "I suggest we keep our options open."

Her eyes drifted shut as he ran a finger over the contours of one cheek. "What kind of options are we talking about?" she breathed. "Dating?"

Maxim's pulse began to speed up. He'd never expected this, not from Adelaide, but she seemed…interested in his touch. Even here in the relative warmth of the valley with no snow or danger around them. Even in the house she'd shared with Mark. "Lovers, at least," he said.

Her eyes opened. "What about marriage?"

He pulled her against him. "I'd want that to be a possibility. What about you?"

"It could definitely be a possibility," she murmured.

"Good." Now was when he should tell her. But she was so open to him. For the first time since he'd met her, the remote Adelaide Fairfax was willing to trust him and accept him—as the father of her baby, maybe more.

"I missed you this past week," he admitted.

"I missed you, too," she replied and stood on tiptoe to kiss him.

Tell her! his mind raged. But she felt so good in his arms, he couldn't. Instead of letting go, instead of breaking the bad news, he deepened the kiss.

"I'm glad you're not upset about the baby," she whispered against his lips.

He wasn't upset as long as she wanted *him,* too. He knew she wouldn't once she learned what he was responsible for digging up about Mark. But somehow he'd stop her from finding out. He'd get hold of Harvey, do whatever he had to in order to prevent it from going public—even if it meant paying the bastard off. The longer he kissed Adelaide, the more convinced he became that he'd do anything to keep her.

"Make love to me," she whispered.

A flicker of guilt made him hesitate. That was a line he shouldn't cross. Not until he'd contacted Harvey and made some sort of arrangement, not until he could feel reasonably secure that she wouldn't be devastated tomorrow.

"I'd like to, but—" he searched for an acceptable excuse "—I'll come back. I've got some things to do."

She guided his hand to her breast. "Are you sure it can't wait?"

Suddenly he couldn't think of *anything* important enough to keep them apart. He'd fix the situation so she wouldn't be hurt, which meant he could stay and make love to her as many times as she wanted him to.

"I guess I can do it later." He could still see Mark watching them from that damn portrait so he swept her into his arms and carried her into one of the guest rooms. No way would he make love to her in Mark's bed.

As their clothes came off, he stared down at her and realized that she was exactly the woman he wanted—the woman he'd wanted for years.

"At last," he said and smiled when she responded so greedily to his touch.

CHAPTER TWELVE

MAXIM WATCHED ADELAIDE in those first minutes after he awoke. He wanted to have breakfast, spend the entire day with her, but he had to talk to Harvey as soon as possible.

"Hey," she whispered sleepily when he kissed her neck.

"I've gotta go," he told her.

"So soon?"

He laughed at the reluctance in her voice. He'd stayed far too long already and was afraid he'd be too late to stop Harvey. "Yeah, but I'll see you later." He got out of bed, then hesitated. His girls were coming home today, which meant he'd be tied up with them. "Actually, Megan and Callie are flying in for Christmas, so…"

"So you need to spend some time with them. Of course." She stretched as she turned to face him. "Have fun."

He wondered what his two daughters would think of Adelaide, but couldn't imagine that they wouldn't like her. He was eager to introduce them, to include her in his family. Would they be willing to accept her? "Any chance you can join us for dinner tomorrow night?" he asked.

"Isn't tomorrow Christmas Eve?"

"Yeah."

She propped herself up on the pillows. "Are you sure that's a good idea?"

"Positive." He wasn't as confident as he sounded. He'd dated since Chloe but not a lot, and he'd never brought a woman home to meet his children. But…he was hopeful they'd be open-minded.

"Okay."

"But just so you know, the baby's a secret. For a while."

"Of course. There's no hurry to tell anyone. I won't even start to show for three or four months." Her eyebrows drew together as she sobered. "But…are you really ready for another woman in your life, Maxim? Are they?"

He smoothed the hair out of her face. "We're all ready, as long as it's you."

She gave him a sexy smile. "I'll be there."

"I'm glad." He bent to kiss her again. "Maybe they'll go to bed early, and we can see if Santa has a little something for you."

Laughing, she fought to avoid him as he chafed her neck with his unshaved chin. "Go home," she complained. "I need sleep. You wore me out last night."

"Call me when you get up," he said and left.

He tried to reach Harvey as soon as he walked out of Adelaide's house, but Harvey wasn't answering. Maxim called him several times before he left for the airport at noon and tried again while he was on his way home with the girls. He knew he couldn't talk freely with them in the car, but he could set up a meeting.

"Shit!" he muttered after his sixth failed attempt.

"What's wrong, Dad?" Callie asked.

Frowning, he hit the off button on his Bluetooth. He hadn't meant to curse aloud. "Nothing." With a smile on his face to cover his growing unease, he encouraged them to talk about their classes, their grades, their friends and the boys they were dating. It wasn't until they got home and Megan and Callie went to unpack that he had a few minutes alone. He used the time to call Harvey again.

Harvey's voice mail picked up. "Harvey, get in touch with me, damn it," Maxim said. "I have a proposal for you. I think it's something you'll want to hear." He started to hang up but brought the phone back to his ear. "I don't care what time of day or night it is," he added, then disconnected.

"Dad?"

Maxim glanced up to find Megan standing on the stairs. With her auburn hair and greenish eyes, she looked like her mother, but Callie, his younger daughter, resembled him. It made him wonder who his new baby would look like—him or the fair-skinned Adelaide? "What?"

"Where's the wrapping paper?"

"I don't know. Did you check with Rosa?" His live-in housekeeper was in the kitchen, cooking one of the girls' favorite meals.

"She thinks we're out." She gave him the smile that told him he was about to do her a favor. "Any chance you'll go get some more? Or maybe a few gift bags? I'd do it myself, but I'm dying to take a shower and Megan's busy primping. She said Ryan's coming by to see her."

"I thought she told me she and Ryan hardly talk anymore," he said.

"I guess they talk enough that she's already told him she's home."

Maxim liked Ryan and didn't want to miss seeing him. But someone had to get the wrapping paper. And maybe Harvey would call while he had some time alone. "Sure," he said. "Be right back."

ON THE DAY BEFORE Christmas the weather dropped to forty-three degrees, bitter cold by Sacramento standards, but the extra chill didn't bother Adelaide. She spent the morning warm and snug in her house, visiting parenting sites on the Internet. She couldn't believe she was pregnant. Just when she'd been feeling most alone, just when she'd given up the hope of ever having a family, she was expecting.

It was almost too good to be true. But a baby meant she had so many decisions to make. Since their crash in the Sierras, her enthusiasm for winning the nomination and then a seat in the state senate had begun to wane; now it was entirely gone. She wondered if she could keep the people who worked for her on the payroll and have them campaign for Maxim instead.

Maxim... He hadn't liked Mark and he didn't pretend otherwise; that wasn't easy to accept. They'd have to discuss it eventually. But for two people beginning a new relationship, they were dealing with enough challenges. They had the baby coming, the public response to what they'd done, the surprise and possible resistance of Maxim's children. Best to adjust a little at a time.

Imagining what would happen when word of her condition reached the media, Adelaide cringed. It would be embarrassing. There was no escaping that. But she doubted it would hurt Maxim's career—especially if she threw her support behind him.

Propping her chin on one hand, she smiled dreamily as she remembered the way he'd reacted to news of the baby. Her life was heading down a path she would've considered impossible just ten days earlier, but the baby she was carrying changed everything.

Would they eventually marry? It wasn't as if she couldn't love Maxim. She was afraid she already did.

Who would've thought—

The ringing of the phone startled her out of her reverie. Reaching for the cordless handset on her desk, she saw M. Donahue on caller ID and smiled as she answered. "Hello?"

"Hey, gorgeous. I've got good news."

"What is it?"

"They were able to recover Mr. Cox's body yesterday. He'll be home for Christmas."

Adelaide wished Cox had made it out alive, but it was a relief to know his family would at least be able to say their goodbyes and lay him to rest. "How'd you find out?"

"The helicopter pilot called me."

"Why didn't he call me? I left him several messages."

"It was only by chance that he returned my calls first. I told him I'd notify you."

"Oh. Do you know when the funeral is?"

"He's originally from Bakersfield, so they're taking his body there and having a small, private ceremony next Monday."

"I'd like to attend, but if it's meant to be private, maybe I should just send my condolences to his family."

"That's what I plan to do. I can give you the address. Are you still coming tonight?"

Forcing aside the sadness she felt about Mr. Cox, she leaned her head against the back of her seat. They hadn't seen each other since he'd left her house yesterday morning. He'd been with his daughters since then, but he'd called several times. "If you still want me there," she said.

"I do. I want to celebrate Christmas with you. And I want you to meet Megan and Callie."

She'd met his children before. She and Maxim had run in the same circles for so long she'd even met his parents. But only in formal situations. Not in this capacity—not as the woman pregnant with his child. "Are you sure they wouldn't rather have you all to themselves? I don't want to intrude…."

"Megan's got an old boyfriend coming over. And Callie has two girlfriends joining us. You won't be intruding. Besides, I've told them to expect you."

"How did you explain our connection?"

"I said we got to know each other while we were stranded, and now we're friends."

"Were they surprised?"

"Of course. But they got over it quickly. Megan even said she thinks you're one of the prettiest women she's ever seen. She said I should've asked you out a long time ago, before you could get it in your mind to run against me."

She laughed. "Already a strategist."

"I wish I'd thought of that."

Closing her eyes, she pictured them all gathered around the Christmas tree. She'd imagined this scene once before, as an outsider looking in. Now she'd be part of it. Until this moment, she'd been afraid that tonight might not work out. She felt self-conscious about barging in on a family's celebration. She felt as if she'd been doing that for years—all the time she was growing up in the system after her parents had died in a house fire. "What should I bring?"

"You don't need to bring anything."

"What if I want to?" she insisted. "What would your girls enjoy?"

"Like most kids, they have a sweet tooth. You could bring a dessert, I guess."

Suddenly, it felt more like Christmas than any Christmas Adelaide had ever experienced. "I'm looking forward to it," she said and got off the phone so she could go to the grocery store. For the first time since Mark died, she felt like cooking.

MAXIM SAT IN HIS living room alone. The area in front of the Christmas tree was now crowded with the gifts his daughters had wrapped. Megan and Callie were in the kitchen, laughing and talking with friends, their voices occasionally rising above the Christmas music playing throughout the house. He planned to go back in and join them. He needed to help Rosa finish cleaning up the brunch he'd made, but…something was bothering him, and he was pretty sure he knew what it was.

He'd gotten hold of Harvey Sillinger last night and been assured in no uncertain terms that there was nothing to worry about concerning Mark Fairfax. But Maxim couldn't put it out of his mind. Harvey's insistence that Maxim should've known him better than to assume the worst set off warning bells in Maxim's head. That statement was so off base it was almost absurd. He'd seen Harvey in action, knew he was ruthless. Usually, Harvey was proud of that trait. So why would he pretend to care about those he might hurt? And why would he suddenly be so amenable to keeping his mouth shut? Harvey hadn't been willing to commit himself to silence the day he'd stormed out of the office.

Something had changed in the past two days….

Rubbing his temples, Maxim went over the conversation they'd had last night.

"I can't believe you think I'd leak information you told me not to, Maxim," he'd said, defensive from the first moment Maxim had managed to reach him. "So what if we haven't known each other long? I did a good job while I was running your campaign. Anyone else would've been thrilled with what I accomplished."

This wasn't about what he'd accomplished, and Maxim had told him as much. Harvey was very dedicated. It was his tendency to forget who was boss that disturbed Maxim—that and the fact that he didn't seem to understand the meaning of the word *mercy.*

"I would've expected you to know me better than that," Harvey had gone on.

"I just want to be sure, Harvey. That's all," Maxim had said. "I just want to be sure."

"What happened to you while you were stranded in the mountains? That's what I want to know, because you certainly haven't been the same since you got back. You don't act like you even care whether you win the primary."

He cared. He loved his job and wanted to keep it, but he wouldn't do it by hurting Adelaide. "I nearly died, Harvey. Coming that close can give you a whole new perspective."

"From *my* perspective, you're losing your edge. But that's none of my business. You have nothing to worry about. Nothing from *me,* anyway."

The clarification had brought a stab of alarm. "What's that supposed to mean? You and I are the only ones who know about the intern, right?"

"Me, you and the intern," Harvey had said.

"The boy wouldn't have any reason to come forward. Why would he risk the embarrassment?"

"He probably wouldn't. So, like I said, you have nothing to worry about."

Sensing an undercurrent in the conversation, Maxim had decided to take that final step, to do all he could to guarantee that this situation wouldn't get away from him. "Is there any way to—" here, Maxim had chosen his words very carefully "—ensure your cooperation on this, Harvey?"

"What do you mean by that, Maxim? I'm an honest guy. I don't take payoffs."

"I'm not talking about a payoff. I'm talking about a *severance* package. To help you along until you find other employment."

"Oh, a *severance* package." After that, there'd been a long pause. "That might be just the thing," he'd said at length. "Especially if you can get it to me tonight."

"If that's how you want it," Maxim had said, and he'd met his former campaign manager at the office.

"This effectively ends our association, correct?" he'd said when he handed Harvey a thirty-thousand-dollar check.

"Sounds fair to me."

Just to be safe, Maxim had asked him to sign a paper saying he was satisfied with the terms of their separation, a paper he'd then locked inside his desk. Harvey had left immediately afterward, and Maxim hadn't heard from him since. As far as he knew, the issue was settled.

Then why did he feel so…*un*settled about it?

"Dad?" Megan called.

He dropped the hand he'd been using to massage his temple. "Yes?"

"Where are you? I want to show you the commercial I had to make for one of my classes."

Drawing a deep breath, he put his conversation with

Harvey out of his mind. It was Christmas, and Adelaide was coming over. He had better things to think about than Mark's affair—and his own hand in discovering it.

"Coming," he called and went to the kitchen.

CHAPTER THIRTEEN

SHE WAS READY and, if she hurried, she'd be on time.

Grabbing the cheesecake she'd made, as well as the wine she'd bought, Adelaide headed for the door. She'd never been to Maxim's place, but she doubted she'd have any trouble finding it. She had GPS on her phone if she got lost. But just as she was stepping out of her house, she saw her friend Ruby pull into the driveway, going far too fast. She came to a screeching halt, and the Escalade jerked back and forth as she slammed the gearshift into Park and jumped out.

Something was wrong. They'd already exchanged gifts over the weekend and hadn't planned to see each other again until after Christmas. Ruby had said she'd be celebrating with her kids and her ex-husband, with whom she was thinking of reconciling. So…what was she doing here?

Adelaide waited on her doorstep as Ruby rushed toward her.

"Adelaide, oh, my God! I'm so sorry."

Sorry? Adelaide didn't know how to react. "For what?"

Confusion descended on Ruby's face and her steps slowed. "You mean…you don't know? It was just on the news. I heard it with my own ears."

The cheesecake and the wine were getting heavy, but Adelaide didn't dare move. "You're not making any sense."

Tears filled Ruby's eyes as she took the wine. Then they stood facing each other, both dressed in their Christmas finery, with Adelaide's heart beating like a jackhammer.

"It's about Mark," Ruby said.

Adelaide couldn't imagine what could be so terrible that Ruby would race over in such a panic. Mark was dead. She'd been dealing with that for two and a half years. Did news get any worse than goodbye *forever?* "What about him?" she asked.

Ruby motioned them inside. "I think you should sit down."

"I don't want to sit down," she said. "I have a dinner date, and I'm going to be—"

"He was having an affair, Adelaide, just as you suspected," Ruby cut in.

This stole Adelaide's breath. After so long, after finally convincing herself that she'd been acting crazy and paranoid and insecure when she'd accused Mark, she was learning that she'd been right from the beginning? "No…"

"Yes."

"With whom?"

"Let's go in," Ruby said and guided Adelaide back into the house.

Adelaide sat at the kitchen table while Ruby took the cheesecake and stowed it in the fridge, along with the wine. "I can't believe something like this would be on the *news,*" she muttered. "I mean, I could see it if he was still in office, but—"

"It's pertinent," Ruby said. "You're essentially running in his place and on his reputation. So anything that blackens his name blackens yours."

"But…an *affair?* A lot of guys have extramarital affairs and it hasn't ruined their political careers."

Ruby frowned. "There's more to it."

"More?"

"Mark also took bribes from local developers."

"You've got to be kidding me!"

Ruby crouched in front of her. "I would never kid about something like this."

Adelaide stared at her helplessly. "He couldn't have. I mean…I would've known, wouldn't I?" She tried to think back. They'd always been well-off. Mark came from money, and she'd built the fledgling business they'd started when they got married into a multimillion-dollar enterprise. Would she have noticed if he had more money in his accounts than he should have? Probably not.

"I don't know," Ruby said, obviously miserable.

He wouldn't have needed the money. But the power might have tempted him. He would've liked doling out favors, being the big man who could make the difference. "How did this come to light?" she asked.

"Luke Silici."

The man who'd wanted to run against Maxim in the primary but backed off when she entered the race? *That* Luke Silici?

"There was a clip of him on the news, condemning Mark for lack of integrity," she was saying.

So he intended to join the race? He must be using this to open the door. But she'd already decided to drop out, hadn't she? Because of the pregnancy? He couldn't know that, of course, but even if he entered the race, there was no way he'd beat Maxim.

"It'll be okay," she said. Somehow, she'd figure it out, come to terms with it. There was a chance Silici had been misinformed. She'd do all she could to fight for Mark's reputation, to preserve her memories of him.

But Ruby wouldn't meet her eyes. "That's not all."

Adelaide remembered the hopes she'd had for this Christmas and felt them fade. "There's more than adultery and corruption?"

"Silici said he has copies of some of Mark's e-mails."

Adelaide let her breath go. "They *prove* he was taking bribe money?"

"I don't know what proof they have on the bribe issue. These apparently have to do with the affair."

Covering her face with both hands, Adelaide tried to calm down enough to think. It was going to be okay, wasn't it? She could live with whatever emerged— because it was in the past. It didn't change the present.

Squaring her shoulders, she lowered her hands. "Who was it? Virna? Or Susie?" She'd named Mark's two most attractive field reps, but Ruby shook her head.

"I wish I didn't have to tell you this…"

What could be left? Proof that he'd never loved her? "Tell me," she said. "If you saw it on the news, I'll find out, anyway."

Empathy softened Ruby's face. "It wasn't Virna or Susie or any of the other aides. It—it was an intern."

Adelaide felt a surge of righteous anger. Those interns were young, some of them just out of high school. "Which one?" she cried.

Ruby cringed. "Phoenix Day."

This was the last name Adelaide had expected to hear.

She was so stunned she couldn't move. "There must be some mistake. Phoenix is a *boy,* the sweetest boy you could ever meet."

Ruby took her hands. "I know."

"You're saying— That can't be true," she whispered. "Mark wasn't gay. Mark…" Remembering his lack of interest the past couple of years they'd lived together, Adelaide fell silent. He'd told her he was too stressed to maintain much of a sex life, too pressured at work, too busy. Was it something else? Something more? An inappropriate attraction to *Phoenix?*

"The boy has agreed to come forward," Ruby was saying. "He's providing copies of the correspondence between him and Mark. At least, according to the news."

Adelaide didn't know how to respond, except to deny it, regardless of any proof anyone claimed to have. "This can't be true. It's a political move, a way to get me to bow out of the race."

"That's what I thought, too," Ruby said. "But…"

"But what?" Adelaide echoed.

"I don't think it's Luke who wants you out of the race. I think it's Maxim Donahue."

Adelaide opened her mouth to argue. Ruby had no idea of the baby or how the situation with Maxim had changed. But Ruby spoke before she could explain.

"It has to be," she insisted. "Silici said Maxim received an anonymous tip, that it was his campaign manager who ran down all the details."

WHERE WAS SHE?

The girls had their friends over. They were chatting happily as they munched on the appetizers Rosa had made, but Maxim had been too busy watching the clock to eat with them. Adelaide was late. She'd said she'd arrive at six, but it was nearly six-thirty. He figured he'd give her another fifteen minutes, so he didn't seem impatient, but when 6:45 p.m. rolled around she still wasn't there. Neither had she called him.

"Dad, didn't you say your friend would be here soon?"

Megan had finally noticed Adelaide's tardiness, perhaps because he'd grown so quiet.

"I'm sure she's on her way, but…I'll check."

Taking his cell phone, he stepped out of the room. But Adelaide didn't pick up. She didn't answer her house phone, either.

Where could she be? Planning to drive over there, he grabbed his keys from the counter and started for the door when he received a call. Assuming it would be her, he pulled his cell out of his pocket and punched the talk button without glancing at caller ID. "Hello?"

"Maxim, you are truly amazing!"

It definitely wasn't Adelaide. That voice belonged to his assistant, Peter Goodrich. Peter kept Maxim's capitol office running smoothly and interfaced with Jan Kenny, who ran Maxim's district office. He also volunteered on the campaign, so they spent a lot of time together. Maxim considered Peter his best hire. But he didn't want to talk to him on Christmas Eve. "Peter, are you drunk?"

"What? Of course not. You know I don't drink."

"You sound drunk." Tall and skinny, with a very deep voice, Peter was so circumspect that Maxim liked to tease him. But he was half-serious tonight. Peter sounded much more animated than usual.

"I'm just…surprised," Peter said.

"About what?" Maxim looked at his watch.

"You did it, man. There's no way she's gonna beat you now."

Slightly irritated because he didn't want to talk business while he was so preoccupied with other things, Maxim scratched his neck. "I don't know what you're talking about."

"I'm talking about Mark Fairfax. How did you know? I mean…what a shocker. I *never* would've guessed he was gay."

Until this moment, Maxim had only been paying partial attention. He'd been too busy watching the clock and keeping an eye on his driveway through the window, expecting Adelaide to pull in at any time. Now every bit of his energy and focus turned toward the conversation. "How do you know about Fairfax?"

"I guess it was on the news. I didn't see it, but someone called Martha and she called me."

Martha Sanchez worked for him, too. She handled all the scheduling for Maxim and the field reps. She wouldn't have felt as comfortable calling him at home, but she and Peter worked well together and had become close friends.

"I mean, it's true, isn't it?" Peter asked. "It's not a joke."

With a silent curse, Maxim crossed the room and sank onto the couch. Damn Harvey Sillinger! He'd taken the bribe money and he'd still gone after Adelaide.

"Maxim?"

"I'm here," he muttered.

"You seem upset."

He *was* upset. If word of Fairfax's affair had been on the news, Adelaide had heard about it, too. They were in politics, for crying out loud. They had people who were paid to watch and listen for any mention of their names in the media. If she hadn't seen it on the news herself, she'd probably received a call very similar to this one. *Son of a bitch.*

"Maxim? Isn't this good news?" Peter asked, uncertain now.

"No. It's not good news," he said and hung up.

CHAPTER FOURTEEN

IT HADN'T BEEN EASY to get Ruby to leave. But Ruby had kids. She couldn't miss Christmas. And although Ruby invited her, there was no way Adelaide wanted to join the party. She loved the children, but this was the first time the family would be celebrating the holidays together in three years. Adelaide refused to interfere with that. Besides, she'd rather be alone.

Bundled up in a wool coat, scarf and gloves, she sat on a bench in Capitol Park, gazing at the building that sheltered California's government. Called the People's Building, it was a domed piece of Greek Revival and Roman–Corinthian architecture resembling the Capitol Building in Washington, D.C. Tonight, the Christmas lights that adorned the building and the trees shone through the fog, making Adelaide feel as if she'd just stepped into the scene portrayed on the Christmas cards they sold in nearby gift shops.

Except she felt no warmth of spirit. She was cold inside, and as empty as the building appeared to be.

Mark had always loved it here, she thought. But not because of the beauty. It was the power that drew him.

Was it the same for Maxim?

Probably. He'd done just about everything he could to retain his seat, hadn't he? And that included making her believe he cared about her. She wasn't entirely sure it was an act, but even if he'd received the anonymous tip Ruby had mentioned and gone after Mark before they'd had the chance to get to know each other, did she really want another man obsessed with his own ambition? Could she deal with a second relationship like the one she'd had with Mark? He'd started putting so many things before her—among them, apparently, his interns.

She shuddered as she imagined what must have happened with Phoenix. Mark had hidden his interest in the boy so well. Or had she merely missed the signs? He'd certainly talked about Phoenix. He'd even had him over to the house. After learning that he didn't have a supportive family, she'd felt sorry for the boy. She certainly knew what being alone was like. But now she saw how effectively she'd been manipulated. It was Mark who'd told her about Phoenix's family. Who knew if it was even true? Had they been kissing and touching in another room while she was right there in the house?

Maybe. Her presence provided the perfect cover, should anyone ever raise any questions. She never would've suspected, hadn't watched them closely at all.

That must've made it pretty darn easy.

But Mark hadn't expected to die and have someone as tenacious and determined as Maxim take over his seat. Would this have come out if she hadn't entered the race? She doubted it. Why would Maxim have bothered with Mark otherwise? Ironically, it was her desire to stand up for her husband because of Maxim's lack of respect for him that'd brought the truth to light.

What did those e-mail messages say? Did she even want to know?

"You're *such* a liar," she told Mark. It wasn't only the

fact that he'd broken their marriage vows that hurt. It was that she'd lost so much self-confidence wondering why she couldn't interest her own husband. "You bastard."

Her phone vibrated in her purse. It'd been going off all night. She would've cut the power, but Ruby had made her promise not to. She wanted to be able to check in. But it was Maxim again.

Adelaide wasn't ready to talk to him. Pressing the button that would shut down her phone, she got up and started to walk around the gardens.

An old man with white hair stood near an American Indian monument. He nodded as she passed him. "Merry Christmas," he said with a smile.

ADELAIDE WASN'T HOME. Maxim had been to her place three different times.

Had she gone over to a friend's? Maybe. But he didn't know the people who were closest to her, wasn't sure who to call. He could understand why she might not want to spend the evening with him, but he was worried about her, worried enough that he'd taken to cruising the streets around her house, hoping to spot her car. It wasn't the best way to give his girls a good Christmas, but he was so preoccupied with this he couldn't go home. And they'd assured him they were fine, that they understood.

So where was Adelaide? She couldn't be in any stores or restaurants.

It was so late that even the businesses that stayed open on Christmas Eve were closed.

He remembered her mentioning Mark's parents and wondered if she'd gone to their home. Maybe they'd heard the news and called her.

After pulling to the side of the road, he used his phone

to check information. Sure enough, the Fairfaxes were listed. But did he dare call them at midnight on Christmas Eve? He was the reason their son's reputation was ruined....

"This won't be easy," he muttered, but he dialed the number, anyway.

After several rings, he heard a woman's sleepy voice say, "Hello." Tempted to hang up, he hesitated. He didn't want to trouble these poor people, especially on Christmas. But he had to know if they'd heard from Adelaide.

"Mrs. Fairfax?"

The sleep cleared from her voice, changing to confusion. "Yes?"

"This is Maxim Donahue."

He could sense her unwillingness to believe him. "Is this some kind of crank call?" she asked.

"No, it's not. I'm looking for Adelaide. I was wondering if you've heard from her tonight."

"You're looking for— Do you know what time it is?" she snapped.

"Yes, ma'am."

"You have no business waking people in the middle of the night, no matter who you are. And after all you've said to discredit my son, why do you think I'd help you?"

Maxim wasn't sure if Mrs. Fairfax's words meant she knew the latest or not. Since Mark had changed and begun to go back on so many of his campaign promises, Maxim had been pretty vocal about his lack of admiration for him. She could be referring to that. "I disagree with just about everything your son did, Mrs. Fairfax. I won't pretend otherwise. But I'm worried about Adelaide. Will you please tell me if you've seen her or heard from her? If you know where she's at?"

"I have no idea. Why?"

Now he was certain they didn't know about Phoenix. She'd still be raging at him if she did. "I'm afraid you'll find out soon enough. I apologize for disturbing your sleep."

"Wait— What do you have to do with Adelaide?"

He told himself to hang up. But Mrs. Fairfax had answered his question. He figured he owed her the same respect. "I'm in love with her," he said and disconnected before she could rebound from the shock.

CHRISTMAS CAROLS WERE the only songs she could find on the radio. Adelaide had heard enough of them for one year, but Christmas carols were better than silence, so she let them play. She'd gone to Midnight Mass at a beautiful church not far from the capitol building. She wasn't Catholic, but when she'd noticed the crowd gathering at the doors, she'd felt drawn to join them.

She was glad she had. The service had reminded her of the meaning of Christmas and given her a sense of peace. It had also reminded her of the baby she carried and the hope that having a child brought into her life. Did the past really matter? Not if she didn't let it, she decided.

But the minute she pulled into her driveway and saw Maxim there in his car, waiting for her, she tensed up again. She couldn't deal with the powerful emotions he evoked—in addition to the disappointment of learning what she had about Mark. She wanted to put Mark behind her and forget once and for all, and she was pretty sure that meant she couldn't have anything to do with politics.

That included Maxim.

After parking in her garage and cutting the engine, she sat in her car for a moment, but Maxim didn't approach.

He got out of his vehicle and leaned against it, waiting. She could see the outline of his body in her rearview mirror.

What would she say to him? As humiliating as it was to admit, he'd been right about Mark. Mark wasn't the man she'd thought he was. But she couldn't blame Maxim for what Mark had done. Maxim's only sin was exposing him. Although that stung, she didn't have the right to be too angry. He'd been her election opponent before he'd been her lover, and any other opponent would've done the same thing.

The radio went silent when she pulled the door latch. She liked the new delay feature that let the music stay on after the engine was off, but the sudden silence felt ominous.

"Hey," he said as she came out of the garage.

"Hi."

He was wearing a heavy coat, a burgundy sweater and a pair of jeans. Just seeing him made her remember what it was like to be in his arms. She'd felt safer there than anywhere else. But she tried to convince herself that was only because he'd saved her life. What she felt was hero worship. Admiration for a handsome man. It wasn't love. She didn't want any part of love, not anymore.

He met her at the walkway leading to the house. "You okay?"

She pushed the button on her key chain that would close the garage door. "I'm fine."

"I've been worried."

"You shouldn't be here," she said. "You've got your girls at home."

"They're not the only ones who matter to me."

Ignoring that statement, she turned on her heel and

marched to the house. "It's late and I'm really tired. Would you mind if we talked another time? It's been a...rough night."

"I know," he said. "I should give you some space. But...can I at least apologize?"

"For what? You wanted to win, and I was in the way. I understand."

"Adelaide—"

Raising a hand to stop him, she donned a polite mask. "Look, I don't blame you. If I were in your shoes, maybe I would've done the same thing. I mean, the object of any campaign is to win. Mark was... Mark was a cheat and a liar, and everything you've ever said about him is probably true."

"I don't care about that. I didn't come over here to rub your nose in what he's done."

"Why not? Enjoy it while it lasts. This was quite the political coup." She knew she was being harsher than she had a right to be. But she'd been wrong when they'd talked about the baby—she couldn't be open to any of the options he'd named. They required too much trust, and trust was something she didn't have anymore.

A muscle jumped in his jaw. "So you're blowing me off?"

"It won't work."

"What about the baby?"

"You get the senate seat. I get the baby." Stepping inside, she closed the door behind her.

MAXIM WAS STILL STANDING on Adelaide's stoop when the porch light went off. He didn't know whether to bang on the door or leave. Memories of the time they'd spent in the mountains, especially of that second night when they'd said so much without saying a word, made him want to insist she come back and talk to him. But he couldn't force her to let him into her life if she didn't want him there. He'd been crazy to think she did. It was Mark she'd always loved, Mark she *still* loved, even though the stupid son of a bitch had been a complete fraud. Mark had never deserved her.

But maybe Maxim didn't deserve her, either.

Thinking of his girls waiting patiently for him at home, he released a long sigh and walked back to his car. He'd been so excited about having Megan and Callie meet Adelaide. Then Harvey had ruined it all.

The radio came on as soon as he started his car and Elvis Presley began singing, "I'll have a blue Christmas without you—"

Quickly changing the station, Maxim backed out of the driveway.

As she watched Maxim's headlights swing out into the street, Adelaide felt like crying. But she choked back her tears. She'd done the right thing. Despite all the years they'd been acquainted, she didn't know Maxim, not really. Maybe he was no better than Mark.

"Getting with me was just another way to protect his political aspirations," she said. But all the things she remembered him saying to her when they were together seemed to dispute that statement. *I can't pretend to be Mark again. If I make love to you, it'll be because you want me... We're talking about a baby, Adelaide. Our baby. My career doesn't come before that... You're the most beautiful woman I've ever laid eyes on....*

Had he meant any of it? It'd *felt* real. Unlike Mark,

Maxim didn't use flattery. He only said what he meant. That was why she'd been upset enough to run against him. He'd told some reporter that Mark had been worse for the district than if it had gone unrepresented, that he'd been one of the most selfish individuals on the planet.

And, as she'd just told him, he'd been right. Why was she blaming him for being right?

The message light blinked on her answering machine. Seeing it, she realized she'd forgotten to turn her cell phone back on after the church service. Ruby was probably going crazy with worry.

Trying to put Maxim out of her mind, she crossed the room and pressed the play button. Sure enough, her friend had called a number of times. Adelaide was about to stop the playback without listening to the rest. She was one touch of a button away from erasing the whole thing when she heard a voice she hadn't heard in a long time—the voice of her former mother-in-law.

"Adelaide? Are you okay? What's going on? Maxim Donahue just called here. Can you believe it? At midnight on Christmas Eve? We don't even know him. I mean, we've met but never really talked. He was looking for you. Only now I'm thinking he must've been drunk, because when I asked him why he wanted to find you he said…he said he was *in love* with you. And then he hung up. That's it. Isn't that crazy? He's the man you're running against, isn't he? The one who never liked Mark? Anyway, give us a call. We'd like to see you this Christmas. You haven't swung by in a while."

Another message from Ruby came on right afterward. "Damn it, Adelaide, this isn't fair. Why the hell won't you pick up?"

Adelaide scarcely heard it. As she hit the stop button, her mother-in-law's message was still playing in her mind: *He said he was in love with you.*

Was it true? Would Maxim really have come right out and said that to Mark's *parents?*

Stunned, Adelaide slowly sank onto the sofa. Was she being as smart as she assumed? Or was she letting Mark ruin what she had with Maxim the same way he'd ruined the last few years of their marriage?

Her hand shaking, she reached into her purse, got her phone and turned it on. She'd missed eighteen calls from Maxim. Why would he spend his whole Christmas Eve trying to reach her if he didn't really care? He couldn't have been doing it simply to neutralize the opposition. The scandal that had broken tonight would cripple her campaign; he wouldn't have to worry about her even if she did keep running.

He said he was in love with you.

Her eyes welled up with tears as she dialed his number. She didn't really expect him to answer. Not after what she'd said to him at the door. But he did.

"Hello?"

"Maxim?"

"Yes?"

"I'm sorry. I—" Her voice broke but she battled through it. "I think I'm just scared."

"I'm not like Mark, Adelaide," he said. "You can count on me."

Recalling the way he'd hauled her out of that Cessna and made her dig that snow cave, Adelaide smiled. He was right. She could count on him.

"Will you come back?" she asked hopefully.

"Are you kidding? I turned around the second I saw it was you. I'm already pulling into your driveway."

Tossing her phone aside, Adelaide hurried to the door—and rushed into his arms as he came up the walk. "Thank God," she said. "I thought I'd lost you."

EPILOGUE

AS ADELAIDE FINISHED arranging the last of the presents under the tree, she could hardly believe an entire year had passed since she'd been stranded in the Sierras. So much had changed since then—she'd dropped out of the race, gotten married, had a baby. But she didn't regret those changes; they'd all been good. She didn't even regret that Maxim was still in politics. Not only had he won the primary, he'd retained his seat in the November election, but the way he handled his job was so different from Mark.

"What are you thinking about?"

She smiled as Maxim walked into the room carrying Connor, their three-month-old. "How close we came to walking away from each other last year."

"We didn't come *that* close," he said.

She arched her eyebrows at him and he grinned.

"I was in love. I wouldn't have let you get rid of me that easily."

Returning his smile, she adjusted the garland on the tree. "Do you think Harvey ever regrets what he did?"

"I would guess he does. He loved California politics.

I'm sure he wasn't happy when there wasn't another politician in the state who'd work with him."

"You have to be able to trust your campaign manager," she said. "It was nice of Luke not to hire him. He could've justified doing it, you know."

"No, Luke's a good man. He didn't appreciate what Harvey did, even though Harvey returned my money." He held up his son and laughed when the baby gave him a goofy smile. "I've been encouraging Luke to run for the state assembly."

"That's a great idea." She reached for the baby. "Here, hand him to me and grab his car seat. We need to head to the airport to get the girls."

Maxim checked his watch. "You're kidding, right? We've got an hour."

The wait was making Adelaide crazy. "Maybe they'll get in early."

"And maybe we'll have to drive around that pickup circle a million times until they show up."

"Come on." She waved him toward the baby's car seat, which was sitting near the sofa. "I can't wait to see them. And I know they can't wait to see the baby."

"They just saw him at Thanksgiving."

"But he changes so fast. And they love having a little brother."

"They love having a mother again, too," he said softly. "Thank you for being so good to them."

Adelaide didn't even have to try. They enriched her life as much as Maxim or Connor. "I never dreamed I could ever be this happy," she said.

He raised her chin to kiss her. "And I never dreamed I could ever be this much in love. Merry Christmas, Mrs. Donahue."

Adelaide closed her eyes as their lips met. She had everything she could ever want, thanks to one snowy Christmas....

* * * * *

THE CHRISTMAS BABY

Day Leclaire

* * *

To Diane Andre, the Tottons' Christmas Baby,
who still brings joy and poignancy to our family,
as well as the occasional Christmas Miracle…
and of course, tons of mayhem!

Dear Reader,

One of my favorite story "types" is family chaos and general mayhem. I don't know—maybe it's because my family has experienced the occasional fits of mayhem over the years. Like the year my family drove to my grandmother's and the top of the roof rack burst open and we distributed our presents all along the Pennsylvania Turnpike during the wee hours of Christmas Eve. My brother was three and when we pulled over to gather up what we could of our soggy booty, he woke up and saw electric towers covered in red twinkling aircraft warning lights and started shrieking, "It's Rudolph!" (Disbelieving gasp.) "Millions of Rudolphses!"

Or there was the Christmas when Santa left a tied-up bundle of cash under the tree—all in crisp new ones— only to have one of our more rambunctious pets distribute pieces of the newly minted bills from one end of the house to the other. Merry Confetti!

Or the time the cat climbed the Christmas tree, chasing one of the twinkling lights, and—in a scene straight out of *Christmas Vacation*—shorted out the power. The cat survived. Barely. But it took a full week before she stopped sticking to the furniture like some giant Velcro puffball.

I have to admit that none of my own Christmases can compare with the one Chaz and Carrie experience in "The Christmas Baby." Prepare yourself for a touch of mayhem, some poignancy and joy, and best of all…a Christmas miracle in the form of one tiny baby.

Merry Christmas!

Day Leclaire

CHAPTER ONE

'Twas the day before Christmas...

AND CARRIE MANNING FELT like a cross between the Grinch and Scrooge.

This was one of the worst days ever, she decided as she dragged herself into her apartment, ranking right up there with the day she and Chaz had broken up.

First, she'd been kept up to the wee hours of the morning by arguing neighbors. Then, when she'd finally slept, it had been right through her alarm, which made her late for work, something she hated. After a mad dash to throw on clothes and grab a breakfast bar that could have been used in a cardboard box as packing peanuts, she'd walked outside only to have the skies spit a nasty combination of rain, ice and sleet into her face. Getting to work through New York City traffic had been a nightmare of epic proportions. But she'd made it and stuck it out all the way until they closed the office at two in reluctant concession to the holidays. At that point, she was handed the truly delightful news that she, along with a solid twenty percent of the staff at her accounting firm, had been laid off.

Merry Christmas, bah humbug. Don't let the door hit you in the backside on your way out. Oh, and that Christmas bonus you were counting on to bring your rent up-to-date? Sorry! Not happening.

Carrie didn't remember much after that, at least not until she returned to the apartment building, where her manager promptly handed her an eviction slip. "Your lease is up," Mrs. McGower cheerfully informed her. "Your apartment and the one next door are being remodeled into a larger unit. The rent will triple and the tenants next door have already said they'll take it. You have until the end of January. Merry Christmas!"

Slamming the door behind her, Carrie wandered over to the wretched little plastic Christmas tree—her one indulgence to honor the season. The management had forbidden live trees—not that she could have afforded one. In the fitful afternoon light struggling to make it through the grime of her window and the gloom of the weather, the tree stood out as a shining example of the truly pathetic. Its sad little boughs dipped under the weight of her handmade ornaments and its fuzzy "needles" were a natty, tangled mess.

"Looks like it's just you and me, buddy," she murmured.

The tree shivered in response and actually shed a few "needles" onto the carpet. If she didn't clean it up, it would end up looking like a green fur ball a cat had left behind. Disgusting, but it pretty much exemplified the way her day was going. Right now all she wanted was to climb into a nice hot tub, fill it to overflowing with bubbles, light the scented candle stubs that were all that remained of the ones Chaz had bought her for her last birthday and pretend that all was joyous in her world. On the positive side, her life couldn't get any worse.

Of course, the desperate wheeze of the broken doorbell

instantly proved her wrong. One more item the landlord refused to repair. It was old-fashioned, granted. Quaint. But she loved that doorbell every bit as much as she despised the five-fingered pounding that others were forced to utilize.

The bell rang again and she eyed the door. Forget it. She wouldn't answer. She folded her arms across her chest to give emphasis to her decision. The way her day was going, it couldn't possibly be good news.

"Open up, Manning. I know you're in there. McGower ratted you out."

Chaz Latimer. Of all the rotten luck. She couldn't take any more today. She really, truly could not. "Go away!" she called to him. "I'm not home."

He responded by shoving a key in the lock. Since she hadn't bothered with the chain, he walked right in. The man she'd once loved with every fiber of her being paused in the miniscule entryway, overwhelming the space just as he overwhelmed most things, including her.

First, there was his height, all six feet two and three-quarter inches of sheer, unadulterated male animal. And his breadth. His college football days had left him with wide, powerful shoulders, a trim waist and hips, and the thighs and butt of a professional athlete. Considering he spent his days working on his start-up dot-com—a computer gaming site—it gave the term "computer geek" a whole new meaning. As if that weren't enough, he sported the face of an angel with a devilish twinkle gleaming in his midnight-dark eyes, the combination of which had the women falling off the sidewalk in their attempt to get a second look. It didn't matter whether they were eighteen or eighty, every last one of them took a tumble whenever Chaz Latimer cruised the city streets.

"Why am I not surprised that the locks were never changed?" he asked.

She struggled to face him with something approaching equanimity, though considering how hard it was just to remember to breathe, her success remained in serious doubt. "Because you know the McGowers?"

"That could be it." He eyed her warily. "I'd wish you a Merry Christmas, but you don't appear in the mood."

She responded with a shrug, hoping her expression didn't betray the traitorous urge to burst into tears all over his big, broad shoulders. "That's because I'm not. You know…Christmas." Her smile wobbled. "Bah humbug."

His attention focused on her with laser-sharp precision. "Now I know there's something wrong. You love Christmas."

The comment rescued her as nothing else could have. She straightened her spine and reined in her emotions. "Since we've never shared one, I don't think you're qualified to say," she pointed out with just a touch of ice in her voice.

He shrugged. "But we talked about it. Childhood memories. Changes we've made to our family's traditions since then. Plans for Christmas future."

The reminder hurt. A lot. They had discussed it, and at the time it had seemed so possible, so shiny and beautiful. Until she'd discovered that his idea of Christmas future was a decade or two further away than hers. "Since we won't be sharing any Christmases, now or in the future, I don't believe you're qualified to comment. So, stop commenting."

He responded with a frown and strode farther into her apartment. His frown deepened when he caught a glimpse of her tree. "That's just sad, Manning."

"Maybe, but it's all mine."

He flicked one of her handmade ornaments, setting it spinning gaily. Unfortunately, it also caused the tree to cough up another needle fur ball and spit it out at his feet. "Aw, hell, no." He took a hasty step backward. "That's just wrong."

"Stop touching it. It doesn't like to be touched. I think it has a cold."

He eyed the disgusting blob of green fuzz inching toward his boot. "More like a stomach virus."

For a brief instant, they shared a moment of levity. Then she remembered. Remembered how they'd first met, how they'd fallen in love, how she believed it would last forever, and how it had, ultimately, ended. Exhaustion flooded through her. "Why are you here, Chaz? What do you want?"

"I heard you were going to lose the apartment and thought I'd check and see—"

"See, what? If I was all right?" He was killing her by inches. "I'm fine. I'll start looking for a new place first thing Monday. You don't have to worry about me anymore, remember? That's what it means when you break up with someone."

"Yeah, yeah. Whatever." He regarded her with heartbreaking sincerity. "If there's anything I can do…"

Love her enough. Believe in them enough. Put their relationship just a millimeter ahead of his dot-com startup. But those wishes weren't the sort Santa could put in her stocking. She forced a cheerful smile to her lips. "Thanks, Chaz. Seriously. I appreciate the offer, but I'm fine."

"You know where I live if you need anything."

"I'll just wave. I'll even use all five fingers."

And he'd probably see her, since he'd moved into the

apartment building directly across the street from hers. His unit was one floor up and two windows to the left. How many hours had she wasted, staring at his shadow moving around the spare bedroom he used for an office? Too many. The Christmas tree had been a blessing on that front, at least, since it obstructed the view. And ever since she'd put it up, she'd been careful to keep the other window—the one in her bedroom—shaded so she wouldn't be tempted to look.

He hesitated. "I guess I should go. It's Christmas Eve and you probably have a full day scheduled."

She upped the intensity of her smile, hoping he couldn't see the grief through the dazzle. "Jam-packed."

"It was nice your company gave you part of the day off." He shot her the sort of grin that had her knees losing their locking ability and kicked her heartbeat up to the full-blown cardio range. "My boss isn't so generous. He has my nose to the grindstone the entire day."

"Cute." Especially considering he was his own boss. "And not surprising. Having lived with your boss I know just how unreasonable he can be about work hours. Is your brother also putting in overtime?"

"Of course. Thad is as committed as I am."

She nodded in complete agreement. "*Committed* being the operative word. Well, good luck."

The dreaded "awkward moment" hovered, one he sliced through with customary precision. He hooked his finger in the front of her blouse and hauled her in close. "Merry Christmas, Carrie."

And then he did what she'd longed for him to do…and hoped would never happen again. He kissed her. Consumed her. Turned her world inside out and tilted it upside down. His body molded itself to hers, the fit sheer perfection. Her body recalled just how to snuggle in and her hands followed the powerful contour of his back with practiced ease. He'd opened his coat when he'd first walked in and the warmth of the fleece lining seemed to close around her like a fist, wrapping her tight against the powerful lines of his body.

His kiss still had the ability to fry her hard drive. Every scrap of memory went off-line and she forgot all the trauma from the past three months. Forgot why she'd broken up with him. Forgot the pain and the sorrow. Forgot how much it would hurt when he left. Instead, her lips parted beneath his and she allowed him in, allowed him to take her one last time.

His mouth moved on hers, hard and thorough, drinking her in with long thirsty gulps. Heat burned low in her belly, softening and melting, pushing outward in hot, greedy waves. His muscles corded beneath her hands, great sweeps of power and strength. She inhaled him, filled herself to overflowing with the delicious scent that was distinctively Chaz. And the taste of him... She couldn't get enough. She'd never been able to get enough of his unique flavor. One kiss and she was gone—wrapped, packed and tied neatly with a bow.

He'd done this to her from the first. It had been a day similar to this, one blasting the city with ice and snow. It had been nighttime and a bunch of revelers had swarmed past her, catching her up in their group just long enough to jostle her and give her a passing grope. When she'd fought free, she'd slipped on ice and taken a nasty tumble. It would have left her vulnerable to further harassment if Chaz hadn't arrived on the scene.

He'd scooped her up and sent the pack on its way with a single hard glare. Then he'd insisted on seeing her safely back to the apartment she shared with two other women. He'd left her at the door with a quip and a smile, and started down the dingy hallway. He took a whole three steps before spinning around and striding back toward her. Without a word he'd made the exact same move as today. He'd hooked a finger into the collar of her coat and tugged her into his arms for a brief, stormy kiss. And that's all it had taken.

They'd exchanged phone numbers and, within two short months, moved in together. Moved in to this very apartment. Their time together had been nine months of sheer heaven, followed by nearly three months of hellish pain. And here she was, back in his arms, inviting him to hurt her all over again.

With a muffled exclamation, she yanked free and took a hasty step backward. She bumped up against her fragile tree, causing it to fling fur balls at her. She could only hope none of them stuck. "Why...?" It was all she could say, all she was capable of saying.

His eyes turned as dark as a winter night's sky. "You know why. Because nothing's changed."

Her chin shot up. "You're right. Nothing's changed."

"I still want you. And you still want me."

"Wanting isn't enough. There has to be more. There has to be a future."

Frustration ate at him. "We'll have a future," he objected. "All I'm asking for is time."

"You're thirty, Chaz. I'm twenty-eight. I don't object to waiting a few years. But you're talking five to ten."

"You make it sound like a prison sentence."

"Because that's what it'll turn into. I've seen it happen. I explained about my mother."

"And I explained that I'm not like your father. I won't make promises of marriage and never keep them. I wouldn't walk out on you, leaving you broke, alone and pregnant. I'd make sure that didn't happen."

"That doesn't change the basic facts. You refuse to marry or have a baby or any sort of real family life until your game site is a success," she argued. "But you've never been able to define what you consider a success. Is it a certain amount of money? A certain level of sales? International recognition? What?"

His jaw took on a stubborn slant. "I'll know when I get there."

She nodded in total understanding. "And that's why I ended things, because there will always be one more condition. One more component you need to achieve in order to consider yourself successful. I had to get out before it was too late and I couldn't—"

To Carrie's horror, her voice broke. Concern flared to life in Chaz's eyes and he took a step in her direction. She held up her hand to stop him. Too many things had gone wrong today for her to gather herself up and remain strong in the face of overwhelming temptation. She was already on emotional thin ice, and her ability to think logically appeared to be on the fritz, as well. If he touched her again, she wouldn't be able to resist. She'd cave. She knew she would. And she couldn't afford to give in to him. If she did, she'd pack up her meager possessions, move them across the street and spend the rest of her life waiting for Chaz to decide to live life instead of planning it.

She gave herself an extra second to recover. When she was certain she wouldn't break, she said, "You need to leave." A silent protest built in his expression and he planted his feet in a familiar stance. A digging-in stance. "Please, Chaz. Please."

The whispered plea did it. A muscle twitched in his jaw and he jerked his head in an abrupt nod. Spinning on his heel, he walked to the door. "Don't forget to put the chain on," he said over his shoulder. "And, Carrie?"

"What?" She prayed he didn't hear the despair underscoring that single word.

"I've given you your space, hoping you'd come to your senses. But this isn't over. Not by a long shot."

CHAPTER TWO

…and all through the house,
not a creature was stirring.
Except, maybe, the baby on the doorstep.

COME TO HER SENSES? *Come to her senses!*

Carrie glared at the closed door in outrage. Was that what Chaz thought? That the fundamental difference in their attitude—one that stretched like a bottomless chasm—was a simple matter of needing some extra space? It just proved how mismatched they were, how right she'd been to end things before he broke her heart. Before she'd gotten to the point where she couldn't pick up the pieces and move on.

There was only one way to handle matters at this point—in the bathtub. After soaking herself into a prune, she'd don her oldest sweats—what she referred to as her security blanket sweats—and burrow into the comfort of a pint of ice cream for her Christmas Eve dinner. Unfortunately, it didn't quite work out that way. Just as she was about to step into the tub, the doorbell wheezed its breathless greeting once again.

She hesitated, torn between ignoring the summons and yanking on her sweats and answering the darn thing. Fragrant steam wafted from the tub, tempting her to climb in. But she was simply one of *those* people—the kind who couldn't screen her calls with an answering machine, couldn't ignore a stranger's beleaguered, "I'm from out of town, would you mind helping me?" and without a doubt couldn't ignore the pathetic buzz of her ancient doorbell, even if it was Chaz again.

The thought of how they'd once been together sent a sharp pain streaking through her. He used to ruffle her hair and laugh about her "Southern Good Samaritan streak." Well, this time he'd hear a few words the original Good Samaritan wouldn't have dreamed of using.

Carrie tugged on her sweats and trotted to the door and yanked it open. "Look, Latimer—"

An elderly woman stood there, wrapped in her beautifully ancient years, with snowy hair and the sort of noble face lined with decades of life experience. Deepset dark eyes stared with disconcerting intensity. "Latimer?" she repeated.

"I'm sorry. I thought you were someone else," Carrie said, summoning up a friendly, reassuring smile. "May I help you?"

"Yes. Latimer. I speak to him?"

Her accent was so heavy, Carrie could barely understand her. "I'm sorry. Chaz doesn't live here anymore." She waved a hand in the general direction of his building, though why she bothered with the pointless gesture, she had no idea. She tried to keep her words simple and clear. "He was here. He left."

"You know Latimer?"

"Yes." She couldn't resist adding a sharp, "Unfortunately."

For some reason, that didn't thrill the woman. "You wife?" she asked suspiciously.

Carrie shook her head, the adamant gesture bringing an expression of relief to the old woman's face. "No way."

"Girlfriend?"

The woman rolled the *r*, filling it with the warmth and flavor of Tuscany at its ripest. For one insane moment, Carrie could have sworn that she could actually smell the heady scent of sun-sweetened grapes bursting on the vine and wild herbs wafting tantalizingly on a summer breeze. Ridiculous.

Carrie folded her arms across her chest. "No, I most certainly am not his girlfriend."

The woman nodded sagely. "Ah, maid. Good. I have present for Latimer. You give, yes?"

Maid? Carrie's mouth dropped open. But before she could vocalize her outrage, the woman turned on her heel and hobbled rapidly away, vanishing around the nearest hallway corner. Okay, granted. Her sweats had seen better days. She glanced down and winced. Far better days. She hovered in the doorway, wondering if she should go after the woman. Something wasn't right. Maybe the woman needed help. It *was* Christmas Eve. And she *did* know Chaz. Perhaps she should take the woman to Chaz's apartment and let him deal with the problem.

Thinking wistfully of that bath she wasn't going to take anytime soon, Carrie headed back into her apartment to collect her purse and coat. She took an extra few seconds to scribble a sign that said: "Chaz Latimer does not live here anymore." She underlined the word *not* twice and added his new address. Returning to the hallway, she taped it on the door and nearly tripped over the giant box sitting on her welcome mat.

It was wrapped in shiny green paper with gold angels on it. For some odd reason, the top sat askew and had a huge red bow on top of it. A small pasteboard tag had been tied to the bow and it fluttered in the draft from the hallway. To: Latimer, it read. From: Santa.

"Darn it," Carrie muttered. "How can I start a new life when the old one refuses to go away?"

Well, this was one gift headed right back to Santa. She picked up the box, surprised by the weight of it, and hastened around the corner of the hallway. The woman stood just inside the elevator door, peering out. The instant she saw Carrie carrying the box, she released the door.

"Latimer," she called. "You give, okay?"

And with that the door slid closed.

"What is it with my luck today?" The question bounced off the walls of the empty corridor, a mocking punctuation point to her frustration.

Spinning on her heel, she marched back to her apartment and closed the door. If that woman thought she was going to carry this box through the cold and sleet to Chaz's, she had another think coming. She was through with him. Today marked the start of her new life. With exaggerated care, Carrie placed the box under the unhappy tree—slightly tempted to peek beneath the crooked lid. She managed to restrain herself. With luck the Christmas tree from hell would decorate the box with globs of needle fur balls. In fact, Chaz's present could sit there until next Christmas, for all she cared. Let the landlord deal with it after her eviction.

That decided, she marched into her bedroom, where she pulled out the sexiest outfit she owned. The maid? She'd see about that. Returning to the bathroom, she stripped and climbed in the tub. The bathwater had cooled to lukewarm and the candle stubs were guttering. She didn't care. She'd sit here and enjoy her bath, even if it meant turning into an icicle and freezing to death. Somehow, someway, she'd recapture the spirit of Christmas even if it killed her. She cranked on the hot water, pleased when the temperamental water heater actually spat some out. Then she settled back and cleared her mind, focusing on the changes she'd make in the New Year.

Number One. Exterminate Chaz Latimer from her world.

Number Two. Repeat Number One until she actually succeeded.

Number Three. Find a job.

She sank lower in the tub at that depressing thought. Jobs were becoming scarcer than hen's teeth. Nor did it look like that fact would improve anytime soon. As much as she hated the idea, she might just have to move back to Raleigh where she'd have family for emotional support and possible job resources. She waved that aside. With luck, it wouldn't come to that. Until it did, she refused to consider the option.

Number Four. Find a new apartment.

A moan escaped her. Just the thought of all the work and hassle that would entail—not to mention where she'd find the money for such an endeavor—heaped panic on top of depression.

Number Five. Make a wish on her Christmas star.

It was something she and her mom used to do every year, and had been the most special part of their Christmas Eve tradition. The two of them would spend endless days beforehand debating just what they'd wish. Of course, having her mom in on the discussion might have something to do with why her wishes came true.

Even so… There'd been that one year when she hadn't revealed her wish ahead of time. No doubt it had been at that crucial age when she'd wavered between belief and disenchantment. She'd been determined not to let anyone know what she wanted until that magical time when they stood in front of the Christmas tree and made their wishes. That night she'd asked for a puppy. And the next morning, much to her amazement and delight, Bella had been waiting for her, complete with a red floppy bow tied around her fluffy neck. After that, she'd believed in Christmas wishes with all her heart and soul.

She and Chaz had never had the chance to honor her family's Christmas tradition, since they'd first met New Year's Day and their relationship had ended nine months later. She stared wistfully at the candles just in time to watch the first extinguish with a faint sizzle and a stream of wispy smoke. And here she was, right back where she'd started…thinking about Chaz. Again.

A thin cry, like the mewling of a cat, had her jerking upright in the tub. Water sloshed over the sides. What in the world…? Heart pounding, she scrambled from the tub and hastily dried off. Snatching up her special Christmas outfit, she scrambled into it before creeping on tiptoe from the bathroom. Cautiously, she peered around the doorway into the main room. Nothing had been disturbed as far as she could see.

A faint rustling came from the general direction of the Christmas tree, and then she heard it again. Only this time it bore no resemblance to a cat whatsoever. This time it emitted the distinct sounds of baby. And the baby sounds came from the huge box addressed to Chaz.

Carrie flew toward the box and ripped the lid the rest of the way off. Rocking back onto her heels, she stared in disbelief. Wrapped in a beautiful Christmas blanket and tucked into the padded box, one accented with feminine lace and frills, lay a baby with a bright red bow nestled in her black curls. She stopped fussing the minute Carrie unwrapped her and gazed with unwavering fascination, all the while chewing on a tiny fist. Then she blinked her huge dark eyes—eyes identical to Chaz's— and offered a toothless grin.

In that brief instant, Carrie melted before that innocent, dewy-eyed look, tumbling head over heels. In the next, the full implication of what the gift meant—that this adorable little mite belonged to Chaz—filled Carrie with a combination of grief and fury.

This little girl was Chaz's daughter. How many times had they discussed the possibility of marriage and children? And how many times had he insisted that he had neither the time nor the interest in either? Yet he'd clearly had time enough to create this baby. Determination filled her. Now he'd find time to take responsibility for her.

It only took her a few minutes to collect her purse and keys, and to scramble into her coat. After an instant's thought, she pulled a knit throw off the back of her couch and carefully wrapped it around the box in order to hold the winter chill at bay. Less than ten minutes later, she'd negotiated the way from her apartment to Chaz's. Setting the box down, she banged on his door.

He opened it, looking attractively rumpled and vaguely sleepy, as though she'd awoken him from a nap. Good. He should be plenty rested to assume his new duties.

"Here. This arrived for you from Santa." She picked up the box and thrust it into his arms. "Merry Christmas. You're a daddy, you SOB."

"WAIT!" CHAZ LOOKED from the box, one that made alarming cooing noises, to Carrie's rapidly retreating back. "What the hell are you talking about?"

Before she got more than half a dozen paces, he tucked the box under one arm like a giant football and snagged her with the other. He marched her back to his apartment, arguing the entire way.

"Let go, Latimer," she demanded. "This is your problem, not mine. I'm leaving."

"No, you're not. Whatever this is, it's now *our* problem." He slammed the door closed, which succeeded in making the box give a high-pitched wail. He stared at it in horror. "What the hell is this? Did you actually wrap up a *baby?*"

Carrie folded her arms across her chest and glared at him. "No, I did not wrap up a baby. She came that way. I found her on my doorstep, addressed to you. That means she's *your* problem, not ours, and for sure not mine."

For some reason, Carrie's anger made her appear positively incandescent. Her light brown hair, piled haphazardly on top of her head, gleamed with rich gold highlights that accentuated the green and gold flecks in her hazel eyes. He could tell she'd been in the tub recently. In addition to the damp tendrils escaping from her topknot, he could smell the subtle perfume of the bath oil she favored, as well as the scented candles he'd given her for her birthday.

Beneath her open coat, she wore a forest-green dress he'd never seen before, a silky slip of a thing that clung to some of the most perfect curves that had ever graced a woman and screeched to a halt midthigh as though knowing better than to hide her incredible, endless legs.

"Focus, Latimer!" she snapped.

He jerked his gaze back to her face, catching a betraying flash of vulnerability. He'd done that to her, he realized with regret. It hadn't been deliberate, but it had happened, nonetheless. "Take off your coat," he said. "You aren't going anywhere until we get this straightened out."

"Forget it. I already told you. This is your problem."

"You are not going to dump this helpless baby on me and then take off. Not without giving me the details first."

She wavered for a brief second. Shooting a regretful glance toward the door leading to the hallway, she released a sigh. "Fine. I'll tell you what I know." She slipped off her coat and hung it on the antique coatrack he'd inherited from his grandfather. "Not that there's much to tell."

He carefully carried the box to the living room and put it on the coffee table fronting his couch. Stripping away the blanket, he peered inside. A baby peered back. A live baby. One who blew bubbles and waved its little arms and legs and did nasty things inside diapers. He said a word he probably shouldn't have. With luck the kid was too young to know.

"That's just sad," Carrie informed him. "Your first words to your daughter and they're swear words."

"She's not my daughter," he instantly denied.

"She has your eyes. She looks just like you. She has your name on her box."

"Where did she come from?"

"I assume she came in the usual manner. Boy meets girl. Boy impregnates girl. Boy ditches girl. Girl has baby, alone and unwed and probably broke."

He shot Carrie a grim look. "You're just full of Christmas cheer and sugarplum bedtime stories." He allowed that to sink in before adding, "I meant…who left her on your doorstep?"

She sank onto the couch beside him. "I don't know. Some woman came to the apartment, an elderly woman."

"Mrs. Claus, I suppose."

"Ha, ha. I'm laughing my way right out the door."

"Okay, okay. Go on."

"She wasn't any relation to Santa, unless St. Nick comes by way of Italy. At least, I'm guessing she had an Italian accent. She asked for you by name. I tried to explain that you didn't live there anymore, but we weren't communicating very well. I thought I'd bring her over to you, but when I went back inside to get my purse, she'd dumped your daughter on my unwelcome mat and high-tailed it for the elevator."

"Why didn't you stop her?"

She glared at him, exasperated. "If I'd known what she'd planned, I would have. But I didn't even know the baby was in there until she started to fuss. By that time, the woman was long gone."

"Did you get a name?" he demanded. "An address? Any information at all?"

He'd put her on the defensive. "How was I supposed to know to do that, Chaz? The package wasn't for me, and Mrs. Claus didn't hang around."

He stared at the baby. It wasn't possible. This couldn't be his daughter. He'd always been scrupulous about using protection. Not only that, but after he'd met Carrie, there hadn't been anyone else in his life. "How old do you think she is?" he asked.

Carrie frowned. "I'm no expert… A couple months? Three, maybe."

Three plus nine equaled a year. He winced. A year ago

plus one week would have been New Year's Eve. He'd been dating… Hell, what was her name? Angel? Annie? Angie. Angie-something-with-a-*C*. He struggled to dredge up an image of her. There'd been a lot of champagne flowing. His brother, Thad, and Dinah were having another squabble. In fact, they'd broken up that night—for reasons eerily similar to the reason he and Carrie had ended their relationship. Thad had climbed into a bottle, while Chaz had chosen to escape in the arms of the luscious Angie. He had a vague memory of brunette and buxom with big brown eyes and a little girl lisp. Nothing like Carrie. His gaze slid to the baby and he frowned. And nothing he'd be interested in associating with on a permanent basis.

It had to be Angie, he decided reluctantly. She was the only woman he'd been with, other than Carrie, during the crucial time frame. "Okay," he reluctantly confessed. This wasn't going to go over well, but he didn't see what choice he had. "There was someone."

CHAPTER THREE

*The stockings were hung
by the chimney with care...
But who'd planned for a baby?
Her stocking wasn't there.*

CHAZ WINCED AT Carrie's expression. He couldn't have hurt her more if he'd slapped her. "It was before we met," he hastened to explain. "Right before."

"None of my concern," she insisted a shade too brightly. She jumped to her feet. "I'll just leave you to get in touch with whomever she is. Merry Christmas, Chaz."

He stood, as well. "Not so fast. You can't leave."

Anger flashed across her expressive face. "Can't?" she repeated.

He lowered his head and thrust his hand through his hair, gathering his self-control. "Please," he said, looking up again. "Don't leave. I don't know anything about babies. So either I call Child Protective Services or the police, and have the baby hauled off on Christmas Eve, or we take care of her until I can get this straightened out."

She shook her head. "What does any of that have to do with me?" She glanced at the baby and her face tightened with something resembling grief. "You didn't want a permanent relationship, remember? Not marriage. Not even a serious commitment. Certainly not a baby. And yet look what Santa's brought you. The irony is—" She broke off and held up her hand. "This has nothing to do with me."

"Carrie, it was a one-night stand."

Brushing past him, she crossed the living area to where he'd put up his own Christmas tree. He'd purchased a real one, whose needles stayed put and didn't fling disgusting globs of green fur at unwitting passersby. She fingered a branch, then wrapped her arms around her waist. "I understand it was a one-night stand. For some reason, it doesn't make me feel any better."

"I'm sorry." He didn't know what else to say. "I wish there were something I could do to change it."

"There isn't."

His gaze returned to the baby. "You're right. There isn't. Which means I should do whatever is in this little one's best interest." He paused deliberately. "And that involves you. I can't do this alone. Not yet. Will you help me? Please?"

She closed her eyes and he winced at the pain etched there. "Do you have any idea what you're asking?"

"Yes," he stated baldly. "I do. I'm hurting you. Again. Still," he hastened to correct. "But this isn't just about us. This is about a helpless infant. Honey, it's Christmas. And you've always been a Good Samaritan. I don't mean to take advantage of that, but I'm just hard-nosed enough to do it if I have to."

An odd smile drifted across her mouth. "At least you're honest." She put him through another minute of hell before nodding. "Okay, I'll help."

"Thank you." He struggled to organize his thoughts. It

all came naturally with computers and business. But with a baby... For some reason, babies engendered a vague sense of panic. "I don't suppose the woman put a name tag on her."

She joined him by the coffee table. "I didn't see one, but I haven't searched the box." Gingerly, she lifted the baby while Chaz examined the padding. "Anything?"

"No. But we can't just keep calling her *baby.* Since it's Christmas, how about Angel? Sort of matches the wrapping paper on the box."

Carrie gave the infant an experimental bounce. "What do you think, sweet pea? Does Angel work for you?" The baby cooed in response. "Alrighty, then. Angel it is."

Chaz searched the box a final time and pulled out two disposable diapers and a can of infant formula. A sudden thought struck. "You know...Angel only came equipped with the minimal accessories. This isn't going to last us through the night, let alone through Christmas."

Carrie's eyes widened in horror. "It's after four now. Most of the stores are going to close early. We'd better get whatever we need and fast."

"Damn it. I've never felt so helpless." He glared in frustration. "I don't know anything about babies. Where do we go and what the hell are we supposed to get?"

"I don't know much more than you. I mean, I babysat when I was a teenager, but not infants." She shot him an apprehensive look. "We'll need diapers, obviously. Maybe more formula. Do they eat baby food at this age?"

"Don't look at me."

She snapped her fingers. "There's an Everything Babies store right around the corner. We could ask them what she needs."

"Right. We'll just say, 'Look what Santa left on our doorstep. We don't know a thing about babies, so why don't you tell us what we should buy.' They'll have the cops on us in five seconds flat."

"Okay, okay." She returned Angel to her little nest. "You're the computer expert. Do a search on Google while I get a pencil and paper, and let's make a list."

A plan. Good. He loved a woman with a plan. It only took a minute to grab a pad and pen from his office, and input the necessary search information into his computer. "Okay, this site says…formula, diapers and baby glop."

"Check, check and check. What else?"

"Hell, look at all this stuff. I swear they need more than the two of us combined."

"Quit complaining, Latimer." Carrie released her topknot and shook back her hair. He watched it glitter and tumble around her shoulders in a sleek waterfall. "Just read it off."

He forced himself to ignore the distraction of all that hair, as well as the way her dress brushed and clung, practically making love to her body. He forced his gaze to the monitor. "Let's see… We need clothes. And there's no way we can keep her in a box. So some sort of crib and stroller." He scrolled down. "Blankets. Toys. You know, it occurs to me that there's a bookstore on our way to Everything Babies. We can poke around for something along the lines of *Baby Rearing for Idiots* and see if we've forgotten any of the basics."

"Good idea."

Chaz checked his watch. "We'd better hurry. We're running out of time."

"Wait, wait," She gestured toward the box. "We can't cart Angel around in that It'll draw attention to us. Why don't I stay here and watch her while you go shopping? You've got a list of the basics."

"True, but that doesn't change the fact that I haven't a clue what I'm doing and I can't risk asking. Besides, we need to make sure we get the right size. We all go together. Wrap her up and we'll carry her. Once we get to the store, we'll stick her in whatever stroller we decide to buy and wheel her around in that."

"Okay, fine. But you carry her. I don't want to risk slipping."

Chaz waited impatiently while Carrie meticulously wrapped the baby in protective layers. Fortunately, the weather had taken a break and, after picking up the necessary child-rearing book, they arrived at the store without incident.

"We close in twenty," one of the female employees greeted them. Her name tag read *Deb*, and she looked less than pleased to see them. Chaz could sympathize. It was Christmas Eve. No doubt she'd hoped to escape early.

"We won't be long, Deb," he assured her with an easy smile.

His smile perked her up and she offered a brilliant one in return. "Hey, no sweat. If there's anything I can do to help you, just let me know."

"I think we're good. But thanks."

"It never fails," Carrie muttered, grabbing a shopping cart. "Eighteen or eighty, it's always the same."

He stared at her in confusion. "What?"

"Forget it. What's first?"

He checked his list. "Stroller. Diapers. Food. Clothes. In that order."

The debate over the appropriate stroller consumed five precious minutes. They finally settled on one that would double as a car seat. On the way to the wall of diapers, they found a portable infant crib and dumped it in the cart,

as well as several of the largest age-appropriate disposable diaper packages they could find. On the food
aisle, Chaz turned ruthlessly efficient and simply scooped
a variety of formula, boxes of cereal and jars of baby food
into the cart.

"Thirteen minutes and counting," he warned as he
steered the stroller toward the clothing aisle. "You grab
clothes. I'll grab blankets. We'll meet at the booties. If
there's time, we'll hit the toy aisle."

Choosing the appropriate outfits apparently took
serious consideration, since he finished with both blankets
and booties without any sign of Carrie. He tracked her
down, still mulling over choices. "If it says three months,
buy it," he said in an undertone. "We're doing boy-style
girl shopping here, not 'does this make my butt look fat'
shopping. Got it?"

"Got it," she replied dryly. "I promise I won't worry
if any of the styles give Angel a serious case of bubble
butt. In the meantime, I suggest you let me finish here
while you do what boys do best."

"I'm afraid to ask."

"Buy your daughter some toys. Stuffed animals, rattles
and teething rings, Chaz. Not trucks, spaceships or laser
guns."

"Spoilsport."

"Five minutes and counting."

He took off, snatching anything pink and plush from
the shelves. By the time he finished there was more critter
in the stroller than baby. Just as Deb announced the
final closing warning over the store loudspeakers, Chaz
wheeled the overloaded cart and stroller up to the check-
out counter.

The impatient manager assigned three people to help

ring and bag. Chaz handed out discreet Christmas tips and then offered an additional wad to the beefiest of the teens to help carry everything back to his apartment.

Once they'd closed the door behind the happy—not to mention financially flush—teen, she and Chaz unloaded their purchases. Winter darkness had settled in by the time they finished and one look at Carrie's expression warned that she was on the verge of bolting, something he'd do anything to prevent. Sure enough, she glanced at him and offered one of her dazzling smiles—the sort that buried her emotions beneath a facade of cheerful affability. The smile served as a warning, one he'd picked up on early in their relationship. It usually meant *I'm not happy, but I'm going to pretend I am while I flay strips off your hide with sweet Southern charm.*

He got in the first word. "Don't."

Her smile faded and she lost some of her balmy South beneath an icy nor'easter. "Don't what?"

"You're going to leave now and I don't want you to."

She spared a glance toward Angel, who slept peacefully in her stroller. "I realize you don't feel equipped to handle your new responsibilities, but you'll catch on. Or if you have problems, call your mom. I'm sure she'll be over here in a New York minute to greet and mother her first grandchild."

"This has nothing to do with the baby and everything to do with us."

She shook her head, refusing to meet his gaze. "There is no us."

"There could be."

Her chin wobbled in an alarming manner. "You're wrong. Now, more than ever, it would be a mistake. You couldn't handle a relationship on top of everything else."

She lifted her gaze to his and her eyes glittered with teary gold highlights. "How are you going to deal with our issues, plus the responsibilities of fatherhood, plus whatever problems are going on with Angel's mother? Not to mention your true love…your Web site."

"We can worry about that tomorrow. It's Christmas Eve, Carrie. Spend it with me. Please."

He didn't give her a chance to refuse. He simply pulled her into his arms again, just as he had earlier that day. He kissed her. And just like earlier that day, she melted. Her lips parted and she sighed. He inhaled the gentle sound, breathed her in. She tasted like Christmas and the advent of spring all rolled into one. She smelled of sunshine and daffodils, Christmas wreaths and mulled cider. And she felt warm as a sunny day and soft as a snowflake on eyelashes.

"Stay," he murmured against her mouth. "Stay for Christmas."

Carrie surrendered. She was lost, lost in a blizzard of heat and passion and uncontrollable need. The rational portion of her brain—a teeny-tiny portion—set off warning bells. But for some reason they sounded like the silver bells in Christmas songs, full of seasonal cheer and joy. Yes, joy. That's what she felt in Chaz's arms. Sheer, unadulterated joy.

Without a word, he swept her into his arms and carried her to the couch. They tumbled, arms and legs intertwined, wrapped together like one of the presents under the tree. All they needed was a bright red ribbon to finish the job.

He found her mouth, ravished it. And she let him. Encouraged him. Parted her lips and met each delicious thrust with a teasing parry. She couldn't even find it within her to protest when his hands skated along the silky length of her dress. He cupped her breasts, running his thumbs across the tips until he'd teased them into rigid peaks. Her gasp caught in her throat and became a moan.

He tore his mouth free and strung a series of light kisses along the length of her neck and into the vulnerable hollow at the base of her throat. His hands began to roam again, finding the hem of her abbreviated dress and slipping beneath. He feathered his fingertips along the sensitive skin between knee and thigh, causing the heat to pump to nearly unbearable levels. He found the seam at the tops of her thighs and traced it, edging her panties aside and slipping inward. Then he cupped her, dipping a single finger inside.

She literally went deaf and blind. It had been so long, so hideously, desperately long. She clenched around him, wrapped her legs tight about his waist, wanting more than this tantalizing foreplay. She wanted Chaz. She wanted him inside of her. She wanted every bit of him possessing her in that wild dance they'd perfected during their months together. She'd never known love could be like that. But something happened whenever she found herself in this man's arms. It was like being granted every possible Christmas wish all in one glorious instant.

He must have felt the same way because he groaned. "It's not enough. It's not anywhere near enough. You know what we want…what we need. Give it to me, Carrie. Don't shut me out again."

"I won't. I can't."

She kissed him frantically, crazed, urgent kisses. He eased his hand out from beneath her skirt and she thought she'd scream in frustration. Until she heard the delicious sound of his zipper being released.

"Hurry," she urged. "Please, hur—"

Nearby, Angel stirred and released a fretful grumble

that escalated into a full-blown cry, and sliced right through the sensual spell that held Carrie in its grip. For a split second neither of them moved.

How could she have forgotten? Chaz had fathered that darling baby with some other woman. As much as she'd love to be the mother—to be involved in a serious, permanent relationship with Chaz—she wasn't. This evening wasn't a scene out of a homey Hallmark special. She could never have that with Chaz. Not without a miracle. And somehow she suspected Santa was fresh out.

"I've lost my mind," she whispered. She ripped free of Chaz's embrace and stood, wobbling as she struggled to get her legs to cooperate with her brain. Not daring to meet his gaze, she yanked at her dress to straighten it. "I can't do this. I won't. I have to go."

"Carrie, wait." He winced as Angel increased the volume of her cries. He picked her up, giving her an experimental bounce. The tears paused and she blinked at him, her mouth hovering between a pout and a smile. He took a single step in Carrie's direction. "We need to talk about this."

"There's nothing to talk about. That baby in your arms says it all."

"Sweetheart—"

She snatched up her purse and whirled to confront him. "What more do you want from me, Chaz? I've done everything you've asked, more than any other woman would have done, given the circumstances. Now it's time for me to leave."

Giving him a wide berth, she darted into his foyer and lifted her coat off the rack. She shoved her arms into the sleeves and yanked open the door. She didn't know who was more surprised—her or Chaz's mother, who stood outside his door with her fist raised, preparing to knock.

She blinked in surprise at Carrie, and then her gaze traveled to her son before landing on Angel. Her eyes widened in shock and disbelief.

Her mouth opened and closed three times before she managed to speak. "Oh. My. God."

CHAPTER FOUR

The baby was nestled, all snug in her crib,
while visions of family danced in her wee head.

CARRIE FROZE, NOT QUITE certain how to handle the situation. "Mrs. Latimer," she said weakly.

"Joanne. You agreed to call me—" She pointed at Angel. "That's a baby my son is holding."

Carrie swallowed. Hard. "Yes, yes, it is. It's Chaz's baby."

Joanne appeared dazed. "I thought you and Chaz had broken up. But instead you had a baby. It's a Christmas miracle, that's what it is." She wrapped her arms around Carrie. "I'm so happy."

"No, no. You don't understand." Carrie threw a desperate look over her shoulder at Chaz. Uh-oh. She knew that expression. He was thinking and thinking fast. That could only mean one thing. Trouble. "Don't you dare!" she warned.

Not that he listened. "I just found out today, Mom." He carefully returned Angel to her stroller where she sat, watching with intense baby interest as the latest drama unfolded. "Carrie brought her over just a few hours ago."

"Why you—" Joanne tightened her hold, choking off the words. "I can't believe this. This is the most wonderful news. Just what I needed today of all days."

"Is something wrong?" Carrie asked at the same instant as Chaz.

Joanne released her hold on Carrie and went over to hug her son. "No, no. Just the usual. This has always been a tough time of year for me." She beamed through her tears. "But not any longer. Now let me see my grandbaby. Come on, give me all the details. Boy or girl—girl by the look of all the pretty lace and ribbons. How old? How did it happen? When did it happen? Oh, tell me everything."

Carrie winced. No doubt the emotions of the season had caused Joanne's logic circuits to overload. Otherwise some quick math would have told her that the baby couldn't possibly be Carrie's. "Joanne—" she began, only to be cut off by Chaz again.

"Her name's Angel, temporarily, at least. And as much as I'd like to tell you it's what you think—" he shook his head "—it's not, Mom."

Her smile wavered. "This isn't your baby?"

"Sort of."

Joanne planted her hands on her hips. "There is no 'sort of' with babies, Chaz. Either she's yours or she isn't. Or are you going to stand there and tell me that Carrie had an affair and you're not sure— Oh. Oh, my goodness." She whipped around and glared at Carrie. "Is that why you two broke up? You fooled around with someone else and now you don't know whose baby this is?"

Carrie's mouth dropped open. "No," she snapped, and shot a glare of her own at Chaz. "Start explaining and do it fast, or I'm out of here."

Chaz held up his hands. "Okay, see, it's like this—"

Behind them, someone pounded on the door. "Hey, bro! It's Christmas Eve. Let me in so we can raise a glass to the old ho-ho-ho himself."

"Sounds to me like Thad's already raised a glass," Carrie muttered as Chaz headed for the door. "Maybe two."

Joanne's face creased in a worried frown. "He isn't handling Christmas any better than I am, I'm afraid. He's never gotten over Dinah. Did you ever meet her, Carrie? She and Thad dated for ages."

"I think they broke up right before Chaz and I started dating," Carrie answered. "But trust me, I sympathize."

It was the wrong thing to say. Their momentary solidarity evaporated. "I guess you're Chaz's Dinah," Joanne said with a hint of censure in her voice.

"And he's my Dinah." Carrie shrugged and pinned a cheerful expression on her face. Damned if she'd look guilty about it. "It happens."

"Usually when it happens there isn't a baby involved."

"True."

Chaz opened the door and Thad blinked at each of them in turn. Then he grinned. "A party. Cool. Dibs on the pretty one."

"Keep your hands off the pretty one," Chaz warned.

Thad winked at his mother. "Forget it. She's all mine." He swooped in, wrapped Joanne in a loving embrace and dipped her backward, planting a kiss on each cheek. "How're you doing, sweetheart? Merry Christmas."

legs. "Whoa-ho. What have we here? Did someone order a baby for Christmas? Mom? Something you want to tell your sons?" angel let out a gurgle and flailed her arms that?" As though in response to mystery

"Oh, get out of here." She swatted Thad's shoulder. "You know perfectly well she's not mine."

"Then that leaves—" He lifted an eyebrow in Carrie's direction. "You've been a busy girl."

She held up her hands. "Wrong again, Thad. She's not mine."

Joanne started. "*What?* What do you mean she's not yours?"

"That's what we were trying to tell you, Mom," Chaz began.

Carrie tapped her index finger against her chest. "*I. I* was trying to tell her."

"Fine. *You* were trying to tell her. Angel was dropped off on Carrie's doorstep with a tag that had my name on it. We're not quite sure who she belongs to."

"Other than you," Carrie inserted smoothly.

Joanne pursed her lips as she studied the baby. "Well, she *is* the living image of you at that age, Chaz, so I'm betting when all this is resolved, you'll find you're a daddy. Which means—" she swooped down on Angel and lifted her gently from the stroller "—I'm a grandmother! Hello, darling girl. Who in their right mind would leave a helpless infant on a stranger's doorstep? Poor baby. Oh, dear. Poor *wet* baby. Would someone like to…?" She held Angel out in Chaz and Carrie's direction.

"I don't have a clue how to change a diaper," Chaz pro-
Carrie g
don't you think, Jo
"I most certainly do.
daughter and change her. Just pa,
off the wet diaper and you should be ab.
to put on the dry one. It isn't rocket science," .... learn

"I'd have an easier time with rocket science," Chaz muttered.

Nevertheless, he took his daughter from his mother and headed for his bedroom, where he and Carrie had set up a temporary changing and sleep area. He put Angel down on the small table, on top of a changing pad—something that, until an hour ago, he'd lived in blissful ignorance of—and popped the snaps on the baby's pretty red-and-green one-piece. The instant her legs were free, she began pumping them like a marathon biker and he found himself staring at her in amazement.

This was quite likely his baby, he realized with a sense of wonder.

He might not have planned to have her, but now that she was here…hell. It wasn't like he'd send her back, even if he could. For the past several hours, he'd been running nonstop, approaching the problem logically. Well… There'd also been that brief time he'd gotten sidetracked by Carrie and the couch. As incredible as that time had been, it hadn't been conducive to considering the ramifications of having a daughter. But now he stood and looked at her. Really looked.

Chaz shook his head. She took his breath away. She was so tiny and overflowing with life. Whoever had been taking care of her had obviously fed her and kept her in excellent health. Granted, she'd been dumped like so much garbage, and someone would be made to pay for that. That didn't change one simple fact.

He was a father.

Just the thought had him fighting for air, and he could guess why the actuality caused such a severe reaction. His own dad wouldn't have won prizes for Father of the Year. But at least, unlike Carrie's father, James Latimer had stuck around until after both his sons were grown and out on their own.

The divorce had been his mother's idea, no doubt an attempt to get her husband's attention off business and on to her. It hadn't worked. Chaz wasn't even sure his father had noticed the end of his marriage. He'd probably signed the divorce papers, along with whatever stack of contracts the secretary had dropped on his desk that day. But his apathy toward the death of thirty years of marriage had wounded his mother beyond measure.

As a result, Chaz had always been determined to follow a different path through life, one where his own preoccupation with work wouldn't cause undue hardship on his wife and children—because he didn't intend to have either until he'd succeeded on the career front and could afford to devote a significant portion of his time and energy to his home life.

Angel paused her pinwheeling long enough to stare up at him, probably wondering why she wasn't papered, taped and snapped back together. He couldn't suppress a grin. "Okay, I got the message. I'm on it."

He two-fingered the dank diaper to one side and examined the clean one. It seemed straightforward. Tab A beneath baby butt. Fold tab B up and over. Fit slot C sticky thing across left side of tab B. Fit slot D sticky thing across right side of tab B. Easy. Of course, the wiggling made it harder than it appeared and after he stuck the sticky tape from slot D onto the right side of tab B, the sucker ripped. Even that he handled. He simply grabbed some duct tape from his office and patched up the problem. No sweat. Then it was down to the rather difficult process of inserting wriggling baby legs back into itty-bitty leg holes of her one-piece and the job was done.

Finished, he lifted her into his arms and found himself inhaling her scent. God, she smelled good. Not Carrie good, but baby good. All new and fresh. And he couldn't get over the softness of her creamy skin. He was a daddy, he marveled again. And this tiny creature, whose heartbeat fluttered against his chest, was part of him and his life, and would be from now on. It was scary. Scary and dazzling. And somehow revitalizing.

He returned to the living room, where he found Joanne and Carrie talking quietly on the sofa. Not good. There was no knowing what the two of them might decide once they had a heart-to-heart. Even worse, Thad was frowning morosely at the tree, no doubt remembering last Christmas with Dinah.

Carrie glanced up and offered an amused smile. Then she gestured toward the bottle sitting on the coffee table. "I don't know when Angel last ate, but I warmed up a bottle in case she's hungry."

If she thought he'd try and palm off his daddy duties on her or his mother, she was dead wrong. He might not have asked for this, but he took his responsibilities seriously. He settled Angel in the crook of his arm, picked up the bottle and offered it to her. Her little rosebud mouth popped open and she latched on to the nipple like a barracuda on live bait.

"So Carrie filled us in on how you ended up in your current predicament," Thad said in an undertone. "I have to admit, I'm surprised. You were always the one preaching about the importance of taking precautions."

"I did take precautions. I've always taken precautions."

Thad lifted an eyebrow. "And yet here you are with a baby in your arms."

Chaz struggled to control a flash of irritation. This wasn't really about him or the baby. He knew his brother well enough to understand that Thad was thinking about Dinah and the life he'd hoped to have with her. "Nothing's one hundred percent," he said. "You know that."

"Your baby is."

Chaz inclined his head. "Fair enough."

Thad stared at Angel, his thoughts buried beneath a scowl. "You do realize this changes everything." His voice had risen just enough to attract their mother's attention, along with Carrie's. "This totally screws our plans."

"Not totally. It just means I have to figure out a schedule that will handle a few additional responsibilities. Since this is my office, as well as my home, I can watch Angel while I work."

"You won't be able to put in the same hours. Do you have any idea how much I've sacrificed for our dot-com?"

"The same as I've sacrificed," Chaz replied calmly.

Stubborn denial built across Thad's face. "It's not the same. It's not the same at all. I loved Dinah, damn you. I wanted to marry her. Have kids with her." He stabbed a finger in Angel's direction. "A kid like you have. But I couldn't. You and I made a promise to each other. You know how important our promises are."

"I know."

Joanne stood, eyeing her sons uneasily. "I don't understand. What's going on? What promise are you talking about?"

Thad spun around and picked up the bottle he'd brought as a Christmas offering. "Ask Chaz." Breaking the seal, he splashed some of the single malt into a tumbler. "It was his brilliant idea."

"Chaz?" his mother whispered. "What's your brother talking about?"

He released as sigh. "He's talking about Dad. And family history. And a promise Thad and I made to each other."

"What promise?"

Chaz regarded his mother, choosing his words with care. "You know how Dad was…"

Joanne waved that aside. "Yes, yes. Work always came first."

Chaz nodded. "Thad and I wanted to go into business together, but we didn't want to turn into him. He'd make promises to us—to all of us—and then break them. You did a great job of covering for him, Mom. But as we got older…" He shrugged. "Let's just say we noticed."

Tears gathered in his mother's eyes. "I'm sorry. It wasn't intentional on his part."

"Don't," Thad broke in. "Don't defend him. Not after all this time."

"He had his priorities mixed up, that's all. I guess he still does." Her chin wobbled. "But what does that have to do with this agreement you two made?"

Chaz spared Carrie a brief look. He could see how she braced herself and it ripped him apart. He'd hurt her. He'd hurt her badly and that had never been his intention. In fact, the entire reason for the agreement was to avoid just that sort of pain.

"Thad and I agreed that we'd put our personal life on hold until after we got our business up and running. We didn't want to do to anyone else what Dad had done to you."

"And yet," Carrie interrupted with such wintry coldness that he cringed, "that's precisely what ended up happening, to both me and, apparently, to Dinah."

CHAPTER FIVE

With mamma all a'tear, while I'm in a funk,
My woman austere, my brother half-drunk...

CARRIE REGARDED THE TWO men. "Am I missing something here, or is that what ended up happening? You made an agreement, but you neglected to warn the women in your life not to expect a 'real' relationship?"

"Dinah knew," Thad muttered.

Chaz met her accusatory look dead-on. "I was up front with you that I wanted to get my business running successfully before committing to a permanent relationship."

She fought to conceal the depth of her hurt. "Funny. Our relationship sure felt permanent. We were living together, Chaz. We talked about the future all the time. And yet you never explained about this promise you and Thad had made to each other. You made it sound more like a business strategy."

"Oh, boys," Joanne murmured. Disappointment weighed heavy in her voice. "I applaud your decision to honor your commitments, but that wasn't the way to go about it. Does it have to be one thing or the other? Can't you find some sort of balance?"

"Apparently Chaz will have to." Thad lifted his glass in

a salute. "He gets the girl, the baby and the home life… everything we agreed to postpone. And what do I get?"

"Drunk, apparently," Chaz shot back.

Carrie stepped in. "Excuse me for interrupting your brotherly spat," she addressed Thad. "But he doesn't have the girl unless he's planning on renewing a close acquaintance with Angel's mother."

Chaz placed his daughter in her stroller and held up his hands. "Okay, that's enough. Time out, everyone."

For some reason, he commanded instant attention. It had always been like that with him. He dominated through sheer strength of personality, an underlying authority that caused most people to bend to his will. And when that didn't work, the rest usually caved when he offered one of those patented Latimer smiles. Even knowing that, she still did as he asked and fell silent.

"It's Christmas Eve. And that means we're not going to continue like this. We're not going to argue." He crossed the room and capped the whiskey before fixing his younger brother with a stern eye. "And we're not getting sloppy drunk. What we are going to do is order Christmas dinner."

"I could live with that," Thad admitted.

"Me, too," Carrie offered.

Joanne shot to her feet. "Well, don't leave me out. I'm fine with someone else preparing a meal."

"Not just a meal." Chaz smiled and Carrie's insides turned liquid, despite the intensity of her pain. "A feast. The best we can drum up on such short notice."

It was as though someone had thrown a light switch and Carrie could feel herself tumbling head over heels all over again. She didn't want to. Now that Thad had explained about the agreement, she knew just how impossible a future with Chaz was. But her heart didn't seem to care if tomorrow meant it would get shattered. She had tonight with the man she loved.

Loved.

The knowledge stopped her cold. She still loved Chaz Latimer. Not lusted—though there was plenty of that. Not admired, although that played a part, despite this agreement he'd failed to mention. She was down to the bones, with every beat of her heart, to the very depths of her soul, in love with this man.

An intense vulnerability swept over her. She couldn't very well leave, though every instinct she possessed urged her to do just that. But she needed to escape, if only for a short time, just long enough to recover her equilibrium. Her gaze fell on Angel and she seized the baby as an excuse.

"I think I'll finish feeding her and then put her to bed where it's quieter," Carrie offered.

She didn't wait for a reply, but left the others discussing dining options. Sweeping the baby into her arms, she disappeared into Chaz's bedroom and closed the door behind her. Now all she had to do was breathe. Breathe and reboot her emotional computer. She crossed to the bed and settled onto the mattress, gazing wistfully at the baby in her arms. Angel latched on to the proffered bottle and gazed right back at her.

If her life had taken a different turn, this adorable little girl might have been her own daughter. Tears filled her eyes at the thought. Great. Just great. This wasn't helping one bit. If she didn't get herself under control, she'd end up in a flood of tears. And then she'd have to climb out onto the fire escape because she sure as hell wouldn't be able to face Chaz and his family.

The door opened and Chaz stood silhouetted for a brief instant against the hallway light. Then he entered and closed the door behind him. "What's wrong?"

She forced out a brilliant smile and cradled Angel closer. "Not a thing."

His eyes narrowed. "Now I know something's wrong. It's that damn agreement, isn't it?"

She dropped the pretense. "It's everything. The agreement. Angel. Thad and Dinah. It's all one huge complication that I could live without." She hesitated. "Listen, maybe I should just go home. I'm intruding. I don't belong here. This is a time for family."

"It's a time for whomever I say it is."

He crossed to the bed and joined her there. Positioning himself behind her, he wrapped his arms around both her and the baby. He lowered his head so his jaw nuzzled alongside of hers and she could feel the warm give-and-take of his breath against her cheek. She shuddered at the sensation, memories piling on top of memories of past moments when he'd held her just like this. Those times were usually a prelude to lovemaking. So passionate. So urgent. A blazing tumble of bodies…and of hearts.

"We'll work through this, Carrie." The memories shattered against his low, rough voice. "Somehow, some way, we'll figure it all out."

She fought to keep her mouth from trembling. "I used to believe in Christmas wishes. But I think I'm a little too old for them now. Santa won't be bringing me a puppy this year."

He eased back and she suspected he was trying to read her expression in the darkness. "I think I'm missing something here. Explain."

She carefully switched Angel to her other arm, a sigh

escaping. "I told you about my mom's Christmas Eve tradition, right?"

"The wishes, sure."

She explained about the puppy. "I believed in those wishes for a long time after that. Right up until a neighbor clued me in a few years later. When Mom found out I wanted a puppy for Christmas, she called everyone she knew until she came across a friend of a friend of a friend who had one poor runt left in the litter his dog had surprised him with."

"Is it important how she pulled it off?" he asked reflectively. "Isn't that what Christmas wishes are all about? Does it really matter whether it's Santa or Mom and Dad, or even a friend of a friend of a friend?"

She considered the question. "I guess I hadn't thought of it in quite that way," she admitted.

"The point is, it happened." She could hear the smile in his voice. "You never know. Maybe Santa pulled a few strings and made sure all the friends lined up so you'd get your wish."

"Aren't you the optimist."

"You're right. I am." Determination threaded through his words.

He took the sleeping baby from her and crossed the room to place Angel in the portable crib. Already, he'd bonded with his daughter, allowing the infant into his life far more deeply than Carrie ever could have imagined. The expression of tenderness on his face nearly broke her heart. Why couldn't he have felt this way with her, experienced the joy of fatherhood with their child? Why did it take this little Christmas miracle for Chaz to find a way to combine the best of all worlds?

He turned to face her. "I like your mom's tradition," he

surprised her by saying. "So tonight, I've decided we're all going to make our own Christmas Eve wishes."

"Don't do that to me, Chaz," she whispered. "I don't think I could handle the disappointment."

He approached the bed. "Who says you're going to be disappointed?"

She squeezed her eyes closed. He was killing her by inches and it took every ounce of willpower to keep from either lashing out or bursting into tears. "It's guaranteed to happen because you can't give me what I'd wish for," she managed to say. "No one can."

"Tell me your wish."

She opened her eyes, startled. He was close. Far closer than she'd realized. And he spoke with a compassion that ripped her to shreds. "It's not time for that," she replied automatically. "That's not the tradition."

He came down on the bed beside her and pulled her into his arms. "Maybe we can start our own tradition."

She turned on him. "How can you even suggest such a thing? You and Thad made a promise to each other that excludes both me and Dinah." She held up her hand before he could argue the point. "There's no working around that. Just as there's no working around Angel."

"I don't intend to work around her. She's my responsibility now and I take my responsibilities seriously."

Carrie fought through the pain. "All the more reason we shouldn't be in here like this. Your daughter is far more important than anything we might have once had."

"Still have," he corrected.

She simply shook her head. "You're wrong."

Chaz lifted an eyebrow. "Am I?"

He didn't give her any opportunity to argue. He chose a far more direct method of proving his point. Without saying another word, he simply scooped her into his arms and kissed her. And with that one kiss, coherent thought evaporated.

She shouldn't give in to him like this. She should push him away, get angry…anything, other than submit. But his mouth seduced her, sliding across hers with a delicious urgency that defied any and all attempts to put an end to the embrace. Instead, she encouraged him with the tiniest of moans, deep and throaty and filled with urgency.

Chaz responded by shifting her backward until her knees bumped against the edge of the mattress. Then he cupped her face and slanted her head to a slightly different angle, just enough so that he could deepen the kiss. And still she made no move to stop him. Just as before, she melted beneath that heated onslaught, falling into him—into his mouth, into his body…and, finally, into his bed. He followed her down, pressing her into the comforter, the dichotomy of softness beneath and hard, masculine strength above had her squirming in reaction.

She wanted this. It had been three impossible months, dark and dreary and lonely. Not a day went by that she didn't think about him, long for him. Wish that Chaz had been just a shade less dedicated to his business—just enough to allow her in. He wanted to. She knew it to the core of her being. Now, finally, she understood why he'd been so adamant about postponing marriage and a family.

His kisses grew more urgent and she threaded her fingers into his hair, anchoring him in place so she could give to him as thoroughly as he gave to her. His hands slid from her face to her shoulders, and then lower, cupping and caressing in their downward path. He lingered at her breasts, tracing the aching tips in a teasing circle until she trembled with need. And then he drifted lower still.

She felt the coolness of the air on her thighs, a coolness in direct opposition to the heated warmth at the very core of her. "Chaz…" His name escaped in a helpless cry. "We can't."

He groaned. "I know. Just let me touch you again. Just for a minute. Then we'll stop."

They were both kidding themselves. He wouldn't stop. Couldn't. Just as she wouldn't do anything to make him. Couldn't. They belonged together, like this. Had been apart for too long to resist what nature had created between them. She lifted against his touch, opening herself to him, quivering beneath an onslaught of overwhelming desperation.

If they could have this single night together, she'd be satisfied. It would almost kill her to walk away, but she'd do it, if only she could come alive in his arms, possess and be possessed, just one last time. He'd worked the hem of her dress up to her waist and hooked his fingers in the elastic band of her panties. His breathing thickened as he inched the scrap of lace downward.

"I've never known a more beautiful woman than you," he murmured. "I've never felt for anyone else what I feel for you."

He was breaking her heart. She slipped her hands over his, preventing him from finishing what he'd started. "This won't change anything. It will only make it more difficult."

His jaw assumed an endearingly stubborn slant. "I don't care. It's Christmas and this is my Christmas wish."

If she were honest, she'd admit it was hers, as well. But it wasn't enough. And it was too much. "Chaz—"

Carrie never finished what she'd started to say and he never knew whether she'd have given him his Christmas wish. A tentative knock sounded at the door. "Chaz?"

Nothing could have dampened his desire faster than the sound of his mother's voice. He levered himself off the bed and straightened first his clothing, and then Carrie's. Helping her up, he pointed to a spot behind the door, where his mother wouldn't be able to see her—or what he'd done to her hair and clothing. Because one look and there'd be no question what the two of them had been up to.

Satisfied that Carrie was out of sight, he opened the door a crack. "We'll be right out. Angel just fell asleep."

"Oh. Oh, good." She caught her lip between her teeth to keep from smiling and Chaz realized the jig was up. "We're ready to order something to eat whenever you are."

"Give us two minutes. Tell Thad to go ahead and order whatever you two decided on, just make sure there's plenty."

Closing the door, he glanced at Carrie, finding he couldn't take his eyes off her. She was the most gorgeous woman he'd ever seen. Her hair fell to her shoulders in a wayward cloud of soft browns and gold, while her lips were still plump and reddened from his kisses. Even without the telltale creases in her dress, her eyes gave her away, the jade and amber highlights slumberous from the banked embers of their passion. In the miniscule dress she wore, every spectacular inch of her was on display. But it was more than just her looks. Far more.

She was also kindhearted. He'd often teased her about being a soft touch, especially living in New York City, but he admired the quality, just as he admired how hard she worked and how brilliant she was when it came to numbers. He didn't know how he'd managed to get through the past three months without the sound of her laughter or the sight of her smile or the soft give of her body whenever he pulled her into his arms. They were made for each other, fitting perfectly in temperament, intellect and strength of passion.

If he were to have made his wish right now, he'd wish that she would bear him a daughter and that his ring glittered on her finger. He'd wish that he and Thad could undo their devil's agreement and that his father would somehow learn that family came first, even ahead of work. And he'd wish that he could find a way to balance the needs of his fledgling business with the desire in his heart—a desire to have it all.

A wife.

A baby.

A family.

And a successful career.

"That bad?" she asked in response to his prolonged scrutiny. Tension crept into her voice.

He blinked, fumbling for a reply. "No, no. You're fine. Just giving us a few minutes to cool off."

She scooped her hair back from her face and ran her hands through the strands in an effort to smooth them. "Better?"

"You look beautiful." His fingers tangled with hers as he helped finish the task. "Are you okay?"

"I'm fine," she reassured him.

"Good. I put some Christmas music on before I came in here. And I've opened a bottle of my very best wine." He nudged her shoulder the way he used to when he was teasing. She smiled in response, though it contained a bittersweet quality. "It even has a cork."

To Chaz's relief, the stiffness eased from her body and she choked on a laugh. "Wow. Now I'm really impressed."

"You should be." He snapped his fingers. "I need to do something real quick before we join the others."

"What?"

"Can't tell. It's a surprise." Aware that their two minutes were up, and then some, Chaz snatched up a pencil and paper and scribbled a quick note before tucking it into his pocket. Then he inclined his head toward the door. "Ready?"

She snatched a deep breath. "As ready as I'll ever be."

They returned to the living area just as Thad flipped closed his cell phone. "Okay, I've placed the order. They promised fast service."

A knock sounded at the door and Chaz grinned. "Okay, I'm impressed. That was really fast." He crossed to the door and pulled it open. Swearing beneath his breath, he almost slammed it closed again. "This was *not* what I wished for."

His father grinned nervously. "Merry Christmas, son. The sign on your old apartment said this was your new place. I guess I missed getting the change of address card." He reached behind him and tugged at someone's arm. "And look who I brought with me."

Dinah peeked out from behind his father's bulk. "Surprise. It's me."

CHAPTER SIX

When, what to my wondering eyes should appear,
But two exes come knocking, one shedding a tear.

AS MUCH AS CHAZ WANTED to turn his father away, he couldn't bring himself to do it. It was Christmas Eve, when families came together in celebration. How many times had his father been around on Christmas Eve? He could count the number on one hand.

He stepped back and waved Dinah across the threshold. Then he shifted in front of his father before James could follow suit. "Mom's here," he warned in an undertone. "She's fragile. If you do anything to upset her, I'm throwing you out, Christmas or not. Are we clear?"

"Joanne's here?" His father's bright blue eyes lit up and his cheeks took on a cherry-red flush. "I've been calling her all day. All I got was her voice mail. I thought maybe she'd gone out of town for the holidays."

"You haven't answered my question, Dad."

Some of his father's good cheer faded, replaced by a hint of pain and sorrow. He released his breath in a gusty sigh. "Yes, Chaz. I understand. I didn't come to start trouble."

Before Chaz could ask why his father *had* come, James brushed past and followed Dinah into the living area.

Dead silence greeted their advent. Then Thad erupted from his seat on the couch.

"What the hell are you doing here?" he demanded, his gaze fixed on Dinah.

"Thad." Joanne whispered a reprimand. "That's no way to greet—" Her gaze shifted from Dinah to James and her eyes widened in shock. Chaz didn't think she'd realized who stood there until just then. "What the hell are *you* doing here?" she asked, confirming his guess.

Dinah's gaze bounced apprehensively from Thad to James to Joanne, and her eyes filled with tears. "Maybe this isn't such a good idea." She took a stumbling step backward toward the door. "Maybe I should go."

Chaz groaned. The evening was growing progressively more challenging. "No one's going anywhere," he announced. "Dinner should be here soon and there's plenty for everyone. We're all going to sit down and—"

"No, we're not," Thad retorted. "If Dinah stays, I'm leaving."

Joanne pointed an accusing finger in the direction of her ex-husband. "And if *he* stays, I'm leaving."

James held up his hands in the exact same gesture Chaz had used earlier that evening, an unmistakable signal for peace. "I know I don't have any right to ask this of any of you, but I'd really appreciate it if—given the season—you would all listen to what we have to say. If you want us to leave after that, we'll go."

Joanne folded her arms across her chest. "Okay, fine. But make it fast so we can get back to enjoying ourselves without you."

Thad's eyes narrowed. "First, I want to know how you both ended up here. Together, I mean."

Chaz winced at his father's expression. Uh-oh. Based on the guilt lining his face, whatever had brought them here wouldn't be anything good. Maybe it was time for a distraction. "Who'd like a glass of wine?" he asked. "Dad?"

His father regarded him with acute relief. "Thanks, I'd love a glass."

"Dinah?"

"Yes, please."

His gaze met Carrie's and he saw a flash of sympathy. While he poured their drinks and succeeded in getting everyone seated in noncombative corners, she distracted them by describing the horror of her day, giving a humorous spin to events that couldn't have been the least amusing in all actuality.

When she got to the part about being fired, Chaz's hand jerked, spilling the wine. "You didn't tell me you'd been fired," he said in concern. That, on top of losing her apartment, would soon put her in dire straits.

She shot him a speaking look. "We had more important matters to deal with at the time. I'll let you take over when I get to that part of the story."

"Some of us have heard this story already," Thad interrupted. "I don't mean to be rude—"

"And yet you're succeeding beautifully," Chaz informed him.

His brother reddened. "You're right. I'm sorry." He glanced toward Dinah and his gaze practically ate her alive. "I just can't wait any longer. What's going on? Why are you here with my dad?"

Sheer panic bled across her expression. "I think James should explain."

"James?" Thad repeated. His eyes narrowed. "When

did you start calling my dad by his first name? The one time you met him, you called him Mr. Latimer."

"That was before Vegas." The whispered confession was barely audible.

"What?" The same question escaped in four different voices.

Chaz put down his wine and unscrewed the whiskey. "Dad? I suggest you take it from there and explain. Fast."

James cleared his throat. "Dinah and I met in Vegas."

"You didn't—" Joanne lifted a trembling hand to her throat. "You can't possibly be—" Her gaze darted to their left ring fingers.

"Married?" he offered dryly. "No, we're not. Though that was the plan when we went."

"What?"

James waved the four of them down again. "Oh, not to each other. Not exactly." He spared Dinah a brief, encouraging look. Not that it seemed to help. She inched backward toward the door, teetering on the verge of making a run for it. "We both flew to Nevada in order to attend a speed-dating party."

Thad frowned. "You went to Vegas to speed date? Why go all that way? You could have done that right here in the city."

Joanne eyed the two of them in disbelief. "Speed dating? You went to Vegas to go *speed dating?*" She eyed the contents of her glass, then knocked back a healthy gulp. "Are you sure there's only wine in this, Chaz? I think I'm hallucinating."

"I'm sure. And you're not." He lifted an eyebrow in his father's direction. "Aren't you a little old for speed dating?"

James took instant exception to the question, bristling at the suggestion. "No, I'm not."

Joanne glared at Dinah. "And aren't you a little young? Just how old are you, anyway?"

"Twenty-two," she replied. "Everyone my age has gone speed dating."

Joanne's mouth dropped open, then she turned on her ex-husband. "James Latimer, how could you? You're a full thirty years older. Not to mention the fact that she's your son's ex-girlfriend. Have you completely lost your mind?"

"I didn't know she was Thad's girlfriend. Not at first."

"Plus, he doesn't look thirty years older," Dinah offered. "I think he's sweet. And he would have made a much better husband than some of the other men there."

Dead silence greeted her statement and Chaz tossed back his whiskey, praying it would help. Thad seemed on the verge of decking their father. Carrie looked shocked, though he thought he caught just the teeniest glimmer of helpless amusement. And his mother appeared as though she were about to pass out. Again.

James yanked at the collar of a shirt that appeared to have shrunk two sizes in the space of two seconds, and cleared his throat. "Did I mention that the speed-dating party was for individuals looking for life partners?"

"No," Joanne snapped. "You neglected to mention that part. And allow me to clarify once again." She leveled a finger in Dinah's direction. "Twenty-two-year-old child." The same finger would have skewered James if he'd been a few feet closer. "Fifty-two-year-old, over-the-hill idiot."

"Oh, there were over-the-hill women there, too," Dinah offered ingenuously. "And they liked him a lot. You should have seen some of the dirty looks they gave me." She broke off with a nervous frown. "Now that I

think about it, they were sort of like yours, Joanne. Um...
Mrs. Latimer. Ma'am."

Chaz headed his mother off before she could take out
Dinah. He exchanged her wine for a whiskey, one she
downed in a single eye-watering swallow. "Easy, Mom,"
he murmured. "They didn't go through with it and they
came tonight for a reason. Let's hear them out."

"Oh, I'll hear them *out*," she muttered. "And then I'm
going to punch his lights *out* before I rip her hair *out*. Is
that *out* enough for you?"

"That should do the trick."

Carrie joined them and wrapped an arm around
Joanne's waist. "Come sit with me. You can whisper rude
remarks to me and I'll snicker. Will that help?"

"That would be lovely," Joanne said grandly. She
splashed more whiskey in her glass before gesturing
toward the sofa. "Let's go."

She tottered off to the couch, making a production of
taking the long way around so she'd avoid coming anywhere near Dinah and James. Dinah was shooting anxious
glances in Thad's direction while he shot infuriated glares
back. James settled for looking patently miserable.

"Well?" he finally said. "Should I continue? Do you
want to know why I went to Vegas?"

Joanne's chin shot up. "I believe you've explained that
part already. You wanted to recapture your youth by con-
ning some poor innocent child into a quickie marriage.
Well, I have news for you, James. The only thing faster
than that marriage would have been the divorce that
would have followed it."

"You're absolutely right," he surprised them all by
admitting.

Before he could say anything further, the doorbell

rang again. "That had better be dinner," Chaz informed the room at large. "I don't think I can handle any more surprises tonight."

Fortunately, it was. The delivery boy was dressed like an elf and was bent double beneath the size and weight of the meal they'd ordered. "Cool Yule, dude. And a merry ho, ho, hernia. Ouch. Mind if I put this down?"

"I'll take some of that off your hands," Chaz said.

The kid handed over the largest two of the three boxes with a sigh of relief. Gulping in air, he wound into a practiced spiel. "Santa couldn't make it. He's a bit busy tonight, as I'm sure you know, so he sent me instead. If you've all been good little boys and girls, I have some delicious treats for you courtesy of Chez Henri." His grin faded when it was returned with stony glares from half his audience. "Whoa. Is this the right place?" He examined the ink scribble on the back of his hand and checked it against the number on the apartment door. "Christmas Eve dinner for Latimer?"

"Unfortunately, you found the right place," Chaz confirmed.

"Hate to be you, dude," the elf muttered beneath his breath. He wrinkled his reddened nose. "This place looks like an asylum for the seriously naughty list."

Thad glared at him. "How about you shut up, put the dinner on the damn table and get the hell out, elf."

"Hey!" The elf cocked a finger in Thad's direction. "That just earned you a place as head naughty. That's a heaping helping of coal for you, little man."

Before the "little man" could launch himself at the even littler elf, Chaz dug for his wallet and thrust a handful of bills into the kid's hand. "Maybe this will help. Merry Christmas."

The elf grinned. "And you, kind sir, just hit the top five on my list of good little boys and girls. Care to try for top dog?"

"Don't push your luck."

"Fair enough. Merry Christmas." He turned and shot Thad a single-digit wave. "And bah humbug to you, jerk."

Of course, that caused all hell to break loose. Chaz managed to get the elf out of the apartment before Thad took him down. Or maybe the elf would have won. He was small, but he looked streetwise and probably had learned to fight dirty to compensate for his size. Chaz sighed. Now if he could only gather up everyone for dinner, let his dad and Dinah finish confessing their various sins and, at long last, get everyone out the door, then he could spend the rest of the night convincing Carrie that they belonged together. That somehow, someway, they'd work through their various problems.

This time he didn't bother holding up his hands. "Okay, listen up." He barked out the command. "I want everyone sitting at the table within the next two minutes or I'm pitching bodies onto the street and it won't be by way of the elevator or stairs. We're all going to sit down and we're going to be civil to one another for the length of one, solitary meal. Anyone who makes even the tiniest nasty crack is going to find himself in the uncomfortable starring role—pun intended—as my new Christmas tree topper. It's Christmas, in case you haven't noticed. And, just this once, we're going to celebrate it the way it's supposed to be celebrated. As a family. In peace and joy and, by God, goodwill toward men—and women—even if the effort kills us. Now let's eat."

A momentary stunned silence followed before everyone made a move in the direction of the table. They funneled past him, each one shooting him looks that varied from hurt to reprimanding.

"That was a little harsh, son," James murmured as he passed.

"Seriously uncool, partner," Thad added.

Joanne simply tsked as she weaved to her chair, a refilled tumbler of whiskey in hand. She fell into her seat with a tiny hiccup.

"You have something to add?" Chaz asked as Carrie approached.

"Just one thing." She leaned in so only he could see the laughter gleaming in her eyes. She mimicked the elf with impressive perfection. "Cool Yule, dude."

CHAPTER SEVEN

Cards on the table, all mysteries for naught,
Out came the truth, whether they liked it or not.

WHILE CHAZ AND THAD unloaded the boxes of food and
placed the various dishes on the table, Carrie and Dinah
carried plates, silverware and glasses in from the kitchen.
In no time, the table was set and the plates passed around.
Before they dug in, James offered a brief blessing.

"For the friends and family gathered here tonight, and
for the food we are about to receive, may we be truly
grateful."

For some reason, the simple prayer changed the mood.
Carrie snuck a brief glance toward Chaz and saw him
studying his parents with an almost wistful expression,
one mirrored by the look Thad gave Dinah. Were they remembering past Christmases, occasions filled with happiness and laughter? She wished she could have shared
just one with Chaz. She couldn't remember him saying
much about those long-ago holidays, other than that it had
been rare for the entire family to be together. It explained
a lot about the agreement he'd struck with Thad, even if
he'd swung the pendulum a bit too far to the opposite end
of the spectrum.

Even so, she refused to give up hope. Maybe, just maybe,

this would be the year everything changed. Maybe when James discovered he was a grandfather, it would make him finally realize the importance of family. And when Thad saw how Chaz combined fatherhood and his work responsibilities, he and Dinah would find a way to work out their differences. As for her... She doubted anything would change. Between work and fatherhood, there wouldn't be any time available in Chaz's life for romance.

The silence continued for a short time while the diners took the edge off their appetites. Taking advantage of everyone's preoccupation with food, Chaz leaned toward her. "Are you okay?" he asked in an undertone.

No doubt he was referring to what had gone on in his bedroom. She offered a bright smile of reassurance. "I'm fine."

"Losing both your job and your apartment on Christmas Eve can't have been easy for you," he surprised her by saying. He captured her hand beneath the table. "I can definitely help with one of those two problems. You can move in here with me while you look for another job."

She closed her eyes, hoping to hide the pain his suggestion stirred. "You know that's not possible."

"You're wrong. It's not just possible, but offers us a chance to work through our issues," he argued. "We could try again. This time we'll put all the cards on the table."

Didn't he get it? "How will that change the basic differences between us, Chaz?" she whispered. "If anything, you have even more pressing responsibilities than you did before."

He nodded in agreement. "I'm not saying it'll be easy. But we can figure it out if we work together." His fingers interlaced with hers, creating an unspoken bond between them. "Aren't you the one who believes anything is possible? That you can make your dreams come true if you try hard enough for long enough?"

"Once upon a time I believed that." Before her world had come crashing down. Before, one by one, she'd been stripped of everything she held most dear. "Listen, this conversation is pointless because…to be honest, Chaz, I'm thinking about moving back home. To Raleigh."

"You're joking."

She caught her lip between her teeth. "What's keeping me here? I have no job, no apartment and no ties—"

"You know that's not true," he ground out. Heads were jerking in their direction and Carrie watched as Chaz gathered his self-control. He spoke again in a softer voice. "This isn't the proper time and place to discuss this. We'll talk about it later, after everyone has gotten the hell out. But trust me, this isn't over."

James chose that moment to set down his fork. He cleared his throat to gain everyone's attention. "I don't want to start another fight, but I think it's important— tonight of all nights—to clear the air. If you'll all be patient with us and listen for a minute, I'd like to explain what Dinah and I were doing in Vegas."

Carrie could practically feel the waves of resistance coming off the others at the table. "Obviously, you were both there looking for life partners," she offered diffidently. "And just as obviously, you didn't find what you were looking for, since you both returned without one."

James seized on her comment with relief. "Exactly. Both of us went there looking for something, something we didn't find." He fixed his gaze on his ex-wife and each son in turn. "I'm not going to make any excuses about my past. I screwed up with you three."

"Yes, you did," Joanne agreed.

He took the criticism with a pained nod before addressing his sons. "I wasn't around when you boys were growing up, when you needed a father most." He swallowed, forcing out the words with difficulty. "Apologizing at this late date isn't going to change that, but I want you both to know I'm sincerely sorry. I was wrong. Dead wrong."

"Why, Dad?" Chaz asked. "Why couldn't you have been both a father and a businessman? Why did you have to choose one over the other?"

"And why business over us?" Thad added.

Carrie flinched. All during her relationship with Chaz, he'd held part of himself in reserve. During their time together, there had been cracks in his control, cracks through which his deeper emotions seeped out. But those moments had been all too rare. Now she was beginning to see the root cause. How many Christmases had he hoped his dad would show up? And how many of those years had he been disappointed? After a while, he'd given up hoping, and buried the hurt and want in a place no one could touch. But here it was, erupting from that secret place, spilling out for everyone to see.

"Why wasn't I there?" James asked. "Or why am I apologizing now?"

"Both," Thad answered for his brother. "We needed you and you were never there."

"Mom did her best." Chaz reached over to cover his mother's hand and give it a gentle squeeze. "But it's not the same."

James didn't spare himself. "I thought providing you with a home and everything money could buy was more important than providing you with my time and attention.

It's what I was brought up to believe and it was wrong. *I* was wrong."

Joanne burst into noisy tears. She snatched up her napkin and buried her face in it. James practically burst from his chair and rushed to kneel at her side. "Honey, please don't."

"How dare you?" she sobbed. "How dare you do this to me now. All those years I pleaded with you. Begged you for just a scrap of your time for the boys. For me. And you never gave it to us. I thought you'd come to your senses when I threatened to divorce you. But you just shrugged it off and kept your nose buried in your work while my world fell apart."

"I was wrong," he pleaded. "I was an idiot."

She slapped the napkin onto the table. "Yes, you were," she told him fiercely.

"I want to change that, if you'll let me."

She shoved him away. "Have you lost your mind? I can't believe you're doing this. Now that the lightbulb has finally gone off, you show up. And what do you admit to all of us? That you've had your midlife epiphany and, instead of coming to me, you flew off to Vegas looking for someone else to share your remaining years with." Her face crumpled, but somehow she succeeded in holding the tears at bay. She faced him down with painful dignity. "How could you, James? How could you do that to me?"

He bowed his head. "I thought you didn't want me any longer. I thought it was over between us."

"Oh, it is! It is *so* over."

"Honey, listen to me. It wasn't until I met Dinah that I realized the truth."

"Dinah!"

Joanne glared across the table at her. Dinah slid down in her seat, distinctly alarmed. Thad inched his chair closer. "Don't blame her. This is Dad's doing," he protested.

"Why not?" Joanne demanded. "She was there, too."

Thad blinked. "Oh. Right." He frowned at Dinah. "What were you doing there?"

"Looking for a husband," she whispered.

Anger exploded across his face. "Why the hell were you doing that?"

Her mouth compressed into a stubborn line. "I had my reasons."

"The point is," James interrupted, "after Dinah and I met and discovered the connection to you, Thad, we realized we were making a huge mistake and we had to come home. Both of us."

"Why?" Joanne asked bluntly.

James hesitated, gathered himself, then admitted, "I don't want just any woman, and definitely not the sort I met in Vegas. There's only one person capable of creating the family I need. And that's the woman I married thirty years ago."

Tears burned in the backs of Carrie's eyes as she watched the transformation to Joanne's expression. In that moment, her resemblance to Chaz was unmistakable. Her dark eyes glittered like jet and the elegant planes of her face softened.

"Oh, James," she whispered. Then she shook her head. "I wish you'd come to this realization years ago."

"Is it too late?" he asked. "Please don't let it be too late."

She hesitated. "I need time," she finally said. "We both do. Time to get to know each other again and learn to trust."

Relief eased the deep lines carved in his face. "Fair enough. As long as you're willing to give me a chance, I'll do whatever it takes to win you back." He glanced over his shoulder at Dinah. "Okay, it's your turn now."

"Her turn for what?" Thad asked suspiciously.

Dinah fixed her gaze on her dinner plate, clearly nervous and a tiny bit afraid. "I don't think I can do this."

"Do what?" he demanded.

"Tell you the truth," she whispered reluctantly. She moistened her lips. "Explain why I went to Vegas."

"You mean…explain why you wanted to marry a stranger?"

She nodded. "Yes."

"You can do it," James encouraged.

"Okay." She exhaled sharply, then swiveled to look at Thad. "There's something I need to tell you, but I think it might make you really angry."

"I won't get angry." He closed his eyes. "Okay, I probably will. But I won't yell at you. Or if I start yelling, Chaz can hit me or something."

Dinah nodded. "That would work. You see—"

Before she could finish her sentence, a faint cry came from the direction of Chaz's bedroom. Carrie shoved back her chair at the same moment that he did. He waved her back. "My kid. I'll get it."

James stared, nonplussed. "Is that a baby? And did he just say 'my kid'?"

Joanne nodded with a hint of a smile. "It is and he did."

"What the hell is going on around here?" he complained.

She patted his hand. "There's a lot you don't know. Things like that happen when you're not around to participate in family life."

He lifted an eyebrow. "Oh, yeah? Well, just wait, sweetheart. You're about to discover there's a lot *you* don't know."

A minute later, Chaz appeared carrying a flushed and sleepy Angel. "Everyone, this is my daughter. Angel, this is everyone."

Instantly, they all started laughing and talking at once, except for Dinah. She shot to her feet, her chair crashing to the floor behind her. "What the hell are you doing with *my* baby?" she shrieked.

CHAPTER EIGHT

But I heard her exclaim, ere she kissed me just right,
"Happy Christmas to all, and to all a good-night."

ALL HELL BROKE LOOSE. Again.

"*Your* baby?" The question came in unison.

"No, it's Chaz's daughter," Carrie attempted to explain.

"She was left in a box on Carrie's doorstep addressed to me," Chaz added.

"That is *my* baby," Dinah said, tears welling into her eyes. "Mine and Thad's. Now, you give her back right this minute!"

Thad leaped to his feet. "Yours and mine? *Mine, mine?*" He dropped back into his chair, his voice shooting up an octave. "I'm the daddy?"

Dinah raced around the table and snatched her daughter from Chaz's arms, smothering the top of her daughter's head with kisses. Angel gurgled in delight, clearly recognizing her mother. Then Dinah turned to confront Thad. "That's what I was trying to tell you. After we broke up, I discovered I was pregnant. That's why I wanted a husband. That's why I went to Vegas to find one."

"And that's why we've spent most of the day tracking

everyone down," James added. "I told her if she needed a father for her child, she might consider starting with the one actually responsible for her predicament."

"And that's you," Dinah informed Thad. "Angela is your daughter."

"Angela?" Carrie repeated. "Is that really her name?"

"I call her Angel most of the time," Dinah confirmed. "But it's really Angela. I named her after my great-grandmother."

Carrie and Chaz exchanged stunned looks. "Weird," she murmured.

Dinah hugged her daughter tight. "And FYI, Thaddeus Latimer, I don't care whether you believe me or not. She's yours."

"I…I believe you," he said. "I thought she looked just like Chaz. But I guess that means she looks just like me, too."

He approached and held out his arms. Dinah hesitated for a long moment before shifting her precious burden into his hands. He stood, unspeaking, just staring down at the baby he held. His jaw worked, making speech impossible. "My daughter. *Our* daughter," he finally whispered. "She's incredible, sweetheart. She's the most beautiful thing I've ever seen."

"Yes, she is." Dinah aimed her momma-tiger gaze in Chaz and Carrie's direction. "What I'd like to know is how you ended up with my daughter."

Chaz shrugged. It felt as though he'd taken a shot to the gut. He'd only just accepted Angel as his daughter, had realized what a miracle he'd been offered, only to have it snatched away.

He suddenly realized Dinah was waiting for an answer to her question. It took him a second to gather himself enough to reply. "To be honest, we don't know a lot. An elderly woman dropped her off outside of Carrie's apartment." He struggled to distance himself, to let go of the dream and face reality. "She was in a padded box with my name attached to the outside."

"You know…" Carrie caught her lip between her teeth and offered him an apologetic look. "The tag simply said Latimer. It didn't specify either you or Thad, and I assumed, since you used to live there, that she meant you."

Chaz glanced at Angela and steeled himself to give up his role as daddy and assume the new one he'd been assigned. "Natural mistake," he replied, though the words came hard.

"This woman…" Dinah frowned. "Fortyish? Blonde?"

"Not even close," Carrie replied. "Elderly, white hair, Italian accent."

Dinah's eyes widened. "Oh, my gosh. Nonna! That's my great-grandmother, Angela's namesake." Her expression hardened. "I can't believe she took such a risk with Angel. How dare she endanger my baby!"

Behind them came another knock on the door. "The way our luck is running, it'll be CPS or the police," Chaz muttered.

Fortunately, it wasn't. He opened the door to find two women standing in the hallway. "Are you Chaz Latimer?" The younger of the two spoke up, a blonde woman, hovering in the plus-forty neighborhood. "I'm Rosalia Luciano. We're looking for—"

"Angela?"

"Yes!" Her knees buckled and Chaz was quick to offer her a supporting arm. "Oh, God, yes. You've seen her? Do you have her?"

He kept one arm wrapped around Rosalia's waist and offered his other arm to the elderly woman he suspected had played Mrs. Claus with Angel. "Come on in and join the party."

Rosalia took one desperate look around and practically exploded across the room toward her daughter. "Dinah!"

"Mom!"

Rosalia made a quick examination of the baby in Thad's arms and fought back tears. "Oh, thank goodness. You have Angela. You have no idea how terrified I've been. I went out to do some last-minute shopping and, when I came home, the baby was gone. It took me a solid hour to find out what Nonna had done with Angela. She flat-out refused to tell me until I threatened to call the police. When we returned to the apartment where she claimed she'd left the baby, no one was there. I totally lost it at that point."

"Aw, hell," James murmured. "Dinah and I took Carrie's note with the forwarding address to help us track down Chaz's new place."

Rosalia simply closed her eyes and shook her head, though Chaz noted that she still trembled from shock. He crossed into the living area to pour her a solid two fingers of Thad's rapidly dissipating single malt.

She smiled with teary-eyed gratitude when he pressed the glass into her hand. "Fortunately, the building manager showed up at that point. She suggested we come here."

Dinah stepped forward to confront her great-grandmother, hands planted on her hips. "Nonna, why did you give away my baby? Mom promised she'd babysit while I went to Vegas to find Angel a daddy. Have you any idea how dangerous that was?"

"Not dangerous. Give baby to maid." She pointed toward Carrie. "Tell maid give baby to Latimer."

Chaz lifted an eyebrow. "Maid?"

"I was wearing my sweats," Carrie confessed.

He winced. "Your security-blanket sweats?"

"Yeah. I guess I looked like your maid."

"Not exactly my image of a maid."

Carrie rolled her eyes. "You mean, not exactly your male fantasy of what a maid should look like."

"True."

Dinah interrupted. "I still don't understand why she would give away my baby—to anyone."

"Nonna didn't approve of your Vegas plan," Rosalia explained. "She felt that Angel's father should take responsibility for his child. But she got Chaz and Thad mixed up and…" She shrugged. "Well, here we are."

"Are you hungry?" Chaz asked the newest arrivals. "Would you like something to eat?"

"No, no. We really should get back home."

"I insist. Please stay."

Nonna didn't wait for a further invitation. She took a seat at the head of the table and, after Thad reluctantly handed Rosalia the baby, allowed him to fill a plate for her. "You father to my Angel?" she asked suspiciously.

"Yes, I am." Then he grinned, a joyous, dazed grin. "Yeah. I really am."

She stabbed a fork in his direction. "You bad boy."

"You're absolutely right, Nonna." He attempted an abashed look, but was smiling too broadly to pull it off. "But don't you worry. I'm going to fix that right now. Hey, bro?"

Chaz had been expecting this, knew what his brother was going to ask before the words were even out of his mouth. And he also knew that he needed to be the one to say them, to let Thad off the hook. "Our agreement isn't working out, is it? What do you say we modify it?"

"Modify it, how?" Thad asked suspiciously.

"I was thinking something along the lines of tearing it up and trying for a little more balance in our lives. It might take us a bit longer to succeed but…" He shrugged. "Family comes first, right?"

"Yeah, it does." Thad made a beeline for Dinah. Gathering her up, he led her to a chair and pressed her into it. Then he went down on one knee. "I've never stopped loving you, Dinah. I was a fool to let you go. All I've ever wanted was to spend my life with you." He spared a brief glance in Angel's direction. "Create a family with you, though we seem to have taken care of that part already. Will you marry me?"

"Oh, yes!" She threw her arms around his neck. "I love you so much."

"Maybe boy not so bad," Nonna pronounced. "Not good. Ring first. Priest first. Then good. But not so bad." That decided, she tucked into her meal.

The next couple of hours passed in a happy haze as everyone cooed over the baby and celebrated Thad and Dinah's engagement. Chaz couldn't help noticing that the joyful couple never strayed farther than a few feet from each other. He even caught his parents exchanging warm glances and stolen touches. Everyone seemed content… except Carrie, who kept the full width of the room between them. No happy endings for them, apparently. Not that it would stop him from trying.

Later that night, Nonna and Rosalia headed off for Christmas Eve mass, while everyone else drifted into the living room. The tree twinkled merrily, offering a promise

that warmed the heart. Chad hadn't forgotten his promise
to Carrie. It was time to continue an old tradition—hers—
and start a new one—theirs. He took a moment to explain
Carrie's Christmas Eve custom, pleased when everyone
jumped at the suggestion. In fact, the only person who
looked less than thrilled was Carrie.

"I'm not sure this is a good idea," she murmured.

"It's a fabulous idea," Joanne enthused, overhearing.
Chaz had never seen her so radiant. "It's almost midnight
and I, for one, can't think of a nicer way to end the evening."

James nodded in agreement. "I think we all have
wishes we'd like to make tonight." He spared his wife a
telling glance. "Wishes that should have been made a
long time ago."

The six of them gathered around the Christmas tree
and joined hands. A hush settled over them as they each
considered their wishes. James spoke up first. "I wish that
I could become the father I never was, and the husband
I should have been thirty years ago."

Joanne smiled with a sweetness Chad hadn't seen in
years. "And my wish is to be with you when your wish
comes true."

"Oh, Jo," he whispered. "Can you forgive an old fool?"

She leaned into him. "Only if you mean it. Really
mean it."

"I do."

Dinah cleared her throat. "I think I already received
my wish. All I've ever wanted is a father for my baby,
only…I realize now, it has to be the right father." She
turned toward Thad. "It has to be you."

Thad tugged her closer. "And my Christmas wish is to
marry the woman I love and raise our daughter with her.

And maybe, someday, have a brother or sister for Angel, as well. Only this time, I want to be there when my baby comes into the world and not miss a single second." He and his father exchanged a brief look of understanding. "I think we've both learned the same lesson, haven't we, Dad?"

James nodded, the muscles along his jaw taut with strain. "I'm just sorry it took me so long to figure out. But I'm relieved you learned it sooner, rather than later, before you lost everything most dear to you."

"Carrie?" Chaz prompted. "Your turn."

She snatched a quick breath and gazed up at the tree. He felt the slight tremble of her fingers. "I…" Her voice broke and she snatched her hand free of his. "I'm sorry. I can't. I can't do this. I hope you all have a very Merry Christmas. But I have to go now."

She darted from the room toward the entryway and snatched up her coat. Before he could stop her, she was out the door. He didn't hesitate. He shot across the room after her. A couple was exiting the elevator just as Carrie reached it and she ducked inside, punching frantically at the button for the lobby. There wasn't a chance he could reach her before the doors closed, so he detoured toward the steps, taking them at a dead run.

He slammed open the security door just as she stepped through the lobby door into the wintry night. He caught her before she'd gone a half-dozen steps. He hadn't bothered with his coat and the cold cut with brutal force. He didn't care. All his focus remained on the single object of his desire.

Carrie.

"Don't go." He caught hold of her arm and swung her around. "Honey, please don't go."

A harsh, frigid wind swirled between them, catching in her hair and sending the silken strands on a frenzied dance. Her eyes were pools of darkness, filled with pain. And her face was pale and cold, empty of all color and vitality. She stared up at him, remote and distant as a winter star. "What's left to be said, Chaz?"

"You haven't told me your wish," he said with a sense of urgency. "You can't leave until you tell me."

"What's the point? It won't change anything."

"Please, Carrie. It can't come true if you don't tell me."

Her face crumpled. "Don't you get it? It can't come true because Christmas wishes aren't real."

He dragged her into his arms. "Don't say that. Not you, of all people. You're the one who believes in the good of those around you. Who helps little old ladies across the street and has a kind word for everyone. You have to believe."

She closed her eyes in defeat. "Oh, Chaz. I can't anymore. I just want to go home." She lifted a hand to his face in an unmistakable gesture of farewell. "You're freezing. You should go back inside."

He shook his head, digging in his heels. "Not until you tell me your wish. I'll go back inside and you can go home just as soon as you tell me."

Debate raged across her face. He could see the resistance, knew that the only thing still holding her in place was her innate kindness. And it was that kindness that wouldn't allow her to leave him standing in the cold any longer.

Her mouth worked for a moment before she managed to get the words out. "Don't you know? Can't you guess?" Her sigh escaped in a soft cloud and her words escaped softer yet. "I wish you loved me as much as I love you."

He closed his eyes as relief surged through him. "Reach in my pocket and take out the piece of paper in there."

She pulled back. "Is that some sort of joke? I tell you I love you and you want me to put my hand in your pocket?"

"Just do it, Manning."

She slid her hand inside his pocket, driving out the cold and replacing it with rampaging heat. She fished out the folded piece of paper he'd put there earlier in the evening and offered it to him. "Is this what you want?"

"That's it. Open it. Read what it says."

She opened the note. *"I wish you loved me—"* she started to read before grinding to a halt and promptly burst into tears. "Oh, Chaz. Our wishes… They're identical."

"That's because we belong together, Carrie." He hooked her chin with his index finger and lifted her face to his. "I love you. I'll always love you. I want to marry you, Carrie. I want to have our own little Angel one day soon."

"Yes, oh, yes. I'd like that, too."

And then he kissed her. Where before their kisses had been filled with urgency and desperation, edged with sorrow and regret, now their kiss became a declaration. A wish both made and granted. Heat flooded through him, first to his lips, then his face, then through his entire body. This moment was all that mattered. Carrie…and the love they felt for each other. He had no idea how long they stood there embracing. He was vaguely aware of the foot traffic flowing around and past and of the honking of horns and swish of cars sweeping by.

Finally, he drew back. "Please come back inside so we can talk."

She didn't need any further prompting. Wrapping her arm around his waist, she returned with him to his apartment building. The ride up to his floor seemed endless. They entered the apartment to find Thad and Dinah curled up together in front of the Christmas tree while Angel slept in her small portable crib at their side.

"Where's your mother and father?" Carrie whispered.

He inclined his head toward the miniscule balcony off the living area. His parents stood there, arms intertwined, gazing out at the city. "It looks like everyone got their Christmas wish tonight."

Carrie studied the scene, misty-eyed. "Do you realize that, if it hadn't been for one innocent baby, none of our Christmas wishes would have come true?"

He tilted his head, considering. "A Christmas miracle?"

She shrugged, offering the sweetest of smiles. "Some could look at it that way. If they choose to."

"And you?" he asked tenderly.

"I choose to believe."

Hand in hand, they headed for his bedroom. There was just enough ambient light to see, so Chaz left the room in darkness. Pulling Carrie into his arms, they exchanged another kiss, this one more passionate than before, a prelude. A promise. A vow. Clothes whispered on their trek toward the floor, the softest of punctuations to their murmurs of love. Just as he was about to swing her into his arms, she broke away and crossed to the window, staring out into the night.

He frowned. "Honey? Is something wrong?"

"No, something's very right." She held out her hand. "Come and see."

He joined her at the window. Snow was falling. Not the harsh icy sleet from earlier that day, but a soft, tumbling snowfall of pure white flakes. A cleansing. In the distance, they could hear bells ringing as midnight struck. Without a word, he picked up his bride-to-be and carried her to bed.

Christmas had arrived. And all through the house, not a creature was stirring. Well, except Carrie and Chaz, who were doing what all lovers do to welcome in such a wondrous holiday.

* * * * *

THE CHRISTMAS EVE PROMISE

Molly O'Keefe

***

To the Gensler family—
all of them, even Jim.

Dear Reader,

I hope you are as excited to read this book as I was to be a part of it! Brenda Novak, Day Leclaire and Christmas—what could be better?

Everyone asks me if I get the ideas for my stories from my own life, and most of the time the answer really is no. My life is far too boring to inspire anything but articles on potty training and 101 ways to cook a chicken breast. But for this anthology, I did find the inspirations in my real life.

The diner in the story is modeled after one of my favorite college haunts in St. Louis—Monroe Diner. I took my husband there for our first date and we watched the waitress, with plastic flowers in her beehive, smoke a cigarette over the soup. Don't worry, I cleaned it up for this story.

Gavin, my hero, got his name because of the endless nagging of a good friend, oddly enough, named Gavin.

And I've been inspired by the friends in my life who worked up the courage to come out to their parents, and by those parents, who handled the conversation with grace and love.

I wish you all a wonderful holiday season!

Molly O'Keefe

CHAPTER ONE

WITHIN MOMENTS of walking downstairs to the diner, Merrieta Monroe was violently assaulted by Christmas.

A giant snake of gold garland over the door had come loose in the night and Merrieta didn't see it and got bonked in the face. Then, while unlocking the door and flipping the open sign, she stubbed her toe on Mom's full-size Santa and nearly body slammed it to the floor.

"God, please don't let Christmas kill me," she prayed and hit the overheads, illuminating in full fluorescent glory the spectacle that was Christmas with the Monroes.

It was as if Kris Kringle had exploded all over Monroe's Diner.

The gold-and-silver garland that covered the ceiling. The full-size crepe-paper Santa, who had been around so long he looked like a victim of leprosy. The twinkle lights. The music...

Wait a second...there wasn't supposed to be any music.

Vengeance in her heart, she whirled and found the culprit. The motion-sensor, sunglass-wearing Rudolph spitting out a tinny version of "Joy to the World," perched, grinning and nodding his mechanical head, on top of her espresso machine.

The one thing she'd begged her mother to leave sacred, uncluttered, unbefouled by schlock—her espresso machine.

And every morning for the past week she'd been home, there he was, proving her mother's devious sense of humor. Or impending Alzheimer's.

Merri backhanded Rudolph into the garbage.

Bah humbug didn't begin to cover her current attitude toward this holiday. *I'll get you, Santa, and your little elves, too,* was really more like it.

Which made her the least popular Monroe in the house. Behind even the cat, who wore her red-and-green collar with only mild disdain.

"Five days, Merri," she told herself. "Only five more days." The countdown wasn't even to Christmas Day. For the Monroes, all this holiday spirit culminated on the night before Christmas, at the Webster Groves Christmas Celebration.

Which, actually, was a fantastic event—the whole town got together to sing Christmas carols and drink eggnog and hot chocolate. Kids got gifts; Mom and Dad went a little nuts for playing Santa and Mrs. Claus. But as far as Christmas parties went, the night before Christmas was about as good as it got.

But the garbage leading up to Christmas Eve made Merri crazy.

On autopilot, Merri put on the coffee and pulled out her mother's banana bread and the whole-grain, low-fat pumpkin muffins she'd made yesterday, after her pants didn't button shut.

Today, she swore, making herself a scrambled egg and a decaf latte. *You have to tell them today.*

Upstairs, the floors creaked and she knew her mother

was up, getting her father a cup of tea. Helping him to the bathroom.

It's a broken leg, he'd yell. *It's not going to kill me.*

Rest, Mom would yell back. *Or I'll kill you myself.*

Merri grimaced. She'd grown up under the constant fear that her parents were moments away from splitting up. It just didn't seem possible that love could survive with all that fighting.

Which is why she took a different tack with her relationships.

And look at you, alone with just your espresso machine to keep you warm.

And forty years later—look at her parents. Still fighting. Still together.

It was enough to have Merri reaching for one of the muffins.

Customers began trickling in, but it was a half hour before Mom came down the steps, looking like Sophia Loren, but better. Lusher, livelier. Red lipstick in place, silver-and-black hair curled and pinned with a festive sprig of holly over one ear, dark eyes flashing.

Mom, as Dad was fond of saying, could stop clocks.

"Merri!" she said, stepping into the diner from the door leading upstairs to the family apartments. She glanced up and down the empty counter. "Have you been busy?"

"Not too bad," she said. "I told you I was fine until nine. You can stay with Dad." She poured her mother a cup of coffee, added two sweeteners and slid the cup toward Lenora without spilling a drop.

Years working in the diner had paid off with surprising but hardly wage-earning skills.

"Trust me, I'd rather be down here," Lenora said as

she sighed heavily and took a sip of coffee. "How are you this morning?"

"I'm fine, Mom." Lenora looked at her dubiously and Merri laughed, because while it was a lie, Mom didn't realize the full extent of the house of cards Merri was constructing. "Seriously. There are worse things in the world than breaking up with your boyfriend."

"Fiancé," Mom said, tsking her tongue. "And treating you like he did, with the affairs and the lies—"

"Mom, stop."

"And right before Christmas, too."

"Well, now I'm getting depressed."

Mom's sharp eyes slid over to her, and Merri, who swore she'd cried her last over Dean Billings on the long drive home with her espresso machine, stared back—dry-eyed.

"You're right, honey," Mom said, flinging her hand in the air. "He's not even worth a second thought."

The silence stretched and Merri felt her face get hot, her news a heavy burden traveling up from her chest to rest uneasily on her tongue. This was it. She was going to do it. Right—

"Why is it so quiet in here?" Mom asked, attempting to look innocent.

Merri nearly sagged onto the counter, a cold sweat breaking across her forehead. *Later,* she decided, relief making her giddy. *I'll tell her later.*

"What did I say about the singing Rudolph, Mom?"

Mom grinned into her coffee mug. "I don't remember, sweetheart. What did you say?"

Merri stuck her tongue out—because it was a brilliant comeback.

Mom turned on the radio under the counter and Bing's voice filled the quiet.

"How is Dad?" Merri asked. "Really?" It was, after all, the reason she was here—not that she had anywhere else to go after the Dean meltdown. Dad had broken his leg and Mom couldn't run the shop, get ready for the Webster Groves Christmas Celebration and deal with leprosy Santa alone. It was just dumb luck that all of this coincided with Merri's life falling apart.

"Still broken and not getting better if he doesn't do what the doctor says." Mom whirled, her brown eyes flashing. "He comes down here last night, after you left, like he's going to work the grill. He asks for the stool, tells me he can sit and flip burgers. I could have killed him."

"Mom, I'm sorry, I had to go—" Apartment hunting. She couldn't even say the words. Apartment hunting in Webster Groves, where she swore she'd never live again.

"It's not your fault your father is stubborn."

"This won't last forever, Mom. Dad will be back on his feet in no time."

"Maybe it's time your father and I sold." Lenora sighed, glancing sideways at Merri. "Or passed it on to you kids."

"Us kids? You mean me, Mom. Jake is in Iraq. And I don't want it." *I don't want to be my parents.*

"But you've had all these great ideas," Lenora said. "With the espresso machine and the muffins. And that café you ran in Kansas City was so lovely—you made it that way. And—"

"I'm not running the family diner," she said. For as long as she could remember, contemplating that particular future for herself was accompanied by the sound of a jail cell door slamming shut.

In a matter of years, after taking over, she'd start

looking, acting and dressing like one of her parents—she could only hope it would be her mother. She'd marry someone she argued with constantly. And then she'd take over the Christmas show. And church choir. She'd complain about bunions and dying business and never go on a vacation—even if the possibility was there.

Just like her parents.

Lenora shrugged an elegant shoulder, but her face had new lines, different shadows, and they broke Merri's heart.

Clearly not the time to tell them her oh-so-cheery news. But maybe it was time for her to take one for the team.

"Mom, without you and Dad there is no Monroe's Diner," she said, searching the garbage for the bane of her existence. She plunked the singing, dancing minion of the devil on top of her espresso machine. "Rudolph needs you."

WITHIN AN HOUR, their regular breakfast crowd was in the door and Merri worked the grill, sweat gathering under the baseball hat she wore to keep her hair out of the way. Despite all of her intentions, she'd ended up exactly where she'd been twenty years ago.

This, she told herself, folding eggs onto a bagel for their signature bagel sandwich—signature because two days ago Merri put a tomato on it—is what happens when you don't have a plan.

She had always decided to let her boyfriends' plans suffice. First Brett, then Dean—she just let herself fall right into step with them, headed wherever they were going. Not making a fuss, certainly never fighting.

Her only plan had been to leave the diner and get

married. A big white dress. Her dad walking her down the aisle to "Canon in D." A party with three hundred guests and ice sculptures and shrimp cocktail.

And she couldn't even make that work.

"Three eggs in a hole," she yelled, slipping the sandwiches into a bag and handing them to her mother. She didn't watch where they went from there; she had pancakes working for Lou at the counter.

The bell over the door dinged as the bagels walked out and she plated the pancakes. She threw on some strawberries instead of the five-pound pat of butter that usually came with the pancakes and slid them in front of Lou.

"Fruit?" he asked, dubious.

"Good for you, Lou, trust me."

She glanced out the front windows in time to see a big man in a black leather jacket carrying the bagel bags to a big black truck purring at the curb.

The truck had a red motorcycle morphing into flames painted on its side, and the man turned slightly before jumping into the passenger seat, revealing his face.

The spatula clattered out of her hand.

It was a face she knew by heart, from the broken nose to the black eyebrows, the eyes like dark chocolate.

Her heart thundered, crashing against her ribs.

It was a face she never thought she'd see again.

Gavin McDonnell.

"Did you know Gavin?" Lenora asked as they watched the truck roar away. The power of the engine echoing through her body.

Know him? She nearly laughed. "He used to be a busboy here, Mom. Remember?"

Hands shaking, she picked up the spatula, rinsed it and went back to scraping the grill as if her life depended on it. Her blood pounded in her ears. She could barely hear her mother.

"That's right. Weren't you in the same grade?"

"He... Gavin was a year ahead of me," she said. Her tongue was too big for her mouth. Her brain too busy trying to handle every memory of Gavin McDonnell roaring free from the box she'd packed them away in. Gavin laughing. Angry. Teasing her. Gavin's mouth. His hands.

"What about the little brother?"

"Sean was in Jake's class," she said.

"They turned out all right." Mom kept talking. "Considering."

"What's he doing back here?" she managed to get out. Because Gavin's plan, much like hers, had been to leave and not look back.

"Gavin moved back to town a few years ago and he and Sean are in business together now. Building motorcycles. Their shop is just down the street. They usually come in here every day."

"Every day?" she squeaked.

"Not so much this week, I guess with the holidays. But usually they're the best regulars we've got."

She could barely breathe. Every day?

Her mind whirled, panicked. If they came in during the rush and she had her back to him, it made sense that she hadn't seen him. And Gavin probably didn't recognize her with her hat on, otherwise he would have said something to mock her untriumphant return to Monroe's.

Gavin, the Gavin she'd known, would love that.

And now she had to face down the prospect of Gavin McDonnell, every day?

Her stomach roiled and quivered.

Merri practically threw the spatula into the tray. "You good for a second, Mom?" she asked. "I need a little air."

Without waiting for Mom's answer, Merri hit the back door that led out to the garbage and the alley. Cold air bit through her thin cotton shirt, raking through her short black hair.

It was all just a tad too much.

A shade overwhelming.

Dean's betrayal. Being home. Christmas.

And now Gavin McDonnell.

It was enough to drive a woman to drink.

If she wasn't three months pregnant.

CHAPTER TWO

AS IT HAPPENED, Merri didn't tell her mother about the baby. Instead, she spent the entire day jumping every time the bell over the door rang.

Please don't be him, please don't be him, she'd pray. And, luckily, it never was.

By five in the afternoon, her heart was so tired of leaping into her throat that she allowed herself a full octane latte.

Sorry, baby, she thought as she sucked the puppy down.

"You all right, honey?" Mom asked, still looking like Sophia Loren. Only now she was afternoon Sophia, lipstick gone, makeup faded, hair looser, but somehow more beautiful.

If she wasn't my mother, Merri thought, *I might be forced to kill her.*

"I'm fine, Mom," Merri said, not quite able to meet her mother's eyes. "I'm just tired."

The bell chimed and her heart was too sore to leap, but still she prayed.

Don't be him. Please don't be him.

Slowly she turned and relief flooded her when she saw the adorable, blond-haired teenager sliding onto the farthest stool. He'd been coming in every day for the past week. Luke was his name, but that's all she knew about him. Which made him an anomaly among their regulars.

"Wouldn't Luke be perfect in the Christmas celebration?" Mom asked, talking without moving her lips, another valuable skill taught by the diner.

"He's a little old for baby Jesus, Mom," she said.

"For the angel, you idiot," Mom said under her breath. And Merri had to admit, throw some wings on the boy and Luke would be the most believable angel in the Webster Groves Christmas Celebration in years. Not hard, considering the angel was usually played by Merri or her brother.

Nobody ever confused them with angels.

Something clattered and banged upstairs and Mom jumped to her feet, eyes on the ceiling.

"I'm gonna kill him," she muttered. "So help me if he's—"

"Go check on him, Mom," she said. "I've got things covered."

Mom practically ran upstairs, and Merri, too tired to stand up from the stool that had been behind the counter since Mom's sprained ankle fifteen years ago, leaned over to greet Luke, the angel boy.

"Hiya," she said.

"Hey," he said with a grin, and her jaded, broken, much-too-old heart skipped a beat. Good heavens, the boy was trouble brewing in about ten different ways. He was tall, shoulders and face filling out a little, which made Merri guess that he was fourteen or fifteen years old. He had a certain air to him, as if he had some secrets that no doubt drove the girls crazy.

"Usual?" she asked.

"Extra whip," he said.

"One of those days?" she asked.

The boy sighed, slouching into the counter. "You have no idea."

Oh, sweetie, she thought. *You don't know the trouble I've seen.*

"Merri's special hot chocolate coming up," she said, forcing herself to her feet in order to build his drink.

"You have any brownies or something?" angel boy asked.

"No, sorry. But we have muffins."

"Not gonna cut it," he said with a wince.

She laughed, deciding that she and Mom would have a little baking spree tonight. They needed some brownies and cookies around here. Maybe some scones.

Luke—a budding artist—set his backpack on the counter and pulled out a long tin from the front pocket. He had pencils in there, and a big notebook in the back pocket.

The girls, Merri thought, *the poor girls in this boy's future. They just don't stand a chance.*

"Hey," she said, taking the mug and the stool down to the end of the counter. "You have to talk to me for a little bit." She wrinkled her nose. "Otherwise, I have to clean."

"Okay," he agreed and took the mug from her. So polite, she thought, wishing she had a younger sister to fix him up with.

"Are you Mary like the Virgin Mary, or Merry like Merry Christmas?" Luke asked. Only the millionth time she'd ever heard that question.

"I'm Merri as in Merrieta." She sighed. "But I think it was just an excuse for my mom." She looked around, gesturing to the Christmaspalooza around them.

"She does seem to like the holiday," Luke said, deadpan.

"All in preparation for the Christmas celebration in the park in five days. My dad dresses up like Santa, and my mom like Mrs. Claus, and we serve hot chocolate and coffee, and people come and sing carols. Kids get gifts. It's a big deal."

"My dad told me about it," Luke said. "Sounds lame."

She laughed. "It's actually…" She thought of that beautiful moment when everyone lit candles and sang "Oh Holy Night." Goose bumps ran up and down her arms. "Pretty great."

The boy shrugged, too cool to commit.

"So," she said, settling in for a good grilling, à la Lenora. "Are you in high school here?" she asked.

"Not yet." He looked down at his notebook, sticking his pinky through the wire edge. "I just moved in with my dad at the beginning of Christmas break. I used to live with my mom way out in the country."

There was something really sad going on behind Luke's eyes and Merri's heart went out to him. Whether it was about his mom or his dad or the prospect of a new school, she wasn't sure. But the boy wasn't happy.

She could relate. In a big way.

"Do you like school?" she asked carefully.

He wrinkled his nose. "It's all right."

Well, that wasn't much to go on.

"Are you leaving behind friends?" She struck on an idea. "A girlfriend?"

"No," he said fast and then shook his head, his eyes on his notebook. He laughed a little. "No."

She wasn't cut out for therapy. She was just making him sadder.

"So what are you doing over Christmas break?" she asked, trying to make things lighter.

"Working with my dad," he said, a certain glow coming on in his blue eyes. Aha, she thought, something he likes. Something he is happy about.

"What do you do?"

"Cleanup, mostly," he said. "But I'm learning a lot."

"Learning a lot is good," she said, smiling at him. She was about to ask him what his father did when she was interrupted by what sounded like an army battalion rattling down the stairs.

She spun on her stool in time to see her father—using his crutch to smack open the door—burst into the room, like an angry chow puppy.

If Mom was Sophia Loren, Dad was Andy Rooney.

He wore an undershirt, under which all manner of white hair sprung. Which made up for his very shiny, very bald head. Anytime strangers met Mom and Dad they seemed baffled until they saw Mom and Dad look at each other. The palpable affection and respect between them after forty-five years was what could really stop clocks.

"Dad? What—" Merri glanced around Dad for Mom, but there was no one there. "Where's Mom?"

"I locked her in the bathroom."

"Dad," Merri moaned, "you can't keep doing that. She's just trying to help."

"I'll let her out in a second. But I need to talk to you."

"To me?"

"Yes—" Dad stopped, noticing Luke. "Who are you?" he asked.

"Luke."

"Nice to meet you," Dad said, shaking the boy's hand before doing a quick double take. "Has anyone asked you if you wanted to be the angel in the Christmas celebration?"

Luke flashed her a blank look.

"I was working up to it, Dad," she said. "Now what's got you riled?"

"You're not going to believe what city council is doing."

They didn't come more evil than city council, according to Dad.

"What now?" she asked.

"Since I've broken my leg, they've decided someone else should be Santa."

"Dad," she said, patting his shoulder. "That stinks."

"Totally right that stinks!" he cried. "Twenty years and they just oust us."

"Well, just you—" His look was murderous and so she changed tactics. "Christmas Eve is five days away. Your leg isn't going to be up to it. Having all those kids sit on your lap will be excruciating."

"That's what your mother said," he told her. "And, for once, she's right. I'm not Santa. But that suit is not leaving this family!"

Merri laughed. "Well, Mom is not about to give up her Mrs. Claus costume anytime soon. She finally put all the sequins on."

"Mom's not Santa, either."

"Then who—"

"You."

Merri and Luke howled. Dad, however, was not laughing.

"You've got to be kidding me," she said.

"It's bad enough they let Starbucks into this town. We're not letting them take Christmas." Dad got a certain Clint Eastwood gleam in his eye. "Not on my watch."

"So *I'm* supposed to be Santa?" she asked. "I'm missing a few key parts for the role."

"You'll be fine," Dad barked. "With the beard on no one will notice."

Wonderful. She was a beard away from looking like Old St. Nick.

"Dad, I don't want to—"

"I need you, sweetie," Dad said, pouring it on thick. Calling her *sweetie* was usually reserved for New Year's Eve when Mom let him have too much of the whiskey she kept under the sink. "With your brother overseas and me in this stupid cast, there's no one else to help. And there's a lot at stake here."

Merri made the mistake of looking in her father's eyes. The past year had been so rough on Dad. Her brother going over to Iraq, the broken leg and now this—it was important. To him, it was very important.

The least she could do was put on the red suit. Besides, at the rate she was going she wouldn't even need the fake belly.

A pregnant Santa—truly the world was falling apart.

"Just for this year, Dad," she said. "Until you're back on your feet."

He whooped before leaning down to kiss her head. She waited for the sound of that trap closing shut on her foot, but all she felt was good. Good that she could help out and return some of the generosity her parents handed out so easily, good that she'd put that smile on her father's face.

"Thank you, Merri," he said, wrapping her up in his smell—Old Spice and Earl Grey. "I better go call Mr. Brooks," he said. "Tell him he's not through with us yet."

"And let Mom out of the bathroom," she said to his retreating back.

"That, too," he agreed, closing the door behind him.

"Wow," Luke said. "Santa."

"Don't you laugh, kid." She shook her finger at him. "My first order of business is drafting you as head angel."

"No way."

She pulled his mug, still half full of cocoa, whipped cream and her secret ingredient, marshmallow cream, across the counter from him.

"You play dirty," he said.

"You be the angel and it's free cocoa every day until Christmas Eve."

"Do I have to wear a costume?" he asked. "Something dorky?"

"You can dress however you want," she said. "You just need some wings."

"I'll think about it," he said and she pushed the drink back toward him.

The bell over the door rang and she was so distracted by her new Santa status that she didn't bother to pray.

And so, because fate was cruel and her hair was a mess, it was him.

Gavin McDonnell walked into Monroe's like he used to. Long legs, loose hips, motorcycle jacket and attitude.

CHAPTER THREE

AND JUST LIKE IT used to, her body tuned right on in. Every nerve, every receptor, every inch of her aware of Gavin.

"Well, well," he said in that rough, dark voice that used to have the power to melt her brain and change her body chemistry. And, damn it, apparently still did. "One week in town, Luke, and look who you dug up. Merri Monroe."

His voice had an edge to it, and so did his espresso-brown eyes, and apparently he hadn't forgotten her, either. Or, clearly, forgiven her.

"Hi, Gavin," she said, her voice a shade too breathy.

"Hey, Dad," Luke said.

"Dad?" she yelped, staring at blond-haired, blue-eyed Luke. Who was absolutely angel to Gavin McDonnell's dark devil.

"I take after my mom," Luke said, his avid attention bouncing between Merri and Gavin.

"So that was you at the grill this morning? I thought they'd hired a new boy," Gavin said with a biting grin.

She sneered at his low blow.

"It's me," she said. "The one and only."

"Never thought I'd see you here again," Gavin said, tucking his hand into the worn black leather jacket she recognized from high school. "What was it you said to me?" He pretended to think.

"Yes," she snapped. Gavin McDonnell got under her skin in a thousand different ways. And time hadn't changed anything. They were still like crossed wires, setting off sparks as soon as the other entered the vicinity. Fighting with him made her crazy—it always did. "I'm home again. I'm working here again. It's all very funny to you, I'm sure."

He smiled and she had to sit back down on the stool, because Gavin's grin was like whiskey. It went right to her knees.

"Let's go, Luke," he said, clapping a hand on his son's shoulder. "Sean is waiting."

"I need to pay—" Luke said and suddenly Merri knew where this was going. Gavin was reaching into his pocket with a wicked gleam in his eyes, and she knew those words she'd said fifteen years ago were about to get thrown into her face and she couldn't bear it. She'd been a kid. A stupid kid. And she'd hurt him on purpose because he'd had the power to tear her apart and set her on fire and she didn't know how to handle it.

"On the house," she said quickly, but Gavin shook his head, his eyes boring into hers. And she could see how what she'd said to him that night, the way she'd dismissed him, still hurt.

"Here," he said, tossing ten bucks on the counter, and she felt a little something in her wither with shame and regret. "You look like you need it."

"Dad!" Luke said, but Gavin hustled him out the door and they were gone.

Merri sagged back onto the stool and watched them walk away.

"You're here one week," Gavin said, watching the road and his kid at the same time, which was giving him a headache. Or maybe it was Merri Monroe giving him the headache. Either way, his head hurt and it was making him surly. "One week and you find the biggest snob in town."

"You acted like a jerk in there."

There was a fight in the air, like lightning in the distance, and Gavin wanted to snap. Everything in him felt about to burst.

He glanced at his son and saw him staring, placid, out the window. Unreachable. Unaffected.

The kid had arrived on his doorstep a week ago, cloaked in this new cool. This new attitude that Gavin recognized all too well, but didn't know how to break through.

It was as if the kid had surrounded himself in ice.

"I was a jerk in there," he agreed, not the slightest bit sorry, but he had to try and set a good example. "And you should never talk to anyone that way unless you have a really good reason. And I have a really good reason."

She crushed me. Annihilated me.

"I think she's nice."

Gavin laughed, ignoring the fact that sixteen years ago he'd thought she was more than nice. He'd thought she was heaven with long legs and night-black hair. God, he'd never been so wrong about something since. Not even Juliet, Luke's mother, and he'd been plenty wrong about her.

"Hardly," he said. "Trust me, I know Merri Monroe and she's not nice."

"How do you know her?" Luke asked, as if it was a challenge. Like after one week of sitting at that counter with the woman his son would know her better.

No one knew Merri Monroe like he'd known her. Not even that boyfriend of hers that she'd chosen over him.

"I used to be a busboy at the diner," he said, which was of course about one-tenth of the story. The other part of the story involved a year of flirting and one night so ridiculously hot it was scorched into his memory.

But the night had been a lie and the girl he thought he was childishly in love with had ended up being a fake.

"You should stay away from her, Luke."

Man, the second the words were out of his mouth he knew they'd been a mistake. There wasn't much of him in the boy that Juliet hadn't managed to force out. But a red flag was a red flag and every McDonnell reacted the same way.

"I'm helping out with the Christmas celebration," Luke said, his chin out. "So I am going to be spending more time there."

Great. Just great. He'd practically asked for that one.

"What are you going to be doing?" he asked, trying to see where a McDonnell fit into that night. He'd gone a few times in the past, admired the lights and the singing, trying to make nice. But he never ever felt like he belonged.

Which was too bad, because as far as Christmas traditions went, it was a real nice party.

"Head angel." Luke's voice had a little sneer in it that Gavin did not like. At all.

"I don't want to fight with you, Luke."

"Who's fighting?" Luke snapped back quickly, like a right hook to the chin.

Oh, kid, Gavin thought, biting back a sudden smile. *We're more alike than you can even guess.*

Silence filled the truck and Gavin watched his boy out of the sides of his eyes. He knew it wasn't the right time to ask questions, but frankly it never seemed to be the right time, and if he kept waiting for the right time he'd be dead before he knew what had brought Luke to his doorstep.

"Your mom said you wanted to leave Salisbury and come here because the kids there were snobs."

"I didn't say that," Lucas barked, looking indignant. And then, as if realizing he'd given something away, he shrugged and slumped into the corner of the truck, staring out the window. "Whatever." He sighed, and Gavin wanted to put his own head through the windshield.

Instead, he took a deep breath, counted to ten and slowed down for a yellow light. "Son—"

"Forget it, Dad," he said, but Gavin wasn't about to forget it. McDonnells didn't forget—it was practically hardwired into them.

"I'm not going to forget it." He clapped his hand on Luke's shoulder. The kid's face didn't look like Gavin's—he didn't have his eyes or hair—but the boy's body was going to be pure McDonnell. In a few years the football coach would be begging him to play.

Luke shrugged Gavin's hand away as if it was poison and Gavin bit his tongue, counted to twenty. Twice.

"I'm so glad you're here, Luke. You know that, right? I've wanted you to live with me for years."

"I know," Luke said, apparently riveted by the strip malls along Watson. The tension was so thick in the car Gavin needed to crack a window.

"But I don't understand why now?" he asked. "Your mom said you were having a hard time fitting in at high school."

Luke snorted hard through his nose and Gavin didn't know how to translate that.

Gavin looked at his son and felt as if his heart was

breaking. Something had happened, either with the boy or between the boy and Juliet, but something had gone down and it wasn't going away.

"Do you want to be here?" Gavin asked, his throat tight, and it seemed like an eternity until Luke turned and answered.

"I do," he said solemnly. "I really want to be here."

Thank God, Gavin thought, his heart pounding hard. *I'm so glad. I love you. I don't want to fight.* All of those were things he could have said, and hell, maybe he should say them. Those books Juliet sent him to read told him he needed to, but looking at the boy staring out the window with a chip on his shoulder the size of the Arch, Gavin didn't think it would work. Luke would laugh and Gavin would be a bigger fool.

So, instead, Gavin said, "Cool."

Luke nodded and maybe, Gavin thought, breathing slowly out of his nose, he'd done the right thing.

But what the hell did he know?

Other than Merri Monroe was back in town, turning his whole world upside down. Again.

"Let's pick up some pizza at Cicero's," he said, hoping food would somehow fill this new hollow ache in his stomach.

Luke nodded enthusiastically, and he turned the truck around, feeling as if he'd dodged the bullet, but the gun was still aimed right at his head.

FORTY MINUTES LATER, he and Luke stepped in the back door of the solid brick house they called home. It wasn't much, but it was McDonnell all the way—the kind of place Mom always wanted but could never afford.

"Lucy," he cried in his best Desi voice. "We're home."

There was a thump from the kitchen and a muttered curse. "We brought dinner, Sean," he yelled, winking at his son. "You can stop trying to cook."

He toed off his black boots and hung his jacket up on a hook that already had two jackets on it.

Sean appeared in the doorway, covered in black grease and tomato sauce. Gavin hoped the grease was from the shop and not from dinner. Sean, as usual, was silent, but after years of practice Gavin could read his brother like a book.

"Sorry, we didn't call," he said. "It was sort of spur-of-the-moment."

"What were you making?" Luke asked.

"Meat loaf," Sean said.

Luke and Gavin shared a grimace.

"You brought something better?" Sean asked, defensive.

"Way better," Luke said. "Seafood pizza."

Sean smiled and took the box from Luke, who quickly kicked off his boots, adding them to the pile at the door. His coat and bag were left in a heap, and Gavin knew he should say something to the boy about it, but Luke was smiling. Teasing his uncle. Joining in the fun.

Being a boy.

"He needs you," Juliet had said when she dropped him off last week. "He needs to be around his father. Around men. He has too many women in his life in Salisbury. Mom, my sisters—we've made him…soft."

Gavin had no idea what that meant. Luke was Luke, like he'd always been. Smart. Quiet. Slow to laugh, but once he got going the kid just got goofy. A crazy good artist. Terrible guitar player. But whatever it was that Juliet thought was wrong, Gavin was glad she'd had enough.

Luke was here.

Finally.

After years of split custody—of battling it out with Juliet over weekends and holidays and summers—Luke was home.

Such as it was.

Their brick bungalow was half repair shop, half movie theater. Without many vegetables.

Heaven really, but he doubted it would pass muster with many women.

"You two wash your hands before you get into that pizza!" he yelled, stepping into the toilet to try and get the grease from under his nails.

Under the sink he had about thirty different kinds of hand soap. He crouched and perused his options. Finally he snagged some natural crap that was supposed to be able to get anything clean and smelled like a forest.

Sean appeared in the doorway, still covered in grease and tomato sauce.

"You're never going to guess who is back in town," Gavin said, trying to work up a good suds between his fingers. That natural crap didn't foam up at all.

Sean blinked at him and shrugged.

"Merri freaking Monroe."

"That's nice," Sean said, leaning against the doorjamb.

"Nice?" Gavin asked, feeling as if his hair was standing on end. "It's hardly—"

"I thought you were over her." Sean's green eyes pierced him. "That's what you said."

That's what I said, he thought. *That's what I said after that night, when she kissed me like she was going to die and I was the only one who could save her.* After that night when she'd pulled her shirt closed over her chest and tossed all her tips onto his bare chest.

You look like you need it more than I do.

Not a good moment. At all.

"I'm over her," he said. He took out the nailbrush and went to town on his nails. "It was years ago. Kid stuff. She's nothing."

But Sean still lingered and finally Gavin snapped. "What?"

"They're clean," Sean said, nodding at his hands. "They always have been."

ON FRIDAYS, SATURDAYS and Sundays, Monroe's was staffed by college students and the family got some time off. Friday afternoon, Mom and Dad argued about the Christmas celebration and Merri got an ultrasound.

She was having a girl.

A healthy baby girl.

Shock was about all that registered as she sat in her car, the photo clutched to her chest like a love letter.

A girl. And just like that, it was real.

She was going to have a little girl, all on her own.

A spasm of joy so powerful it nearly brought her to tears was followed quickly by a fear so intense she had to gasp just to breathe.

She pressed the photo to her lips, the slick paper cool in her hands.

"Hi, baby." She sighed. "I'm your mommy."

All the ways she could ruin this opened up around her like a minefield.

She'd made a mess of her own life. Why in the world did she think she could make a better life for her daughter? What kind of example was she? She couldn't make relationships work. She trusted the wrong kind of men.

Negative thoughts like that had been attaching themselves like leeches and she tried desperately to shake them loose.

Things wouldn't be easy, she knew that, but they never were. And this baby was loved by her, and as soon as she told her parents, they would be in love, too.

And Dean could rot.

He didn't want this baby and he definitely didn't want Merri, and so he would get none of this. None of this joy. None of this happiness and excitement. None of the little girl growing fingernails and eyelashes inside Merri's belly.

Oddly, a half year of hating herself for staying with Dean when she'd known what he was up to—the shame of having been taken for such a fool, the bitter residue of that night three months ago and the heartache of pinning all those big wedding dress dreams on such a lousy man—vanished.

Gone.

This was a new chance to get things right. For her little girl.

It meant, of course, that apartment hunting had to happen for real, rather than in theory. She would need her parents' help.

She waited for the sickening trapped sensation to close in around her, but all she felt was relief.

Relief that she was here and that they were able to help. Relief that she had them.

And joy.

I gotta tell my folks, she thought and slipped the picture into the back pocket of her jeans before climbing out of her Jeep.

She took the fire-escape steps straight up to the apartments and opened the window to her bedroom. Mom had taken down the Johnny Depp posters and repainted the lime-green walls a cheerful yellow almost the moment Merri had left for college. Jake had it worse—his room was turned into the Christmas celebration storage closet.

"Mom!" she yelled, stepping from her old room into the hallway. She followed the sounds of an argument into the kitchen.

"You're not going!" Mom yelled at Dad, who was shrugging into his red-and-black-checked jacket.

"Someone has to," he said. "Since you decided our costumes were better left in storage."

"We had moths!" Mom cried. "What did you want me to do?"

"Hey!" Merri shouted, getting her parents' attention. *I'm having a baby,* she thought, but didn't say. Hardly seemed the kind of thing to spring on them right now— Dad would have a heart attack. "What's going on here?"

"I'm going to the storage unit to get our costumes," Dad explained, trying to fish his keys off the hook. Mom had smacked her hand over them and wasn't moving it.

"The man can't drive with a broken foot."

"And you can't drive at all!" Dad yelled at Mom, who hadn't ever owned a driver's license.

"I'll go," Merri volunteered.

Bawk, bawk, bawk, bawk, she thought. *You want some fries with that chicken?*

She held out her hand for the keys to the storage locker and Dad reluctantly handed them over.

"Costumes," she said. "Anything else?"

"Our big percolator," Mom said. "Can you fit that in your car?"

"I should," she said and headed toward the steps leading to the diner. She suddenly had a craving for a hot chocolate and some saltines. Together. Weird.

Downstairs it was fairly busy with people coming in for the all-day breakfast. Heidi at the counter gave Merri a bright, former-cheerleader smile that made Merri's teeth ache with its sweetness. Joe at the grill just grunted.

Luke sat at his usual spot, finishing up a hot chocolate.

"Hey," she said to him. "I'll make you one of my specials to go if you come with me."

"Where?"

"Christmas land," she said. "Your first duty as angel is to schlep."

"I haven't told you I'd be the angel."

"Will you?"

He drained his mug and shrugged. "Sure."

"Like there was ever any question," she joked, secretly relieved and thrilled to have the help. Merri crumbled saltines on her cocoa and put a few on Luke's just for fun.

Luke shrugged into a leather jacket that looked a lot like Gavin's but newer, and she led him out back to her trusty Jeep.

She started the car and cranked the heater.

"So my dad doesn't like you," Luke said as soon as he was buckled in.

She paused for a moment, about to take a sip of cocoa. But with his words, her stomach twisted.

"I know," she whispered, pushing her cup into the holder on the console.

"Why?"

She backed up and headed down Lockwood toward old Webster Groves where her parents had a storage locker.

Why? Why does Gavin McDonnell hate me so much? Because I was awful to him? Because he let me past every single one of his boarded-up windows and locked doors and I turned around and stabbed him in the heart?

All that and more, she was afraid.

"Dad says you're a snob."

It stung slightly—like all things about Gavin McDonnell did. Even after all these years, the thought of his dark hair under her fingers, the sound of his low laugh, the heat of his sideways glances, were all pinpricks to her heart.

And talking about him, with his son no less, was incredibly painful. She just wasn't into pain today.

"You know, I think I've changed my mind about you being the angel."

"Too late," he said, smirking. "Christmas Eve is three days away and I've already figured out my costume."

Wow. She was impressed.

And suddenly ravenous for a hamburger.

"You hungry?" she asked.

"Sure."

She pulled into McDonald's and counted out the change in her console to get them two hamburgers and a supersize fries.

Luke watched her, no doubt wondering why she had to scrounge for change, but since she was buying she figured she didn't need to explain.

"So," Luke said once they were past the drive-through, the smell of processed meat and cheese like ambrosia in the air. "About you and my dad…"

"You're like a dog with a bone," she grumbled.

"So I've been told." He hogged some fries. "My dad?"

"I wasn't very nice to him," she said, taking a handful of fries before he ate them all. Not totally true, considering that night and how very, very nice to Gavin she'd been before saying what she said. And remembering that reminded her of how nice he'd been. A blush built from the center of her body, a sudden heat between her legs.

He'd been *very* nice.

"And the next time I see him," she said, "I'll apologize."

Luke nodded.

"We used to be friends," she said, wondering why she didn't just shut up. "He was a fun guy, your dad. Funny."

"Dad? Funny?" Luke asked, as if the idea was preposterous, and she remembered her own shock of finding the deep river of teasing and sarcasm that lived under his gruff, screw-the-world attitude. It was like finding chocolate under concrete.

"Not at first," she said, remembering those first few days working with him. It had been like standing next to some kind of storm cloud. She'd been attracted and nervous and a little scared all at the same time. And the arguing... Lord, those were some epic battles. "But once he got going—"

He'd been relentless; she smiled, remembering. Making her laugh until she begged him to stop. Making her laugh until she ran for the bathroom.

"He's not much of a laugher these days?" she asked, wondering about the changes in Gavin, when she'd be so much better off keeping her mind away from him.

"I guess," Luke said. He took the lid off his hot cocoa. "Are these crackers?"

"Makes the Merri special more special." She laughed, and he scowled, shoving the lid back on.

"Working with him and my uncle is a blast."

"You guys build motorcycles?"

"The best bikes," Luke said. "Dad's been on the Discovery Channel like three times. The *Great Biker Build-Off,* and he's never been beat."

Merri didn't know the show, but there was something bittersweet in the back of her throat. Something like pride for the hard-luck McDonnell boys who managed to turn everything around.

"You guys must be really good," she murmured, watching the boy's face and eyes light up.

"Well, Dad and Uncle Sean are. I mostly clean, but lately I've been helping do some design stuff..." Luke kept talking about handlebars and fabrication while she pulled into the storage-locker parking lot.

It took them a few minutes in the maze of buildings to find the right one.

"Here we go," she said, shoving the last bit of hamburger into her mouth. "Let's see what we can find."

What they found was a mess: old furniture, decorations, leprosy Santa's forebearer—Ebola Santa, his foam guts bleeding out onto the floor. There were two percolators and she had no doubt that the one she picked would be the wrong one, so she had Luke take both to the backseat of her Jeep.

Costumes were easy. Two garment bags and they were done.

"I need these," Luke said, pulling a pair of giant wings with a two-foot span and missing most of their feathers from the very back of the closet.

Her Christmas celebration costume her senior year of high school.

"Wow," she said. "I haven't seen those in ages."

"They're awesome," Luke said, glowing at the sight of them.

"Yes," she agreed, having spent weeks building them in shop class. "They are, but incredibly awkward," she said. "You won't fit through doors, or in cars or—"

"I'll make them work," he said.

"Christmas Eve is three days away," she said. "You sure?"

"Totally."

"All right," she said with a shrug and they locked up the unit behind them just as snow began to fall. Rainy, cold snow.

She hurried to put the costumes and wings in the Jeep, but with the percolators there just wasn't enough room.

"We can make two—"

"Nah," Luke said, grinning at her in a way that made her more than a little nervous. "I'll call my dad—he'll come get us. Unless you think that would be weird."

If she said no, she'd look like the jerk Gavin no doubt thought she was. She wasn't a jerk, and she was an adult and she could own up to her mistakes.

No matter how awkward.

"Not weird at all," she said, resigning herself to her fate. "Give him a call."

Luke stood under the eaves of the storage building and pulled out a sleek black cell phone. Merri sat back in her Jeep and pulled out the picture of her baby.

If she needed any more proof of her adult status, that little amoeba was it. Merri ran her finger across the little girl's curled feet. She would clear the air with Gavin, tell her folks and start looking for a place for her, the baby and the espresso machine to call home.

"Hey! What's—" The front door opened and slammed shut and Luke was sitting beside her in the Jeep, all before she could thrust the picture back in her pocket. "What's the photo of?"

Merri didn't think. She didn't even consider. It was the most thrilling, terrifying news of her life and she wanted to tell someone. Anyone. Except her parents.

"Can you keep a secret?"

Luke's eyes went dark and he nodded solemnly. *Secrets,* Merri thought, *are clearly a big deal.*

"I'm pregnant," she said, and saying the words made it even more real. More wonderful and scary. "I'm three months pregnant with a little girl." Well, now it was a little more scary than wonderful and she felt as if her lungs were filling up with cement. "I'm all alone. My boyfriend is an ass and I'm going to have a baby. By myself. By—"

She couldn't breathe. Suddenly the world didn't have enough air. "Holy cats," she gasped, her hand fluttering over her chest. "I can't—"

Luke pushed her head down, knocking her forehead into the steering wheel and blasting the horn once.

"You're hyperventilating," he told her and she recognized it herself. She popped open the driver-side door and scooched around so she could put her head between her knees.

I've got to get used to this, otherwise I'll never survive the pregnancy, she thought, staring at the wet gravel of the parking area.

Feeling better, she sat up, ruffling the tips of her short black hair.

"I have a secret, too," Luke said, and Merri glanced over her shoulder at him.

Uh-oh. Something about the boy seemed about to break and she reached out and grabbed his shoulder. "Luke? Are you—"

"Gay," he said, his voice thick, his eyes wet with tears and anguish. "I'm gay."

CHAPTER FOUR

MAN. OH, MAN. What do I say? she thought, blinking at Luke, who looked as if he'd been tied to a rack that was getting pulled tighter and tighter.

"I think that's cool," she said and he rolled his eyes at her. *Okay,* she thought, *not exactly right.*

"Trust me," he said. "It's the furthest thing from cool. I told my mom and she totally freaked out and dumped me on my dad."

"That's her problem," she said fiercely, and he started at her sudden vehemence. "If your mom couldn't accept this or is too small-minded to get that you are still you, then that's her problem. Not yours." He stared at her, openmouthed. "Got it?" She gave him a little shake.

Finally, he smiled ruefully. "Yeah," he said. "I got it. I mean, I always sort of got it, but…she's my mom…you know? I didn't think she'd…"

He sniffed hard and looked out the window, quickly brushing away his tears. She wanted to hug him; she wanted to bundle him up and put him in her pocket so no more bad things could happen to him.

"Does your dad know?" she asked carefully.

"Are you kidding?" Luke barked. "Gavin McDonnell? Tough guy, motorcycle man? Like he's going to be cool with a gay son?"

"Your dad loves you," she said, without a whole lot of proof. But Gavin was loyal—until crossed.

Surely he could handle this.

Couldn't he?

Oh, no. Poor Luke. She wasn't Gavin's son or gay and *she* was worried. "You need to tell him sometime."

"Like when I'm fifty," Luke scoffed.

"What if you meet someone?" she asked quietly, and he tensed, clenching his hands together in his lap. "What if your mom tells him before you get a chance? You don't want that, do you?"

"No," he whispered, "that would be the worst."

He huffed a big breath and they both watched icy snow gather on the windshield.

"This sucks," he said.

"I know."

"Have you told your parents about the baby?" Luke asked, and she could feel herself blush. *Way to practice what you preach, there, Merri.*

"Not yet, but I will."

"When?"

"By Christmas Eve," she said, being honest. "Before the celebration." Three days gave her plenty of time to think of the right way to say everything she had to say. "What about you?" she asked.

"Tell my dad I'm gay by the Christmas celebration?" he asked, and while that wasn't totally what she meant, she supposed it would work. "That should make the holidays special."

"Well—" she smiled "—it will make them unforgettable, that's for sure."

Luke chewed his lip and then stuck out his hand. "It's a deal," he said. "Secrets out by Christmas Eve."

She shook on it, feeling a tide of inevitability at work. Like going on a diet pact with your best friend, she couldn't back out of this now. "By Christmas Eve."

The roar of a truck could be heard in the distance getting closer. "That would be him," Luke said.

Merri gathered the scattered ends of herself, ready to face one of the worst things she'd ever done. But as the big black truck turned the corner, eating the distance to her Jeep, she felt fifteen all over again.

Like she was playing with fire.

The truck stopped a few feet from her tiny Jeep and Gavin hopped out. Snow dotted his close-cut dark hair and the shoulders of his black leather jacket, and through the windshield his warm chocolate eyes found hers.

Oh. Wow. Her hormones sighed.

He stepped closer, his long legs encased in black denim, the metal tips of his cowboy boots gleaming in the snow, and her whole body pulsed at the sight of him.

There was a good chance she was about to hyperventilate again, so she threw open her door and jumped out onto the gravel.

"Hi, Gavin," she said brightly. "Thanks for coming to our rescue."

"No problem," he said, polite as could be, but he wasn't there. Not really. It was as if the fire in him was banked, reserved. She pulled the collar of her coat up higher because he made the cold colder.

Then Luke hopped out of her Jeep and Gavin's smile was real. Warm.

"Dad!" Luke said, and Gavin's smile got even brighter, like the word *Dad* infused him with a glow.

Why does that make me want to cry? she wondered.

"Come look what I found." Luke led him around to the

back of the Jeep where the wings stuck out awkwardly, a good third of the white feathers falling to pieces in the snow.

"Nice," Gavin said, checking a weld that she knew was as strong as could be. "They're put together right," he said. "What are they for?"

"Angel wings," Luke said. "For the Christmas celebration. Head angel, remember?"

"Christmas celebration," he said with an expression she couldn't quite read, until he glanced at her from the corner of his eye.

Anger—she read that loud and clear, all directed at her. Wonderful.

"The feathers won't make it in the back of the truck," Gavin said, stroking a damp white feather between two of his big fingers. Merri swallowed and looked away, stupidly reminded of being stroked by those big fingers.

"I don't need the feathers," Luke said. "I've got a better idea. I, ah, might need some help."

Gavin looked over to his son, surprised, and then he quickly covered it, nodding like it was all to be expected. "All right, then, let's get them in the truck."

The guy was going to help his fourteen-year-old son make two-foot angel wings. Gavin was a cool dad; it warmed her to see it. And surely such a cool dad could handle a gay son, and at this particular moment he could handle an apology from a woman who'd hurt him.

Ah, humble pie. Delicious.

"Luke," Merri said. "Could you give us a second?"

Luke looked panicked and Merri tried to shoot him a reassuring look. Jeez, the guy needed to give her a little more credit. He'd just told her his secret; she wasn't about to turn around and stab him in the back.

The message must have been received because he grinned.

"Sure," he said, lifting the lightweight wings easily from the back of the Jeep and leaving her alone with Gavin McDonnell and all the mistakes she'd made.

GAVIN WATCHED HIS SON walk away because he couldn't quite stand to look at Merri.

"Gavin?" she said, her soft voice like a freaking feather over the nape of his neck. He was thirty-five years old, for crying out loud. He was a father. This woman—this girl from high school—shouldn't have this effect on him.

"Gavin." Her fingertips landed on his elbow and, even though it was impossible, he could swear her touch burned through the leather of his jacket.

"What?" he snapped, pulling away. Her arm fell back to her side.

"I don't want to fight," she snapped back, her eyes sparking, her cheeks going flushed.

And like it was sixteen years ago, all his blood headed south.

"Come on, Merri," he said, keeping the antagonism going because that he could handle. Anything else and he'd be lost. "Fighting is what we do."

"It's what we did," she corrected. "We're adults, Gavin. Let's act like it."

"Fine," he said. "What do you want?"

Merri licked her lips and he looked heavenward. *A dog on a string,* he told himself. *You're no better than a dog on a string for this woman; you always were.*

"I'm so sorry for the way I treated you," she said, her dark eyes wide and liquid and gorgeous, and he was so caught up in those eyes it took him a second to process what she said.

"Sorry?" he said.

"For what I said…that night…you know." Yeah, he knew. The tip of her tongue touched the very center of her Kewpie doll lip and he wanted to bark at her to stop it. But he knew she didn't get her attraction. The sexiness that she had been so oblivious to throughout high school still lingered around her, like exhaust. And looking at her, he knew she still didn't get it. Why women looked sideways at her and men stared blatantly. It was the sparkle in her eyes, the lush curve of her upper lip, the way her legs moved and her hips swayed and the way she laughed. God, when she laughed—

"I handled things all wrong," she said. "That night."

He laughed because he didn't know what else to do. Sixteen years later she apologizes.

"Handled having sex with me or handled me telling you I loved you?" he asked, the words thick and awkward out of his mouth. No wonder he didn't say it anymore—it was just too damn hard. "Because you handled the sex part just fine."

She blushed bright red to the tips of her hair and he smiled. "Don't worry about it," he said, enjoying her discomfort. "It's been forgotten."

"Right," she snorted. "You're acting like you've totally forgotten it."

"Okay," he snapped at her. "You're forgiven."

He turned to leave but she grabbed his arm again, and he clenched his teeth against the sudden and exasperating urge to haul her up on her tiptoes and kiss her. Just to see how she handled it. Just to get the need out of his system. Surely it wouldn't be as good as he remembered.

Surely that mouth and those hands and the things they made him feel had been embellished in his memory. His years of fantasy.

Why, he wondered, *haven't I grown out of this? It's sick to still feel this way for her. Suicidal.*

"Come on, Gavin." She smiled a lopsided grin that only made her look like a Kewpie doll with dirty secrets. That urge to kiss her revved up a few rpm. "It was a long time ago. And I..."

He waited but she stalled, an insecurity in her eyes.

"Haven't forgotten, either?" he asked, stepping forward, diminishing the space between them because he was reckless and stupid and dying for the smell of her. After so many years, he wanted just a taste.

She nodded, her dark eyes so sweet and deep. "I was scared, Gav," she whispered.

He reeled back, stunned, feeling like a hole had been blown through him. "Of me?"

"Of what you made me feel. It was so—"

He remembered; he'd been there. That night with her had been like nothing he'd ever experienced before. It felt real. Adult and significant, when every girl before and, frankly, every girl after, had been diminished by his earth-shattering hours behind the counter with Merri Monroe.

"Scary," she finally said. "To me. To feel what I felt for you."

It was weird but what flooded him felt like relief. He hadn't been wrong. That night had been what he'd thought—powerful. Powerful enough not to be forgotten. By either of them.

His fingers burned with a sudden desire to touch her, to slide across that velvet cheek into the heavy silk of her hair.

"I'm sorry," she whispered again. "For what I said. And how I acted. I wish that was enough to make it better, because I know how mean it was. I knew how much it would hurt. I said it not because I believed it—"

He held up his hand, stopping her. An old burn lit up in him, an old fire that beat back the cold air creeping into his coat.

"I'm over it," he said. If Sean were here he'd laugh, but Gavin didn't have that luxury. He had to believe this. He had to believe that he didn't love this girl anymore, that what she'd said didn't have anything to do with what he'd done with his life. Why he'd come back to this town, proving to every person who didn't think he'd rise above his mother's sins that he was more than Lynn's wild boy. "Very over it."

"I'm not," she whispered. "I'm not over it at all."

He put his hand onto the Jeep, trying to look nonchalant, but his knees didn't seem to work. His heart was beating too fast.

"Dad?" Luke called from the truck.

"Coming, Luke," he said. Turning away from her was like turning away from the sun. "I, ah—"

She smiled, sad and wise, somehow. "Have to go." She finished his sentence. "I know."

Gavin was torn, like he'd always been, right down the middle, by all the things he felt for her. And again, despite what he knew could happen—the way she could ruin him with a glance, a word, a kiss—he found himself wanting to risk it.

She was here. She'd apologized, and she was looking at him like she used to—part desire, part hero worship, part boxer on the other side of the ring—and, frankly, it still got him. He'd been coming in every day for the

And Gavin wasn't so oblivious to second chances that he couldn't see this.

"Would you like to come back with us? To our house? Not the old house, it got torn down. We have a new one. Sean, Luke and I." He was rambling like a teenager. "Have dinner?"

Her eyes dilated and her mouth went tight, a sadness so profound and so utterly surprising he could taste it rolling off her.

She tucked her hands into the pockets of her coat, a black curl falling over her forehead, and he wanted to tuck it behind her ear. Ease whatever this sadness was that gripped her.

A snowflake landed on her cheek and burned away as he was held, stuck, in suspense.

"I can't," she finally said, looking up. Tears, big and real and heartbreaking, pooled in her eyes.

CHAPTER FIVE

CRYING? MERRI THOUGHT, slamming the door shut on her Jeep. Frantically she wiped away tears that would not stop coming. *Really, Merri? Crying? In front of Gavin? This is what you've come to?*

Wow. She could not have looked like a bigger fool. Maybe if there had been some snot involved? Or if she'd just come right out and said, *My life is such a huge mess right now, I can't see straight, much less...* What?

What had he meant about asking her to his house? For dinner. What was that? A date? No. Not— Was it a date? If it had been any other man there was no doubt it would have been a date. But with Gavin? She just could never be sure.

I. Can't. Do. This. Again.

Gavin was not what she wanted, no matter how he made her feel.

Holy cats, did he make her feel. So much so, she broke up with Brett right after that night. So much so, that, years after that night, she used to lie in bed with Dean and think about Gavin, her body flushed, her mind agonized.

So much so, that she sat here, having made the biggest fool of herself, and she was still turned on for the guy.

She thunked her head down on the steering wheel.

What's wrong with wanting him? a voice asked. *You're*

here now, in Webster Groves. For a long time. What would be wrong—

Brutally, she ripped the thought out at the root.

You, she told herself, *have terrible taste in men. Look at where you are. Alone. Home. Pregnant. All because you trusted a man not to knock you up and still choose the cocktail waitress.*

You need to get your life together.

A life she didn't want to spend fighting, like her parents did. A life, that no matter how Gavin made her feel, didn't include him.

Me. The baby. Espresso machine.

That's my life now.

Christmas Eve, she thought, resolute and terrified. On Christmas Eve, everything would fall into place. She'd tell her parents and get her act together.

IT WAS TWO DAYS before Christmas Eve and Gavin couldn't wait anymore. Sean and Luke were out test-driving the last custom job before delivering it to the Busch family, so Gavin practically ran to the scrap room.

Luke had been back in this room with those wings for the past twenty-four hours and he'd even enlisted Sean's help. Gavin tried not to be hurt that he wasn't asked, particularly since his son seemed so excited about "making it a surprise."

But he was a little jealous, and he was eaten up with curiosity.

"You have to wait until Christmas Eve," Luke had said, grim and serious, as if he were planning on storming Normandy that night.

This Christmas celebration thing was turning into a big deal around his house.

The shop was empty after that custom was out the door, and he didn't have anything to occupy himself. No work. No wings. And so he spent nearly every waking moment trying not to think about Merri. About her lips. Her tears. Whatever it was that was making her so sad and why she couldn't have dinner with him.

Another man, probably, was the answer to the last question. But then why the tears? Another man she didn't like? Another man who didn't deserve her? Because that would be Merri's style. That idiot she dated in high school—who spent more time worrying about his hair than on what Merri was doing behind the counter with a guy like Gavin—had never deserved her.

And Gavin liked to think he did. He did back then and he did now. An attraction like what he'd felt the other day at the storage place? An attraction that hadn't died or faded or changed into something else in fifteen years? An attraction—

"I should just forget about!" he nearly yelled, his voice echoing through the empty building.

Good God, he thought, this needs to stop. The Merri obsession needed to be put aside, once and for all. The woman said no. Who cares why?

"She said no!" he said, just to remind himself.

He opened the scrap room door, pushing the heavy steel with his shoulder, and a cool draft blew through since they never bothered to extend the ductwork this far.

He reached for the light, seeing nothing but the constant gleam of metal in shadows and—

"Hello? Luke?"

If he'd conjured her out of thin air, he wouldn't have been more surprised.

"Anyone home?" Merri's voice carried from the front

door, the sound of her footsteps loud in the empty building, like cannon shots, and Gavin stood, dumbfounded, in the doorway.

She was here? At his shop? A moment he'd fantasized about like crazy—a chance to show the woman who'd stomped on his pride just what he was capable of. What he'd made of himself.

"Back here!" he yelled, his voice cracking slightly, like the teenager he'd been.

He heard her rounding the corner and he stepped out of the doorway to the scrap room, striding down the big center aisle between the four work spaces.

They nearly collided at the door that led to the reception area.

"Hi," she said, laughing and stepping back. "Sorry."

"It's all right." He smiled, feeling awkward, while at the same time noticing everything about her in a single glance. A red scarf and pink cheeks, windblown hair and bright eyes. "I didn't mean to run you down."

"I didn't mean to barge in on you." She laughed, looking around the room. "Look at this place, Gavin." Gavin tried to see the shop through her eyes, but all he saw was blood, sweat and tears, his and his brother's.

All the shining chrome and orderly red toolboxes. The state-of-the-art hydraulics and metal-working equipment. All he saw, in total honesty, was his beating heart, put on display for her to see.

"I like your Christmas spirit," she said, pointing to the singing and dancing Rudolph that he—for reasons he didn't want to examine—found so entertaining.

"It's no Monroe's," he said. "But we do what we can."

She smiled, but was silent, taking in the rest of his shop, and he felt that beating heart speed up. He told himself that Merri Monroe's opinion of him, like the opinions of anyone outside of his brother and son, didn't matter. But his suddenly sweaty palms told a different story.

"This place is totally amazing!" She sighed, spinning in a circle.

"Thanks," he said, feeling a very unmanly blush build up from his chest. For crying out loud, he built hogs for a living; he shouldn't go around blushing.

Thank God a tool tray, slightly disorganized, sat beside him and he could clean that up, focus his attention on anything besides her.

"How long have you been open?" she asked.

"I left town for a while and when I came back Sean and I went into business together, fixing bikes. Once we got a little cash under our belts, I tried my hand at making an original and it all seemed to work out." He tucked the loose ratchets back into their snug Styrofoam homes.

"Worked out?" she asked, quirking an eyebrow at his understatement.

He shrugged, unable to say more, but feeling a grin curl his lip as he lined up pliers according to size.

"Is it just you and your brother?" she asked. "Doing all this work?"

"We've got one other mechanic and another fabricator, plus we run an internship program with a couple of the different high schools and community colleges."

Her eyes settled back on him and he suddenly remembered all those things he'd said to her behind the counter at Monroe's. Those wishes he'd cradled so hard against his chest. Those dreams he'd nurtured among the weeds of growing up the way he did.

"That's incredible," she said, her voice gruff, her eyes serious.

"Well." He coughed, supremely uncomfortable. "It keeps us out of trouble. What about you?" he asked, shoving the attention over on to her. "What are you up to these days?"

Those cheeks of hers went white; a subtle tension creased her lips. "I'm between jobs," she said. "But I was managing a café in Kansas City."

"Ah." He smiled. "A Monroe doesn't fall far from the tree? Or, I guess, the restaurant business?"

"It's in the blood," she said with a shrug.

"How long are you home for?" he asked, fondling the last plier like a lifeline.

"A while," she said, running a hand over the stainless counter, clearly as unnerved as him. "I just rented a place off Kingshighway. I move in after the New Year."

"That's…incredible."

She's moving back? Part of him howled. She's standing there looking at you sideways and she's moving back to town?

Hold on there, killer, his common sense chimed in. She already said she couldn't.

He smiled, remembering Merri of old, and wondered if maybe she just needed to be convinced. And man, oh, man, weren't those nights of convincing her etched into his memory.

"Look at us," he said, checking his watch. "Five minutes and no fighting."

She laughed, bright and cheerful. "That's got to be a Christmas miracle. Quick, let's talk politics."

Suddenly they lapsed into silence. A very uncomfortable silence. She reached out and stroked the handlebars of one of his show bikes—a custom job that got about two feet per gallon but looked like something he saw once at the Met.

Her being here, smelling like sugar and french fries, her fingers stroking the bright chrome—it was a wet dream.

"You, ah, looking for a bike or something?"

"No!" She laughed. "You cured me of any curiosity that night you took me home from that graduation party. Remember?"

Remember? Her pressed against his back, nothing but T-shirts between them, her hand burning a hole through the skin at his waist. Her breath like fire against his neck. They'd left that party together because her date had gotten drunk and rude and, when Gavin arrived, only because he was sleeping with the older sister of the guy throwing the stupid thing, she'd been in tears on the front step.

He'd felt for the first time in his life like Galahad, or something. He'd whisked her away on the back of his bike and gone too fast, showing off, trying to show her how cool he was, and all he'd done was scare her.

"I'm sorry," he said. "I'm so sorry about that night. Your first ride should have been a great experience. You should have felt safe and exhilarated and—"

"Oh, it was exhilarating."

He caught her sarcasm. Man, he wished he could take back that night. He'd give up the touch of her hands and the burn of her breath, just so she wouldn't have that memory.

"You should go again," he told her earnestly. "Give it another try."

She stared at him for a second too long, her tongue at

the corner of her mouth, and his whole body tensed and twitched. "Maybe," she said, meeting his eyes. "Sometime."

"Right now," he said, stepping toward her. Hungry for the touch of her hands on his waist, the heat of her body at his back, the cold of the wind on his face. He got hard just thinking about it. "Let's go right now. I swear, I promise, I'll make it great for you."

The minutes seemed to drag on, spread out to fill the room, the whole world, and he couldn't look away from her. And she couldn't look away from him, and again he felt that pull, that gravity, that was Merri Monroe.

"Merri—" He sighed.

She blinked and jerked, glancing down at her hands. The moment popped and dissipated. "While I love the invitation, I'm here on official Christmas Eve business. Where's, ah, Luke?"

"Luke?"

"He's supposed to help me put lights up at the park."

"He's out with Sean. They—"

The back of his neck prickled. Luke volunteered to go with Sean for that test-drive and delivery. Luke, a McDonnell who never forgot anything, had either forgotten his plan with Merri or was trying to set them up.

Devious, Gavin thought, fighting a smile. *The kid was devious.*

"They won't be back for a while," he said and Merri's face fell.

"All right." She sighed and then forced a bright smile. "Thanks, Gav, I'll—"

"I can help," he said, falling cheerfully right into what his son must have planned, because she was so irresistible with the red scarf and chrome-stroking fingers.

And because he was, deep down, suicidal. A total reckless idiot.

She hesitated and he smiled, feeling wild. He hit the lights and plunged the warehouse into darkness. "Come on," he said. "I won't bite."

HOLY CATS, THE JEEP was so small. The Jeep was actually, at this moment, filled with Gavin McDonnell's slightly combustible scent, the smallest space in the world. Minuscule.

Merri couldn't breathe without tasting him on her tongue, in her throat. She could feel him, like static electricity, all along her right side.

"So," Gavin said, shifting slightly in his seat, his mahogany eyes on her in a way that made her skin feel like dancing. "Luke tells me you're wearing the Christmas Eve Santa suit."

She groaned. "With Dad's broken leg—" She gasped and turned to stare at him. "You could do it." But he was already shaking his head. "Why not? It would fit. Sort of."

"If word got out that Gavin McDonnell was Santa, no mother would bring their kid down to sit on my lap."

She went cold at his words. "That can't be true," she whispered.

He smiled ruefully. "Sadly, my reputation and that of my mother lives on."

Merri chewed on her lip, considering carefully the intelligence of bringing up this topic. But she was never very smart, particularly where Gavin was concerned, and as she turned left on Big Bend toward the park, passing the university, she just asked the question burning on her tongue.

"Why did you stay here?" she asked. "You always

told me you were going to go west, build motorcycles out in California."

He didn't answer and she could feel the heat of his gaze. Finally, unable to resist, she glanced at him and he sat there, grinning at her. "You remembered?" he asked.

I remember everything, she thought, burning with memories, all of them.

"Well, you talked about it enough," she joked.

"I guess I did," he said. "That was my plan but then I met Juliet—Luke's mom. She was a student at SLU, but when she got pregnant she headed back to her family. I went with her but we just couldn't make it work. So I moved back to Webster Groves a few years ago and it was as far away as I was willing to be from my son."

Stupidly her whole body tuned in, waiting breathlessly for more from him, but of course he was silent. "He's talked about her," Merri said when Gavin didn't add to his story.

She parked behind the amphitheater where the celebration would be held and turned off the Jeep, plunging them into a darkness that blended with the darkness outside. A few lights reflecting off snow, a moon that took up half the sky and the fire in Gavin's eyes were the only illumination. But it was enough. More than enough to see the cold shock on his face.

"What did he say?" Gavin asked, his voice shadowed with anger and surprise.

Oh, no, Merri thought, *bad territory. Unwise move, Merri. Retreat. Retreat.*

"He said he's happy to be here," she answered quickly.

"I can't believe I'm asking Merri Monroe for information about my kid," he said bitterly, and Merri's pride roared at his insinuation.

"Then don't," she snapped, unbuckling her seat belt and throwing herself out of the Jeep. She stomped to the back, pulling out the box of tangled white lights.

Détente was over, apparently. She yanked out a coil of lights, lifting a snarl that she tried to shake out. It was back to crossing wires with Gavin. Back to antagonism and yelling. Nothing ever changed, certainly not between them.

She heard his car door slam and he was out in the dark and cold with her. He charged around the Jeep, his breath like smoke in the air.

"What do you know, Merri?"

"How about you try talking to him."

He lunged forward, not touching her, not laying a finger on her, but she felt touched all the same—by his breath, his eyes, his anger.

"You think I haven't?" he asked. "You think I haven't tried a hundred times to get Luke to talk to me? Tell me what happened with his mom?"

Her anger popped, vanished. This wasn't about her. It was about Luke and Gavin and the pain they both carried in their faces.

"I'm sorry," she whispered. His face was illuminated by the one streetlight ten feet away and his eyes were shadowed, filled with questions and concern.

He's a parent, she realized. He's a father and he feels something's wrong and doesn't know what to do.

It was all right there on his handsome face and it was all she could do not to reach out and touch his lips, soften the stress and pain that had settled over him like a mask.

Instead, she looked down at the lights, trying with shaking fingers to pull the knot free.

"If you know something…" he said and swallowed.

She couldn't tell Luke's secrets, no matter how much Gavin needed answers. No matter how much she felt his pain.

Their Christmas Eve pact was unshakeable. It had to be.

"Merri," he whispered. "Look at me, please."

She squeezed her eyes shut and dropped the lights. Gathering her courage, she looked at him.

"He said he's happy to be here," she said, her voice a scratch in the intimate darkness. "He loves working with you and Sean. He loves you."

It wasn't a lie, but it wasn't the whole truth, and they both knew it.

His eyes flared and his breath came out like a hammer. "You know something more," he whispered. "He told you something—"

She put up a hand between them as if pushing back the heat that radiated from him. Never in her wildest dreams did she ever imagine this much pain from Gavin. The depth of his feelings astounded her and she realized she'd seen glimpses of it as a teenager. That night when he'd told her he loved her—his lips against her neck, their sweat cooling on her body—she'd been unable to look him in the eye, to see all that raw, naked feeling.

It had been scary to have those emotions directed at her when she didn't know how to handle it.

Such an idiot, she realized. *I'm such an idiot for throwing all that love away.*

Gavin would never cheat or lie. But he also wouldn't hide himself away like she had, making safe choices with her head instead of her heart.

For Gavin, love was love and it was the whole thing.

And here it was, intensified and magnified for his son,

and she totally understood Luke's fear of hurting or disappointing his father.

"I won't break a promise," she said. "And I promised Luke I wouldn't say anything. But if you ask him and give him time… Christmas Eve—"

Gavin threw himself away from her, pacing the dark shadows under the pine trees around them.

"Christmas Eve," he muttered. "What is with you two and Christmas Eve?"

"You have to talk to him," she said and he continued pacing. She watched for a while, feeling slightly sick to her stomach with anxiety, and then finally turned her attention back to the lights at her feet.

The terrible tangle, that with time and patience she could unravel. Unlike her and Gavin.

They were a mess destined to stay messy.

"Why are you back here?" he asked.

"I'm helping my—"

"Why aren't you married? Living in some suburban fantasy with a Ken doll and two kids like you always wanted?"

Oh, well, that hurt, and she threw the lights to the ground, charging the darkness. "Maybe I am," she snapped. "Maybe I have a wonderful life, with a wonderful man. Maybe my children—" Her voice broke, her facade cracking, but she pressed on. "Maybe everything is perfect!"

She punched him hard, right on his chest, but he didn't move. His heartbeat thundered under her touch and she was too slow to move her hand and he grabbed it, flattened it, so her palm was sandwiched between slick leather and his hot skin.

"Then why are you so sad?" he asked, his eyes boring right through her skin, right into her confused heart.

Too much, she thought panicked. *He sees too much.*

She jerked away, but he didn't let her go; he held on to her hand while she pulled, like a fish on a line.

"Let me go," she snapped furiously, trying hard not to fall apart but failing in so many ways. Her nose was running, her eyes wet; her heart, already battered, was in danger of splitting wide open.

He didn't say anything, he just pressed her hand harder to his body, and she swore she could feel his shirt beneath the leather and his skin beneath that. She could concentrate and feel his blood and muscle and the fierce, passionate loyalty that pumped through Gavin McDonnell like gasoline through an engine.

Her whole body seemed to shake, bounce between memory and the present. "I'm not sad," she insisted, defiant, proud and lying.

"You're about to cry right now," he whispered, pushing and pushing her to places she didn't want to go. "What's wrong, Merri?"

The sound of her name on his lips, rolling off his tongue, was the last straw, and suddenly everything seemed to collapse around her.

"What's wrong?" she asked, swallowing down a sudden hysteria. "What's right? Look at me. I'm thirty-four years old. Alone. Living with my parents again in a room that smells like french fries. I'm stupid about men, stupid about relationships. My life was supposed to fall into place by now, not fall apart."

"Merri." He looked baffled. "Life doesn't fall into place for anyone. You have to work and sacrifice—"

She snapped her hand back. "Don't tell me about work, Gavin," she said. "Or sacrifice. You have no idea—"

"You're right," he said quickly, his hands cupping her

shoulders, running down her arms to find her fists. "I'm sorry."

He petted her fingers, coaxing her hands to open, placing his palms against hers, where she wasn't sure if the pounding she felt was her heart or his.

"You don't know me," she said, wanting it to be true.

"Don't I?" he asked, smiling just a little, just enough to seem sad. "I always thought we knew each other better than most people. It's why I loved you," he said, his honesty so humbling she could barely breathe. "And why you gave me your virginity, right?"

"Yes," she said, unable to deny the fact that they did seem to share an understanding, even now, years after teenage infatuation should have worn off. She thought about his shop, about how he'd watched her as she looked around, about how badly he liked to pretend that he didn't care what people thought about him.

But he lived here. He'd stayed here and proved everyone wrong, because it mattered to him.

And she knew that. In her bones, she got it.

"But you don't know my life," she said. "You don't know what's happened to me."

"Then tell me."

The words, her secret, this new burden she carried like stones around her neck, were right at the tip of her tongue and she found herself wanting to open up to this man.

It's because you're alone, she thought. *It's because he's here, close enough to touch, and your body is on fire.*

"What happened to that Brett guy?" he asked. "In high school."

"We broke up."

"When?"

"A few weeks after—"

His eyes flared as if he knew how she was going to end that sentence.

After I handed you my virginity. After you told me you loved me. After all the fear you made me feel wore off and I realized how cold Brett was. How he could never be you. How no one could ever be you.

"We were kids," she whispered, not sure who she was talking about. "It wasn't real."

He tugged on her hand, pulling her in, and she went, her legs stiff, her head screaming in protest and her heart shutting it out.

"I'm not a kid anymore," he whispered, his breath feathering her face, brushing her eyelashes, feeding a sudden internal fire.

She opened her mouth, wanting to breathe him in. Wanting to eat him, suck him, taste him. And there he was. His mouth. His tongue. Those teeth and lips.

And she was starving. Starving to feel him. To feel like she did that night, as if she was right on the edge of the world, being pushed off. He held her so hard, his arms so strong, his hands so big, it was like being caught in a storm.

Exhilaration flooded her, every nerve ending flared, and she groaned into his mouth, leaned into his heat. It was as if the past fifteen years had been silent, and being kissed by Gavin, held by Gavin, was one big long laugh—a scream. Something wild, barely in control.

He lifted her slightly, her toes brushing the ground as he stepped toward the Jeep, bracing her there. He arched against her, pinning her with his hips, and she felt every rigid inch of him. His chest and torso, the growing wonder between his legs.

Her body melted and sighed. The hard rock of his

thigh slid between hers and she could have cried at the electrical pleasure that ran through her body.

This was sex. This was passion. This is what a man should make her feel. This was…

A total mistake.

She was pregnant.

And this was Gavin McDonnell, the last thing she needed right now.

"Gavin," she breathed, pulling away, bracing her hands on his shoulder, trying to leverage herself away from that thigh.

"Merri." He sighed into her neck, licking her skin, biting at the pulse in her flesh.

"Gavin." Her voice was only slightly stronger as her body and will battled it out. "I…can't."

He leaned back, his eyes hooded, wary. A question burned there and she shook her head. "I can't," she repeated.

She stumbled when he stepped away and his hand lifted as if to brace her, but she couldn't risk more touching. She was another kiss away from having sex against her Jeep, for crying out loud.

"Is there someone else?" he asked, and she nearly laughed.

Oh, how to answer that kind of question. How to answer it when her body throbbed and her heart ached and all she really wanted to do was fold herself up against that chest again.

"You could say that," she whispered and he jerked as if she'd punched him.

His bitter laugh cooled the rest of her passion, and as he turned away, pushing his hands through his hair, she wished her life was different. That she'd been smarter somehow. More realistic.

"Then why are you here?" he yelled, his arms flung out in the park as if he were asking the universe.

Because I have nowhere else to go, she thought.

"I'm here to put up lights," she said, lifting her chin in the air, faking a bravado she was far from feeling.

She expected him to leave. Hell, if she were him, she'd leave. But as she picked up the coil of lights, black against the snow, with numb, fumbling hands, he was right there with her, careful not to touch her. Exuding a hurt anger that she always seemed to bring out in him.

I'm sorry, she thought, feeling an awful lump in her throat. *I'm sorry we're always so wrong for each other. I'm sorry I keep hurting you when it's the last thing I want to do.*

In electrified silence, they strung the twinkling white lights through the trees, creating, in the winter air, the appearance of stars—that, unlike Gavin, were close enough to touch.

CHAPTER SIX

GAVIN THREW OPEN the back door, gratified when the brass knob banged into the wall with a nice thunderous punch. He'd like to punch some walls, behavior he knew he was too old for, but still—fist meeting drywall would be really satisfying right now.

Frustration ate at him like a thousand piranhas. After hanging lights, after kissing Merri and feeling her melt against him, after talking about his son—who apparently trusted the totally untrustworthy Merri Monroe more than he trusted his own father—after the unbearable ride home with Merri in that too-small Jeep, he was ready to take his frustration out on someone.

"Sean!" he bellowed.

"We're back here, Dad!" Luke yelled from the front TV room, and Gavin, breaking his own rules about shoes in the house, stomped through the hallways to find them.

The room was dark, *Batman Returns* playing for perhaps the eight hundredth time on the big-screen TV, and both Sean and Luke had their feet up on the coffee table next to an old catalytic convertor Sean was trying to salvage.

Gavin flipped on the lights, pounded the off button on the remote.

"Hey!" Luke yelled.

"Uh-oh," Sean muttered.

"Right, uh-oh," Gavin said through clenched teeth. "What's the big idea, Luke?"

Luke for just a second looked like a fish out of water, but then realization lit a match in those blue eyes and he tried too hard to look innocent. "What big—"

"Don't lie," Gavin said. "Don't lie to me. I can handle lots of things in this house, but we don't lie!"

Luke swallowed and nodded his head.

"Were you supposed to hang lights with Merri?"

"Yes."

"Did you forget?"

Luke glanced at Sean, who burrowed a little deeper into his side of the couch.

"No," Luke answered. "I didn't forget. I was hoping…" Luke trailed off, stared down at his hands, and Gavin didn't know what to do with himself. His son was trying to fix him up with Merri Monroe, and he'd gone with it. Like an idiot, he'd jumped at the chance.

"What?" he asked, feeling a weariness climbing his spine. He was too old for all this crap. "What were you hoping?"

"She's really cool, Dad," he said. "And she's sorry for the way she treated you in the past."

Oh, fantastic, she told Luke what she'd said. Wonderful. Really. Was there no privacy anymore? Couldn't the past just freaking stay in the past?

Well, a little voice whispered, *not when you press the past against the side of her Jeep and shove your leg between hers.*

"I suppose this was your idea," Gavin said, whirling on his brother, who of course simply shrugged.

"I don't need your help with my love life," Gavin said.

Sean snorted.

"You have something you want to say?"

"Yeah." Sean stared at him from beneath his omnipresent cap. "What love life?"

"Yeah, Dad," Luke jumped in before Gavin could reach out and knock that stupid cap off his brother's head. "What love life?"

"This," he said, pointing his finger at Luke, "is none of your business."

"Don't get mad at him," Sean said. "It was my idea. You've never gotten over Merri Monroe, and when she came back into town it just seemed like it was time to get you off your ass."

Gavin reached for his stupid, meddling brother.

"It's not like you're dating anyone," Luke said, cutting in before Gavin could get in one good punch. "You haven't for years and she's all alone—"

"She's not. She's got someone," Gavin spit out, the words like hot coals falling from his lips into a stone-silent room.

"Did she say that?" Luke asked, appearing stunned.

"Yes," he said, wiping a hand over his face, wishing this whole night would just go away. "So next time, before trying to fix me up, why don't you do some more research."

"She's lying, Dad," Luke whispered.

But Gavin refused to be interested. He refused to ask any questions, no matter how badly he wanted to. If her rejection stung, then this was like being dipped in boiling oil. She'd lied to get out of that kiss. She'd lied to stop what was happening between them.

Which was worse?

"It doesn't matter, son," he said. "Merri doesn't want anything to do with me."

Just like before.

"I'm sorry, Dad," Luke said, his eyes big and earnest, and Gavin's anger melted away, leaving only confusion about what Merri knew about Luke.

He cupped the boy's head, remembering him as an infant, when his whole body fit into the palm of his hand like some kind of miracle.

"She told me I need to talk to you," he said.

Luke's whole face shut down, every emotion gone, nothing but suspicion and closed doors. *Wow,* he thought, *such a McDonnell.*

"About what?" Luke asked, as if he didn't know.

"About why you're here?"

Luke was silent, and Sean, an idiot but no dummy, stood and left the room.

"What did you tell her, Luke, that you can't tell me? What's going to happen on Christmas Eve?"

Hurt and confusion and a panic that seemed like a scream in the silent room filled Luke's blue eyes and Gavin was ready to rip off his skin to take that away.

"I don't want to hurt you, Dad," Luke said, standing and stepping away, putting a distance between them that was bigger than this room. Bigger than Gavin could cross alone.

"Hurt me?" he whispered. "How in the world could you hurt me? I swear, son, whatever it is that you're keeping a secret isn't going to change the way I feel about you."

I love you. He should just say it. Just put it out there and see what happens. The kid has to know.

"Just give me some more time," Luke said. "I swear. Christmas Eve and I'll tell you."

Gavin shook his head, baffled by how Merri Monroe and the holiday figured into all of this.

THE DAY BEFORE Christmas Eve day dawned like a Burl Ives song. Sunshine, blue sky and lots and lots of snow. Big fat flakes hit Merri's bedroom window, clung and gathered in heaps at the corners.

Looks fake, she thought.

She could already smell cookies baking in the kitchen, and the sound of Dad singing along with Springsteen on the radio about Santa Claus coming to town.

Wanting to throw a shoe at the door, she knew, was not the proper response to such holiday cheer.

She thought of the gifts she was going to get her parents today, and the fancy pencil set she'd picked up for Luke on a whim. Imagining their delight and surprise didn't even lift her spirits.

She was Scrooge McDuck, all the way.

But since Monroe's was going to be packed today with shoppers looking for sustenance, she was Scrooge McDuck with a grill to manage.

Better get the show on the road, she thought sourly, throwing her blankets off her legs.

Downstairs, as soon as she flipped the sign to Open, the bell over the door didn't stop ringing. And all the old regulars braved the snow to come in for free coffee and some Monroe Christmas cheer. The booths were packed. The counter had a few open slots, but not many.

"Hey, there, Paula," Dad said, greeting old Mrs. Phillips from his spot on the stool closest to the door. He took her coat, hobbled over to the coatrack and stuck his tongue out at Mom, who glared at him.

"It's Christmas, Lenora," he said, bussing her cheek, wrapping his arms around her and swaying slightly, as if he was about to do a little Fred Astaire in the packed diner. "Lighten up or you'll scare away all our customers."

"You should be resting," Mom said, but her eyes were smiling and her hand, when it patted his cheek, was tender.

Dad pulled a ratty sprig of mistletoe from his back pocket and held it over his head, wiggling his eyebrows at Mom. Which, frankly, made him look as if there were white caterpillars dancing on his forehead, but Mom leaned in to nuzzle his neck in front of God, Mrs. Phillips and everyone.

It was ridiculous, really, but Merri's throat got tight. The coffeemaker was never going to nuzzle her neck. Never. And, she realized, she wanted what her parents had. She'd take the fighting and bickering and Christmas fascination if she could just get someone whose neck she'd want to nuzzle when she was sixty years old.

Gavin's neck was good for nuzzling.

But it was simply the last of her many worries.

She stared down at the omelets on her grill. Omelets adorned with red and green peppers, tomatoes and broccoli. Mom would have thrown in garland, once she saw what Merri was doing, but Merri had to draw the line somewhere.

This was her effort at Christmas spirit—appropriately colored vegetables. Wasn't she just a little Christmas elf?

As it was, customers were stunned to see vegetables arriving in their food and Merri decided salads to replace some french fries wouldn't be a bad thing for her, her parents or the customers.

Imagining her father's reaction made her smile.

"Merri!" someone whispered, and she turned, flinging a red pepper onto the far wall.

"Over here!"

A cold draft swirled around her feet and Merri faced

the door to the alley where Luke stood, looking more and more like his father every day—from the leather jacket to the pissed-off attitude.

"What are you doing?" she asked. Where's your father? Is he still mad? Have you two talked?

"Can you talk to me for a minute?" He waved her over, his fingers and the tip of his nose bright pink.

Merri remembered she had a beef with the boy for standing her up last night with the lights and thus setting in motion the whole scene with Gavin.

For crying out loud, she was about to be a mother; she had no business being involved in all this drama.

"Merri!" Luke cried, his eyes stony, and she wondered what had gotten the boy all riled up. Then she remembered their Christmas Eve pact.

Maybe Luke told Gavin and it didn't go well.

"Mom," she yelled, plating the omelet and sliding it to Mr. McGee at the counter. "I'm outside for a second."

She grabbed her mother's old green cardigan that had hung on a hook by the door since the dawn of man and stepped outside into a gusty blowing wind.

"What happened, Luke, did you tell him?" she asked, wedging herself between the fire escape and a stack of empty milk crates.

"Tell him?" Luke looked stunned for a second. "Oh, you mean *tell him* tell him. No, of course not."

"It's Christmas Eve," she said.

"Tomorrow."

"Close enough."

"Have you told your parents?" he countered.

"No," she answered pointedly. "I haven't had the chance because I was hanging lights all last night. You were supposed to help me, remember?"

Luke ignored her and leaned right into her personal space, forcing her to step backward, colliding with cold metal.

"Why did you tell my dad that there was some other guy in your life?" Luke asked, looking not at all like a fourteen-year-old angel boy, but like a McDonnell out for blood. She gaped at him.

"I didn't tell him any such thing."

"He said you did. He said you wanted nothing to do with him."

It was so far from the truth she couldn't even think about it. To dwell on all that she wanted and couldn't possibly have with Gavin would make her heart break. But she'd given him that impression, and she could understand why he'd feel that way, but what else was she supposed to do?

Even if she told him the truth, the result would be the same, except perhaps it would be Gavin wanting nothing to do with her.

"Merri?" Luke asked, appearing baffled and hurt. "Why did you lie?"

"I didn't lie," she whispered, hating that she'd hurt Gavin like that again, without even trying. "I said I have someone in my life—"

"Who?"

"I'm pregnant," she whispered, glancing behind her to make sure Mom wasn't listening in at the door. "Have you forgotten?"

Luke blinked at her. "So?"

"So?" She laughed. "Look, Luke, you're what, fourteen? I don't expect you to get what a big deal this is—"

"Do you like my dad?" Luke asked, crossing his arms

over his chest. His breath made plumes in the cold Christmas air.

Her skin felt too tight and Luke's bright eyes seemed to look right through her.

"It's irrelevant right now, Luke," she whispered.

"Not to him, it's not."

She sat down hard on a stack of milk crates. "What are you doing?" she asked. "Last night with the lights and now this? Are you trying to fix us up?"

He shrugged. "My uncle Sean said that Dad never got over you."

She couldn't argue with that—last night pretty much proved they weren't over each other. But there was nothing that could be done—life had moved on.

She stood, angry with Luke and Gavin and the whole situation. "We're adults and we don't need your help," she cried. "This is my life you're playing with."

"Oh, yeah?" he asked, his face going pink to match his cheeks. "What are you doing telling my dad to talk to me about why I'm here? Why are you playing around in my life? I thought we had a deal."

"Your dad is really hurt—"

"And telling him I'm gay is going to make him happy?" Luke looked nearly wild and Merri cooled off slightly, understanding the kid's anguish.

"You know—" Luke's face screwed up, everything about him dismissive "—maybe this whole Christmas Eve pact thing was a mistake. I don't need to tell him anything and maybe you should just stay away from my dad."

"Luke, come on—"

"No." Luke backed away, his hands up. "Just stay away

from both of us." And then he was gone, running down the alleyway, his shoulders hunched against the cold.

She sat back down on her milk crates—feeling as if she'd just been abandoned by her only friend.

CHAPTER SEVEN

GAVIN WOKE UP early Christmas Eve day. This is it, he thought as he made eggs and bacon. He wondered what the revelation would be as he watched Luke eat breakfast.

"You okay, son?" Gavin asked as Luke pushed away from the table, breakfast decimated in front of him.

"Great, Dad. Thanks for breakfast."

No revelation. No nothing.

Sean left to do his annual last-minute Christmas shopping. Luke and Gavin worked on the painted electric guitar they were getting Sean. But they talked about the Cardinals' hopes for next season, of all things.

Morning turned to noon, clear turned to snowy, and eggs and bacon turned to ham sandwiches, and nothing sprang from Luke's mouth.

Nothing more life changing than he was thinking of being a Red Sox fan.

It's Christmas Eve! he wanted to shout, but he didn't. He was playing it cool, letting Luke decide when he was going to talk. But the hours passed and the stress of waiting, of playing it cool, of not grabbing his son and shaking him, was giving him a heart attack.

"Come on, Luke," Gavin yelled, checking his watch. "We've got two hours before we have to be at the park and, if you need some last-minute help with these wings, we're running out of time."

"Okay. Okay. Just give me a second." Luke's voice was muffled from behind the heavy door of the scrap room and so was the sound of something crashing to the ground.

Gavin leaped off the worktable he'd been sitting on. "Luke?"

"I'm good. Just—" Luke groaned and then yelped. "Ouch. Wow. Okay. You ready?"

Gavin scrubbed his hands over his face and nearly laughed. He was so nervous, so excited, about seeing these wings of Luke's.

"Come on out," he yelled.

Gavin's mom had not been what one would call a good mother, and when times got tough with Luke, he only had his mother's poor example to go on.

Which made parenting the equivalent of traveling in space with a map of Ohio.

When he'd been ten, Gavin had brought home a science project he'd gotten an A on—a basketball he'd painted up to look like Earth. He'd worked after school with the art teacher for three weeks on that ball, wanting to get Australia and the colors just right.

Mom wasn't home when he came home from school, triumphant with that grade, so he left the ball on the kitchen table with the grade next to it. In the middle of the night he'd woken up to the sound of his bedroom door slamming open, and his mother, drunk and weaving in the doorway, launched the ball into his room.

"What did I say about leaving your toys around?" she'd yelled and slammed the door.

He wanted to be the opposite of that kind of parent to Luke.

He wanted to be encouraging. Loving, even.

And he got the sense that these wings were a big deal. Gavin didn't want to blow it.

"All right," Luke said and the door creaked open, revealing his son, but not his son.

His son as a custom-built motorcycle angel with purple, red and gold flames painted up the front of two-foot chrome wings.

"Holy…" he breathed, stepping toward Luke, wanting to hug him. Wanting to throw his arms around him and cradle him against his chest and tell him how proud he was. How loved Luke was, how talented and smart and clever and amazing.

But that ice was there—those brick walls between them that didn't used to be there.

Gavin's eyes burned and he blinked, leaning close to study the detail on the flames.

"You did this?" he asked, his voice gruff, full of a thousand unsaid things.

"Uncle Sean helped with the fabrication."

"But the paint…?"

"Yeah—" Luke cleared his throat "—that was me."

Gavin couldn't speak through the dam in his throat.

"You like them?" Luke asked, trying to sound nonchalant but only sounding painfully young.

"They're—" he searched for the right words, the right thing to say to a cool, secretive fourteen-year-old boy "—righteous."

Luke's face broke into a wide, beaming grin.

"How are you wearing them?"

"I've got a holster on under my shirt. I had to cut holes—" Luke swiveled slightly, nearly taking off Gavin's head.

"Crap," Luke whispered, laughing. "I have to be careful."

"Yeah, you do." Gavin laughed, too.

Gavin finished inspecting the wings, finding no fault in them whatsoever. "Merri is going to freak when she sees these," Gavin said, wishing he wasn't thinking of her even now.

"Who cares what she thinks," Luke spat, his face a thundercloud.

"But," Gavin said, shell-shocked, "it's Christmas Eve."

"It's just another night, Dad. Help me take them off so we can just get it over with."

"I thought you—" But Gavin didn't finish the sentence. It worked in his favor that Merri was no longer Luke's best friend. But still, he had to wonder what Merri had done now.

And if his son was ever going to tell him what was bothering him.

Two HOURS BEFORE having to be at the park, Merri stared at herself in the full-length mirror in her room.

Pregnant Santa coming atcha.

"Mom," she said, pinching her nose against the headache taking root behind her eyes. "Can you turn off the radio?"

"It's Christmas music, honey. It's Christmas Eve."

"I know, but we've been listening to it for a month."

"Fine," Mom said, pretending not to be peeved as she switched off the radio on the bedside table with a definitive click.

Mom kept fussing with her and Merri kept wishing this holiday was over.

"You look darling," Mom said from over Merri's shoulder.

"I look ridiculous," Merri said, twitching the long beard over her face, trying to keep it out of her mouth. It tasted like old gum and coffee.

The suit was too big and the giant black belt that she'd hoped would keep things cinched in made her look like a red velour sausage. Luckily Dad was short and the pants weren't too long, but the arms of the jacket hung over her fingertips.

"It's too bad we don't know what Luke will be wearing," Mom said, lifting Merri's hand to try and make the sleeves work.

"Yeah," Merri said, rubbing her eyes. "About that."

Mom perked right up, her nose for trouble honed to perfection. "About what?"

"I don't know if Luke is going to be there."

"Why? Is he sick?"

"No." Merri took a deep breath. "He's mad at me."

"Merri." Mom sighed, disappointment wafting off her like sour perfume.

"Who cares, Mom? We can get someone else to be the angel."

Mom's stony glance slid over Merri as she stepped back, sticking pins back in her pin cushion.

"Maybe we should find someone else to play Santa," she said.

"Yes!" Merri cried. "Finally, someone in this family seeing reason. Me as Santa is a stupid idea." Merri groaned. "The whole thing is stupid."

Mom, her face folded into stern and angry lines Merri hadn't seen since she was a child, stepped in front of her. And Merri realized she'd gone too far.

"What is wrong with you?" Mom asked.

"Nothing!" Merri snapped. "I'm fine."

"No," Mom corrected, "you're not. You're petulant and childish."

Merri stepped back, stunned by the vehemence in her mother's voice.

"I understand you've had a rough time of it, but so has your father, in case you've forgotten. And so, frankly, have I."

"You're right," Merri said earnestly, but Mom held up her hand, cutting off the apology.

"We love you and are patient with you but I have had enough of your black cloud, Merri. I have had enough of your barely contained disdain for our home and our life and our celebration."

Oh, my Lord, this was worse than she'd thought. *Am I really that bad?*

"Well, guess what, kid, it's your life, too. And you can be angry about it or you can get your act together and see how lucky you are." Mom checked her watch. "I need to get ready. We'll meet you at the park in an hour."

Oh, man, Merri thought, watching her mother go. She'd just washed her hands of me. First Gavin and Luke, now Mom.

Merri faced herself in the mirror and didn't recognize herself, and it had nothing to do with the red suit, white beard and pregnancy. This person staring back at her— sad and out of control and angry at the world for the decisions she did not make—wasn't even a person she liked.

Her parents were nothing but good to her. Loving and caring and generous and she treated them as if she was constantly doing a favor for them. They liked their life, their community, and the diner was the center of that. The hub around which all things they loved revolved.

Things she loved, too.

Maybe, she thought, the diner wasn't the trap.

Maybe it's my own sick head.

She groaned, thinking of Luke who had only looked up to her, trusted her, and she'd stepped all over him. And Gavin…well, how many times could she stab that man in the heart?

"I don't like you," she said to the Santa in the mirror. "You better get your act together."

She did the best she could to shorten the Santa sleeves on her own with safety pins and duct tape, and she grabbed the gifts for her family and Luke.

Night had fallen on Christmas Eve and the moon and stars outside her bedroom window were white and dazzling. She knew that the town, her family, friends and neighbors would be gathering up gifts and heading out their doors for the park. For Christmas and this celebration that Mom and Dad cared for and cultivated out of love and friendship.

It's Christmas Eve, she thought, searching through herself for courage, honesty and some genuine Christmas spirit. Maybe Santa would bring something good for all of them.

Stranger things had happened.

"DAD," LUKE SAID, pulling the tarp off the wings from the back of the truck. "You don't have to stay."

"Not stay?" he asked, stunned Luke would think Gavin would drop him off and leave him there. "Why?"

"You know." Luke shrugged. "She'll be here."

Gavin sighed. "The day a girl scares me away from watching my kid in these freaking amazing wings is seriously the day I die."

Luke's eyes flared with gratitude and something that seemed just slightly respectful. Maybe, Gavin thought, the ice was thawing.

"Cool," however, was all he said.

They were parked behind the main park. The small amphitheater where the party was being held stood behind some trees and down a hill about thirty feet away. But wafting up the hill through the cold crisp air were the sounds of talking and some very bad group singing.

Gavin felt the ties of his past and the reputation of his mother close around him. A lot of people who remembered his mother and the trouble he'd caused growing up would be at this thing—and he wasn't really up for the sideways looks. The rehashing of those not-so glory days.

From the din down the hill, Merri's laugh suddenly rang out, clear and unmistakable, like a bell, only adding to his general crappy mood.

The truth was that if Luke wasn't here, Gavin would be far, far away from this park and this celebration.

He'd been burned by Merri twice, and twice was enough. Twice, actually, was enough to make him angry and he hoped she had the good sense to stay far away from him tonight.

"Dad?" Luke asked. "You all right?"

"Fine," Gavin said, sounding unconvincing even to his own ears.

"You know, Dad," Luke said, mimicking Gavin's own voice and the words he'd said a thousand times since Luke had moved in. "You can tell me anything."

Gavin laughed, rubbed a hand over his short hair.

"I'm, ah, just a little nervous about this Christmas thing."

"You scared of Santa?"

Gavin looked at his son and realized he'd kept a lot of

his past a secret from the boy because it was bad and he didn't want any of that bad to mix up with the perfection that was his son.

But, he thought, if this secret the boy kept was along the lines of all the secrets Gavin had kept over the years, maybe telling him would pave the way.

"I wasn't a good kid," he said, and Luke's blond eyebrows snapped together, laughter leeching from his face, and with that look Gavin felt even worse about the things he'd done. "I mean, I did some bad stuff and some people in town like to remind me of that when they see me."

"What kind of bad stuff?"

"I drank and I smashed stuff up and was basically a jerk."

"You?" Luke asked. "Why?"

Oh, man, why did he open his fat mouth? "Because I was angry." He sighed. "Angry at my mom and angry at being poor and angry that everything I wanted never seemed to be within reach."

"Come on." Luke laughed. "You're not like that anymore."

"I'm not?" he asked, thinking of Merri and the way they fought. The way she felt constantly out of reach and how mad that made him.

"You're like one of the coolest bike builders in the world."

Gavin's chest went hot and he breathed down big gulps of cold air. As compliments went, it was the best he'd ever gotten.

"Besides, Dad," Luke said, "you know what Uncle Sean would say…"

"Yes, I do, and that's hardly appropriate—"

"Screw 'em," Luke finished with glee.

Laughter poured out of Gavin's chest. What good had

he done? What profound kindness did he perform in another life to deserve this boy?

"You're right," he said, palming the boy's head and giving it a shake, about the only touching Luke would allow these days. "But watch your mouth."

Luke had to strip down to a long-sleeved T-shirt and Gavin helped him with the holster and then to shrug into two old sweatshirts he'd cut holes into.

Luke pulled on mitts and a hat but still Gavin worried.

"You gonna be warm enough?" he asked, taking in the fairly thin ensemble and the cold air swirling with snowflakes.

"Sure," Luke said with a grin, "I'm a McDonnell."

Ah, words to warm a father's heart.

"Well, then," Gavin said, giving the amazing magical wings a little tug. "Let's go have some fun."

It was Christmas Eve, after all, his first with Luke, and he was determined to enjoy it. Merri Monroe and the past couldn't ruin everything.

THE AMPHITHEATER WAS filling up with neighbors and laughter. Mom and Dad handed out cookies and hot drinks while Merri handed out sheet music and candles that everyone would light at 9:00 p.m.

Kids ran around screaming, drunk on Christmas spirit, and it was spreading to the adults. Lots of hugging. Lots of good cheer. Lots of flasks pulled out of winter coats.

"It was good of you to fill in," Mr. Johns, her high school science teacher, said as she handed him "Oh Holy Night" and a candle. "It means a lot to your dad. To everyone."

She glanced over at her parents. Mom looked like a combination between Mrs. Claus and a disco ball, and Dad had fashioned a very terrible set of antlers out of what looked like wire coat hangers in brown socks attached to an old hat of Mom's.

Mom and Dad were bickering by the coffee machine, surrounded by friends and family and community members who adored them. Then suddenly Dad kissed Mom and the fight seemed to be over. As usual.

I am a Monroe, she thought, really trying to understand what that meant for her. It meant family. And tradition. It meant lots of fighting, but lots of kissing, too. And suddenly, stupidly, because she'd never actually thought of it before, she realized her baby girl was a Monroe, too.

Her hand went to her waist, the small bulge of her baby Monroe.

She looked around at this glittery beautiful event and realized there was a lot to be proud of being a Monroe. A lot to relish. Being a Monroe meant something in this town, and it meant something good.

I'm such a fool, she thought, denying it for so long.

"It's the least I could do," she told Mr. Johns, feeling her smile grow in sincerity. "I'm a Monroe, after all."

But sadly it seemed her realization was too little too late. Mom and Dad were ignoring her. She'd tried to apologize and she'd tried to give them her presents but they simply smiled right through her.

"Later, kiddo," Dad had said, but it lacked its usual warmth.

There was a loud chorus of gasps and Merri turned to see Luke step into the clearing under a banner of twinkle lights.

"Holy cats," she murmured, absorbing the boy and those wings in all their glory. Merri could not believe the industrial beauty of them or the fact that Gavin was right there beside him. The combination of the painted two-foot wings, like something out of a metal dream, and Gavin's totally uninhibited pride, made her throat clog with sudden emotion.

"Look at them," she whispered.

"I see them," Dad said, hobbling over to Luke with land record speed. Dad shook Luke's hand and then Gavin's. He must have said something funny because Gavin tipped his head back and laughed, the sound floating through time and space to reach right into her chest and stroke her heart.

Soon there was a small crowd around the McDonnells, everyone gaping at those wings. But, more importantly, including Gavin and Luke, wrapping the long arms of the community around them.

Gavin was so surprised, she could see it on his face. He wanted to be guarded, careful. Ready, perhaps, for a fight. But the town wasn't giving him one.

She watched as they beat back his suspicion, his years of hurt feelings, with love. Acceptance.

"Look at them," Mom said from behind her.

"Incredible, huh?" Merri breathed.

I want them, something in her cried.

I want the right to go up and throw my arms around the both of them and tell them how proud I am to know them.

She wanted that, and so much more.

"Seems like with you back in town, maybe you'll have another chance with Gavin," Mom murmured, and Merri whirled to face her.

"What do you mean another chance?"

"Please, Merri." Mom sighed, tucking some silver garland behind her ear. "I'm not blind or stupid." She cupped Merri's cheeks. "But sometimes you are."

And then she left, taking coffee to the masses.

One of the kids came over and asked if it was time for the gift giving, and Merri snapped into motion.

"Hey, Luke," she said, cutting through the small throng of teenagers that hovered around the boy. "I'm so glad you made it," she said.

"I told you I would," he said, slightly sullen.

"Okay, then, you, ah, ready to get to work?"

"Sure," he said, stomping off to the center of the amphitheater where the Santa chair and sack of toys were waiting, leaving behind him a draft of cold air and disdain sharper than any winter.

"Not sure what you did," Gavin whispered in her ear, his breath lighting every nerve south of her hairline on fire. "But it worked. Luke is good and mad at you."

"I know," she whispered, hating to face him. Hating to see the anger and disdain in Gavin's face, too. But she did it, anyway, because she was that kind of idiot.

There was no disdain on his face, no anger. His face was carefully, painfully blank. As if she were a stranger. As if she were nothing to him.

Perversely, now that he didn't want her, she wanted more than ever to throw herself against that leather chest and be welcomed there. Cradled there.

"The wings are amazing," she said.

"They are."

"So are you," she said, the words slipping out like indoor cats seeking freedom. "Ah, I mean, with the town. I thought you were still the black sheep of Webster Groves. Persona non grata."

"I guess everyone's forgotten or something," Gavin said, looking around him as if slightly surprised to be there.

"Or," she said, just laying herself out on the line, "they finally see what a good guy you are."

Gavin sighed heavily through his nose, his eyes searching her face. Emotion flickered across his face, his lips tightening with regret, his eyes shadowed with confusion. "You're killing, me, Merri," he whispered. "I never know, from one minute to the next, who you're going to be."

She didn't have an answer, considering she didn't know herself. But she knew she liked herself better when she was with him; she liked the opportunity she had to be the person he thought she was—someone he could love. Someone he wanted.

"Hey, Santa!" Luke yelled.

"I have to go," she said, reluctant to leave Gavin's side.

"Story of my life," he answered and then he simply turned around and left her.

An hour later, Luke hadn't said so much as boo to her and they were done handing out gifts and taking pictures. Luke had been a total pro, though, especially considering that most of the kids wanted their pictures taken with him, and the photographer had to set up farther back to accommodate his wing span.

"We done?" Luke asked her when the last dollar-store toy had been handed out.

"Not yet," she said, the pencil set she'd gotten him tucked into her deep pocket. "Follow me?" she asked, trying not to let on that this was as important as it actually was.

He glanced at her and shrugged, but he followed her around the amphitheater, where she quickly ditched the incredibly itchy beard and Santa hat.

"Oh—" she sighed, rubbing at her face "—that's better."

"What's up?" Luke asked, not dropping the attitude for a minute.

"Luke, I'm so sorry for talking to your dad about you," she said. "I honestly didn't mean to upset you."

Luke blinked and then shrugged. "Fine."

She smiled. "Your wings are amazing."

His lip curled in a reluctant half smile. "Thanks," he said.

"Seriously, they're like art. The paint—" She touched the purple flame closest to her. "You must have worked so hard."

His eyes widened slightly. "I did," he agreed. "But I wouldn't have been able to do it if you hadn't given me the frames."

"No problem," she said, knowing there was still a ways to go before she was cool, but it felt like maybe she was on the road. "I wanted to give you something else," she said. "A Christmas gift."

She dug the pencils out of her pocket and held the red wrapped box out to him. He stared at them, his mouth gaping.

"You, ah, didn't have to do that," he whispered.

"It's Christmas," she said, smiling, feeling her heart start to mend and grow. Feeling parts of herself that had withered in the past little while grow flush with living again. This is why her parents loved Christmas, because it allowed you to be the best of yourself. It allowed you to let go of all the garbage and hold on tight to what it meant to be decent. Kind. Generous.

Christmas felt good. That's all there was to it.

"And you were a fantastic angel. The best we ever had."

He took the box and carefully opened the paper, gasping when he saw the expensive art supplies. "Wow." He sighed. "Wow, Merri, these are amazing."

"Well, kid—" she sighed "—you're pretty amazing."

He cleared his throat and shuffled his feet and she wanted to laugh and tell him that if they just hugged it would be less uncomfortable than pretending that they didn't care. But he was fourteen.

And she didn't know how to hug him with those wings on.

"So," he asked after a long moment, "have you told your parents?"

Right. Reality. "Not yet," she answered. "Have you told your dad?"

"Told me what?" Gavin asked, standing at the corner of the amphitheater.

The panic in Luke's eyes was staggering. Heartbreaking. Merri opened her mouth to say something, anything, just as Luke blurted out, "Merri's pregnant."

CHAPTER EIGHT

THERE WAS A ROARING in Merri's ears as all the blood in her body stopped in its tracks and fell to her feet.

She stared blankly at Luke, wondering if he'd said what she thought he'd said. Surely he didn't just blab her secret to Gavin McDonnell, the last person she wanted knowing she was pregnant. Surely she just heard wrong. Perhaps he said—

"I'm sorry," Luke mouthed and then, as if his wings worked, he just vanished into the darkness beyond the lights.

"Merri?" Gavin asked and, slowly, reluctantly, she turned to face him, her mind scrambling for some kind of lie, some kind of distraction, but once she saw his face her mind went numb.

Gavin was smiling.

"Is it true?" he asked, his eyes alight.

Shocked, she nodded.

"Aren't you happy?" he asked, as if the possibility of her not being happy seemed crazy, and her respect for Gavin grew. Babies were good. Period.

So different from Dean's reaction. So different from her own that she felt guilty for her weeks of worry.

"I am happy," she said, her voice hoarse.

"Wow!" he cried, laughing a little. "That's incredible."

He reached out as if to haul her into his arms, but then stopped and simply patted her on the thick shoulder of her Santa suit instead. "Congratulations," he murmured, his gaze warm, his smile so sweet she wanted to cry. The silence stretched and she felt the world turning so fast she got a little dizzy.

His eyebrows lowered, the hand on her shoulder stopped patting and grabbed her as if to hold her up.

"Merri? You okay?"

She shook her head.

"Do you need to sit down?" he asked, looking around for some kind of seat. Finally he just pushed her down onto the cement step of the amphitheater. "Should I get your parents?" he asked, turning as if to go, and she grabbed his hand.

"They don't know," she murmured.

"You haven't told them?" he asked, and she shook her head.

"Oh," he said. And then sat beside her on the step, the heat of his body filtering through the red velour of her Santa suit to seep right into her skin.

"What's going on, Merri?" he asked.

Here it was, her great moment for honesty. The chance to just set down the giant snarl of her life right in front of Gavin. Show him every mess. Every mistake.

"I'm pregnant," she said. "With a little girl. My fiancé," she said, picking at the white faux-fur cuff that had come loose from her tape job, "has been cheating on me. And when I found out about the baby and told him…well." She sighed and looked up at the stars, cold and white in the thick black sky. "We broke up. I'm alone. Pregnant. Broke and back in Webster Groves."

Gavin didn't say anything, and as the mortification

grew she pulled herself together as if to stand, as if to walk away. This, she told herself, was why she'd been keeping it a secret. Because her own disappointment in her life was hard enough to deal with. Heaping everyone else's on it was just asking for pain.

And she'd had enough. Truly.

"Well, Gavin, it's been—"

As she shifted her weight onto her feet, she felt his hand slide around her, cup her shoulder and pull her into the hot cradle of his body.

"That," he said, pressing a kiss to her forehead, "totally sucks."

Laughter, like sunshine, like bright clear water, like a thousand showers and hot baths and everything clean and good, bubbled up from her chest—from underneath her misery and embarrassment—and popped out of her mouth.

"The baby doesn't, though," he said, leaning back to look into her face. He was so close she could see his eyelashes, the scar at the corner of his lip. Her laughter stalled and something warmer took its place. "Babies are blessings," he whispered. "No matter how they come about."

"You're right," she said, nodding. "But sometimes, with the rest of it, I forget. It doesn't totally seem real."

"That's all right, Merri. It didn't seem real to me until I was holding Luke in my hands and he was screaming his head off."

She rested her head on his shoulder and soaked in his heat, the comfort of his presence, the special zing that traveled through her body at his closeness.

"I can't believe some idiot out there is letting you go," he said, his voice low and burning. "Letting you and his baby go." The grip on her waist tightened. "He has a chance at everything..." He trailed off and Merri shut her eyes against hot tears.

"The other night," she said, figuring if she was going to be honest, she might as well go all the way, "in the park. When I told you there was someone—"

He put a finger over her lips and she gasped at the sensation. "I understand. You've got a lot on your plate without me running around like an idiot."

"You're not an idiot. You're not at all. You're everything I wanted Dean to be. Everything any man should be. Passionate, caring, smart, hardworking. Sexy as all get out."

"But?" His hand slid away and she felt nothing but cold where he'd been touching her. Cold to her bones without his warmth.

"Gavin, trust me, if things were different..." She trailed off, feeling as if her body were starving for him, thirsting for him. She reached for him, but he pulled away.

He stared into her eyes, as if reading her, studying her.

"Different?" he asked. "How?"

"Different in every way," she said, feeling hysterical laughter building in her like steam.

"But they're not and that's what's stopping you," he whispered with a soft, sad smile. The disappointment in his eyes lanced her, and when he leaned down to press a featherlight kiss to her lips it felt like the keys to the kingdom, the chance at everything she ever wanted or could dream of wanting—and then he was gone.

"You should tell your folks," he said, squeezing her shoulder before standing up to leave.

She grabbed his hand, a pregnant Santa holding on to

a motorcycle man—the idea was as ludicrous as the idea that he could possibly be suggesting there was still a chance for them.

"We fight all the time, Gavin," she said.

"I like fighting with you," he said with a shrug.

"I'm terrible with relationships," she said. "Terrible. I'm passive-aggressive and moody and I have all these expectations—"

"I'm not very good with relationships, either," he said. "I'm argumentative, sometimes irrational. I'm a total neat freak."

"I'm three months pregnant with another man's baby," she said. "You can't possibly want me like this. You can't—"

"Merri," he said, his voice sharp. "You have no idea what I want." He thrust his fingers into her hair, cradling her face with barely contained violence. His eyes were on fire, his face hard, and he took her breath away. "I have wanted you from the moment I saw you. I will want you pregnant, alone, broke, happy, sad, angry, smelling like french fries—however I can get you. And I get that you're scared, but, Merri, you're always scared."

"Being alone and pregnant is pretty damn scary," she snapped.

"And I'm telling you, you don't have to be alone," he whispered. "I'm right here—all you have to do is reach for me. It takes courage to be happy."

He paused, as if waiting for her to do it, and her fingers burned, her hands pulsed, her body ached.

"We don't know each other." She sighed. "It was one night sixteen years ago."

"One night sixteen years ago that neither of us has ever forgotten. And, if we do this your way, we'll never

get to know each other," he said, the question floating between them.

"Gavin," she said. "It's not that simple."

He let go of her face, his fingers leaving tracks of sensation across her skin. "It is, Merri. You've just never seen
it that way."

With one last long glance, Gavin walked away, melting
into the shadows, taking with him what felt like every
possibility for those dreams of hers to come true.

GAVIN WALKED. People called out to him and he waved.
Maybe he smiled. He didn't know. The Christmas celebration went on and he just walked through the trees,
hoping that if he walked long enough, far enough, he
might be able to shed a little of this pain, like a skin he
didn't need anymore. Because, seriously, he did not need
this Merri-inflicted agony anymore.

He felt like every bone and nerve ending had been
scorched by the exposure, by the tearing off of his skin
and revealing his heart. Only to have it ground to dust
under her careless feet, once again.

Ah, Merri, so damn close and still so far away.

"Dad?"

Luke appeared from the dark trees to his left. He'd
taken off his wings and put on the leather coat Gavin had
given the boy last year for Christmas.

This year, Gavin had a bike for him. A little souped-
up scooter. He couldn't wait to see Luke's face tomorrow morning.

"You okay?" Luke asked, catching Gavin's shoulder.
"You look…sick."

"I'm…" Gavin stopped, tired of pretending. "I'm
really pretty sad, Luke."

"Because Merri is pregnant?"

Gavin breathed hard through his nose. "No, because she's too scared to see that she doesn't have to be alone if she doesn't want to be."

"Do you love her?" Luke asked.

"I did," he said, "a long time ago. And now with her back in town I think I could probably be in love with her again in about five minutes, but it doesn't matter. Not if she's too scared to try."

"I shouldn't have told you," Luke said, tucking his hands back into his pocket. Snow dribbled off a tree and dusted his shoulders. "It was her secret."

Right. Christmas Eve secrets. "Seems to be a lot of that going around these days."

"We made a promise," Luke said, swallowing audibly. "That we would tell our secrets to our parents on Christmas Eve."

All the hair on the back of Gavin's neck stood up as if lightning were about to strike.

Gavin had called Merri a coward for not taking what she wanted, and maybe he wasn't much better. Maybe he was a coward, too, letting this ice take over their lives.

"I love you, son," Gavin said, his eyes blazing through the dark distance between them. "Whatever it is that's bothering you, I'm with you. I'm here for you. No matter what."

Luke stepped back into the shadows, his face obscured in the darkness, and Gavin had the terrible sense that he was losing him. He reached out for his son.

"Luke?"

"Stay there, Dad," Luke said, his voice so different, so old and young at the same time, it nearly stopped Gavin's heart.

Gavin paused where he was, feeling something in the

air, things at work, and he waited, his heart in his throat, for the world to fall down around him.

Please, God, please let him be okay...

"I'm gay," Luke whispered.

Gavin felt the world tilt under his feet; the stars twirled, a wild kaldeiscope above his head.

"Did you hear me, Dad?"

Gavin nodded and he couldn't catch his breath much less talk.

"I told Mom and she freaked out," Luke said, his voice getting hard, his hands turning to fists beside him. "You're freaking out, too, aren't you?"

Gavin shook his head, but Luke wasn't buying it, and Gavin could feel the kid's anger and frustration like a thousand hornets coming after him. "She sent me to you, so what are you going to do, Dad? Where are you going to send me?"

Luke's words cut like razor blades and Gavin needed a second to process everything, but he didn't have one. The future was in the balance and Luke was slipping away, heartbeat by heartbeat behind a wall Gavin would never be able to get around if he didn't do something *right now.*

Gavin couldn't feel his own face. His arms. But he reached for Luke, anyway, curling numb fingers around his son's shoulders.

Luke slapped at his hands. "Don't—"

"I'm not sending you anywhere," he said, pulling Luke out into the light, and the tears in his son's bright blue eyes nearly sent him right to the ground. "You're my son and I love you."

Luke's shoulders caved a little and the boy pitched forward. But Gavin was there. Gavin was there to hold him, hug him hard to his chest.

"You don't care?" Luke asked.

Gavin blinked. "Of course I care. I care about everything about you. But I'm not mad." He cupped the boy's head in his hands. "I thought you were going to tell me you were sick or something." Gavin sighed, relieved that it wasn't the case.

"Mom said this is worse," Luke whispered against his jacket. "She said sickness could be cured."

Gavin's heart broke wide open and he blinked back hot tears of anger that Juliet could be so callous.

"Your mother, I'm sorry to say, can be an idiot."

Luke smiled and leaned back, making eye contact that Gavin felt deep in his chest. This, Gavin thought, was trust. This was love—unconditional. And it felt like Gavin was flying.

"Merri said the same thing about Mom," Luke told him.

And with the mention of Merri's name he crashed back to earth.

"Well." He sighed. "Merri's smart about some things." He kept his arm slung over Luke's shoulder, reluctant to let go of him. "Should we head home?"

"Not yet," Luke said. "I want to see the 'Oh Holy Night' thing with the candles."

"Okay," Gavin agreed, girding himself for more of Merri Monroe.

He and Luke walked arm in arm toward the amphitheater, the gravel and snow crunching under their boots.

"So," Gavin asked, realizing he was about to embark on a conversation he never saw coming. "Is there a guy in particular…?"

Luke patted his shoulder. "One step at a time, Dad. Let's go one step at a time."

CHAPTER NINE

MERRI STEPPED AROUND the edge of the amphitheater and all the voices were too loud. All the lights too bright. There were so many people and it all began to hum and whirl in front of her.

Gavin was gone. She'd just pushed away any chance she had with him, all because she was too damn scared.

"I'm pregnant," she said softly.

Her mother, glittering three feet away, didn't hear her. Dad, the antlers curling down around his shoulders, didn't even glance at her.

"I'm pregnant!" she yelled.

And everyone turned to her. Conversations stopped midsentence. Candles and cookies were dropped. One lone voice carried on with "Little Drummer Boy," but it, too, was shushed as everyone's attention focused like a laser on the pregnant Santa standing on stage.

There was expectation on these faces, but there was also love. She knew every single person in this clearing. She'd served them breakfast and coffee; she'd spent the night as a child in their homes; she'd sat in their classrooms, growing up learning things that changed her life and things she'd already forgotten.

Two nights ago when she and Gavin strung lights in the trees, she'd thought she had no other place to go, but the reality was…there was no place she'd rather be.

That trap she'd been so afraid of—turning into her parents—it was gone. It had been in her head all along.

There was only love here, and that could never be a trap.

"Honey?" Mom asked, coffee running onto the ground from the pitcher she had tilted. Mrs. Phillips took it out of her hands.

"What did you say?" Dad asked, climbing onto the stage as best he could with his cast. "Lenora, what did she say?"

"I'm going to have a baby," Merri said, her voice cracking under the weight of everyone's stares. Well, she thought, in for a penny… "By myself."

A few people gasped and she wanted to roll her eyes, but suddenly at the edge of the crowd she saw Gavin and Luke staring at her with their mouths agape. Gavin gave her a very discreet thumbs-up, and she was buoyed by his strength. By his presence.

"I'm three months pregnant with a little girl," she said, loud and clear, a smile on her face, joy in her heart.

"A baby girl!" Mom cried, clapping her hands and wrapping her arms around Merri. "Oh, my goodness, what a Christmas gift."

"I'm going to need help," Merri said.

"You've got it," Mom declared, tears rolling unchecked down her cheeks. Funny, but for the first time since finding out she was having a baby, Merri didn't feel like crying, she didn't feel as if she were standing at the edge of disaster. She was almost, just about, exactly where she needed to be.

Laughter bubbled up, like some hidden spring.

"I've rented an apartment," she said. "I move in after the New Year."

"That's great," Mom said, nudging Dad. "Isn't that great?"

"I sort of like having you around," Dad said with a smile.

"Well, I'm going to be around, because I have some ideas for that diner. Big ideas." She gave her father a stern glance. "They include vegetables."

"Hallelujah!" Mom cried. "We can go on a cruise."

"Aren't we forgetting something?" Dad asked. "Where the hell is Dean?" Dad looked both thunderous and endearing with his ramshackle antlers.

"I don't need him, Dad," Merri said, reaching out to straighten the lopsided coat hangers. "I don't want him."

And then, because truly this was the hard part, the last few inches to get to where she really needed to be, she turned to Gavin. She met his eyes across the ten feet that separated them and tried to convey how sorry she was, how scared she'd been and stupid. "I want you, Gavin," she said to him, in front of a hundred people. "I always have."

Time ground to a halt—a dog barked somewhere, the earth turned, people cried and laughed and some of them were whispering behind their hands, but it didn't matter. All that mattered was Gavin, his brown eyes warming, doubt turning to a bright happiness.

Luke shoved him toward her and she watched, spellbound, as Gavin leaped up onto the stage, his long legs eating the distance and years between them. His eyes so warm. So happy. He was transformed, a different man somehow.

Gavin, complete, she realized. He was a happy man.

"I have no idea how this is going to work," she whispered as his hands slid around her, the world falling away as he leaned down to kiss her cheek and breathe into her ear.

"That's the fun of it, Merri," he said. "No one does."

Oh, wow, his arms felt like home. All these years, all these mistakes, and here she was, right back where she started—in Gavin McDonnell's arms.

"Hey," Luke said, having followed his father up on stage and Gavin leaned back, throwing an arm around Luke's neck. "You guys getting married or something?"

"Whoa, there," Merri said. Though she had to admit, those wedding dress dreams were complete with Gavin at the end of the aisle. "Let's go one step at a time."

"Yeah?" Gavin asked, a wicked glint in his eye. "What's the first step?"

"A date," she said, pretending to be prim, pretending that the first step wasn't going to be getting naked and quick. "A real one."

"Great," he answered, his eyes hot as he bent to kiss her nose. "I know this great counter…"

She howled with laughter and threw herself into his arms.

"Hey, look," Luke breathed and they unfolded themselves from their group hug to see the whole park awash in candlelight. A hundred pinpricks in the velvet night, a hundred faces, a hundred bright smiles illuminated.

It was miraculous, the kind of thing that only happened on Christmas.

Those first haunting strains of "Oh Holy Night" filled the air, her father's stunning baritone leading the charge, and Merri flung her arms around Gavin, kissing his cold cheek.

"I'm so happy," she said and then she threw her arm around Luke. "You are such a good angel."

"I told him my secret," Luke said and Merri pushed away from their hug.

"And…?" she asked, searching for hidden currents between father and son but finding none. Instead, Gavin just grinned at Luke.

"He's my son," Gavin said, tears in his eyes. "I don't care if he's green."

Oh, wow. "Good answer," Merri said and had to reward such excellent parenting with a big kiss.

"Merry Christmas, Gavin," she whispered against his lips.

"Merry Christmas, Santa."

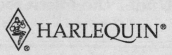